THE
MORTAL
KNIFE

D.J.McCUNE

DEATH & Co.

THE MORTAL KNIFE

HOT
KEY
BOOKS

First published in Great Britain in 2014 by Hot Key Books
Northburgh House, 10 Northburgh Street, London EC1V 0AT

A CIP catalogue record for this book is available from the British Library.

ISBN: 978-1-4714-0231-9

1

This book is typeset in 10.5 Berling LT Std using Atomik ePublisher

Printed and bound by Clays Ltd, St Ives Plc

Hot Key Books supports the Forest Stewardship Council (FSC),
the leading international forest certification organisation, and is
committed to printing only on Greenpeace-approved FSC-certified paper.

www.hotkeybooks.com

Hot Key Books is part of the Bonnier Publishing Group
www.bonnierpublishing.com

For Ellen, our bright light, with love

Prologue

verywhere he looked, the dead were waiting.

Luc Mortson sighed and stared around the Hinterland, allowing himself one moment to stop and breathe, before he resumed his work. Anything longer than that was a luxury he couldn't afford when hundreds of souls stood beside him in the Hinterland, staring at their own bodies and trying to understand that their physical lives were over.

Why did these jobs always seem to happen at night? Luc stifled a yawn and watched his father Nathanial working, dressed in his usual suit and camel-hair coat. A landslide had engulfed an Italian village overnight, killing hundreds as they slept. The Mortsons had been at home in London, tucked up in bed when their death senses flared. There was no choice but to get up, get dressed and get out of the door. After all, they were Lumen – the guardians of the souls of the dead.

Nathanial had his hand on the shoulder of a middle-aged man, his mouth close to the man's ear, chanting the directions the soul needed for his journey onto the Unknown Roads. Luc

3

could see the soul's face relaxing and knew that any second the man would step through his Light and say goodbye to the physical world. Sure enough, a moment later the man moved forward and disappeared, leaving only his crushed body behind.

Luc winced at the sight of the bodies, fidgeting with the keystone round his neck. Most humans couldn't see the Hinterland until they were dead – which was just as well really. It would only freak them out. The Hinterland was another realm, a borderland between physical life and the next life. It lay on top of the physical world like a clear film covering a map, allowing souls a one-way view of the world they were leaving behind. Most souls were happy enough to go, once they realised their souls had plenty of life in them yet.

Nathanial came over and gave him a brief smile. 'We're getting there. Most of the fast-response Lumen are here now. You can rest when we're finished. Go and help Aron.'

Luc nodded and searched for his older brother. When a big disaster like this struck, specialist Lumen had to get there fast and give directions to the souls before they wandered into their Lights, confused and frightened. None of them had expected to die tonight; none of them were prepared mentally. If they went through their Lights without directions it was easy to get lost on the other side. Fast-response Lumen came from every part of the globe to prevent this.

As Nathanial moved away, Luc called after him. 'Where's Adam?'

Nathanial's jaw tightened. 'He's over there sitting down. He's . . . indisposed.'

Luc's eyes roamed through the crowd until they locked on a

4

small figure huddling by what used to be a house. His younger brother was bent double, retching. 'Oh right. Nothing new there then.' He grinned. What was it with Adam? He was a Mortson like the rest of them. He had the same blood and the same keystone but somehow the Mortson talent had missed his younger brother out. Adam was fifteen but he was still at *school* – and what self-respecting Luman stayed at school after the age of eleven?

'Get back to work, Luc.' Nathanial sounded sharper than usual.

Luc frowned as his father walked away. He turned his attention back to Adam, watching him wipe his mouth on his hoodie sleeve and edge towards another soul. His brother was in disgrace. Adam had done something major a few days earlier – a solo job. Guiding a soul into his Light all alone, without supervision from a full, Marked Luman.

Luc couldn't understand it. What was Adam trying to prove? He hated coming on jobs at the best of times – so why would he go and do one on his own? Breaking Luman law was a big deal. It was the kind of thing that could bring your physical life to a fast end.

Luc shrugged. It wasn't his problem. Adam was a moron at times but he was all right. He searched for a soul and found a girl about his own age. Dying at seventeen didn't seem fair but Luc pushed away the unexpected pang of sadness he felt. Lumen didn't decide who lived and died – they just dealt with the fallout.

He moved towards the girl with his biggest smile. He was good at being a Luman. He was even better with the ladies.

Chapter 1

he holidays were over. All over London, thousands of alarm clocks were ringing, beeping and blaring into life while owners muttered, cursed and battered them into silence, creeping deeper beneath the covers for a few more minutes in bed.

Not Adam Mortson. He'd been up for hours, pacing round his bedroom, watching the digital numbers on his clock flicker and change, heartbeat by heartbeat. Now he grinned at his reflection in his bedroom mirror, uniform immaculate, shoes gleaming, hair . . . under control. Half-term was over. He was finally going back to school. *Brilliant!*

He skipped downstairs and into the kitchen. No one else was there and he hummed under his breath while he waited for the toaster to pop. It would be nice to eat without having an angry audience. Meals had been a bit tense for the last week.

It hadn't been a typical half-term holiday, even by his standards. In fact, on the first day of the holidays he had thwarted a suicide bomber and saved lots of innocent bystanders. He'd followed that up by doing an underage soul guiding, sending the bomber's soul into the afterlife before he had come of age and without a Marked Luman present. He'd known he was going to be in trouble. What he *hadn't* realised was just *how* angry his father was going to be.

Was it really only a week ago? He'd been with Melissa before he got home. As soon as he opened the front door a not-so-welcoming committee was waiting for him. Nathanial and Elise were standing, arms folded, faces grim. Auntie Jo was there too, just behind, and for once she wasn't smiling. There was no sign of his older brothers, Aron and Luc, or his younger sister Chloe – but he was pretty sure they were lurking nearby, ears flapping like radar dishes.

The toaster popped and Adam's cheeks burned at the memory of the conversation that had ensued. He'd been grounded of course, just as he'd known he would be – but the direst threat of all had been made; that he wouldn't be going back to school. Only Auntie Jo's arguments had saved him, although she'd seemed reluctant, as if wondering whether she was doing the right thing.

Auntie Jo had always been Adam's ally in the fight to stay at school – something no one else in the family could understand. The Mortsons were Lumen, guardians of the souls of the dead. They didn't need to go to school. Most Lumen – like his brothers and his sister – had left at the end of primary school, having learned to read and write. Besides, they got plenty of lessons at home, taught by their mother Elise and a reluctant Auntie Jo. The boys learned all about guiding souls, while Chloe was taught how to be a perfect wife and hostess.

The Mortsons were expert Lumen, specialising in helping the most tricky souls, those who had died suddenly or unexpectedly.

7

In fact, Adam's father, Nathanial Mortson, was High Luman of Britain, overseeing all the souls and Lumen in his Kingdom. Aron and Luc were both showing signs of the Mortson talent – and everyone expected Adam to show the same promise.

The problem was that Adam was pretty much the worst Luman in history. Every time he swooped – stepped into the Hinterland and travelled to a newly dead soul – his nose would start bleeding madly. He never knew what to say to the souls other than, 'Erm . . . sorry, you're dead.' And worst of all his stomach had a habit of getting upset in the Hinterland. No soul wanted their last sight on earth to be a fifteen-year-old throwing up on his trainers.

Adam knew he wasn't meant to be a Luman. He wanted to be a doctor. Unfortunately this was the maddest thing anyone in his family had ever heard. During their teen years Lumen children were normally 'home-schooled' – not that the authorities knew what kind of 'education' they were getting. Adam had fought tooth and nail to stay at Bonehill Charitable School and hang out with his friends and Melissa – but he knew his parents were starting to have second thoughts. They'd put up with it so far but their patience was running out . . .

Adam sighed and smeared marmalade on his toast. He had just lifted the first slice to his mouth when the back door opened and Nathanial and Luc walked in, obviously back from an early morning call-out. Adam froze. Nathanial stared at his uniform, gave him a stiff nod, then stalked out of the kitchen, leaving Luc and Adam alone.

'All right, leper?' Luc said cheerfully, snagging one of the pieces of toast. 'I keep meaning to get you a bell so you can ring it and shout "*Unclean, unclean!*". At least we'll know when you're in a room – no nasty surprises for anyone.'

Adam scowled. *I did the right thing,* he told himself for the millionth time. *The people I saved were innocent. They didn't deserve to die! And the bomber didn't deserve my help onto the Unknown Roads.* He was in trouble for the bit his family knew about – the underage guiding. If they knew the rest he would be dead right now. Literally.

Luc pulled out a chair, interrupting Adam's thoughts. 'You know, you should be welcoming me with open arms. I'm pretty much the only one in the house who doesn't hate you.'

'Sam and Morty still like me,' Adam muttered.

Luc sniggered. 'Yeah. They're *dogs,* Adam. I was thinking more about the human occupants.' He swiped another slice of toast, ignoring Adam's curses. 'So . . . back to school. You'll get to see your girlfriend again!'

'She's not my girlfriend,' Adam said. *Yet.* His heart sang a happy song, remembering how it felt to finally kiss Melissa Morgan. She'd liked it too! Well, OK, she'd given him a six out of ten but he reckoned with a bit of practice . . . He threw more bread in the toaster, humming to himself.

'Ahhh, Adam's in lurrrrve,' Luc trilled. 'You enjoy it, seriously. It's only a matter of time before you get caught and then you'll be more in the doghouse than the actual dogs.'

Adam glared. In a world of arranged marriages, having a girlfriend was just one more forbidden thing for a Luman. Lumen tended to get betrothed at an early age (to other Lumen of course) and married young – not that Luc ever had any problems with ignoring the rules and impressing the opposite sex. 'Why would I get caught? It's not like *you* never go out with people. *You* never get caught.'

Luc snorted. 'Yeah, but I'm me and you're you. It's like comparing something really clever with something . . . really not clever. Plus I don't go all goggle-eyed over girls. I'm like James Bond. In, complete the mission and get out while the going's good. You're more like Romeo – and that story didn't end well.'

Adam applied a vicious smear of peanut butter to his toast and grabbed his schoolbag. 'I don't care what you think. Everything is going to be fine.'

He could still hear Luc's laughter ringing in his ears as he stalked out of the back door.

Adam's anger faded as he sat on the bus to school. There was no point getting mad at Luc – or indeed any of his family. None of them could understand why he wanted to go to school, even Auntie Jo. Why would they? They didn't *want* to be normal. In fact, the very idea of being normal left Luc cold! Luc *liked* being a Luman. He liked not going to school and swooping and guiding souls – but then he didn't throw up or get nosebleeds every time he did it. Aron, Adam's eldest brother, was planning to follow in their father's footsteps and become the next High Luman. Chloe wasn't allowed to be a Luman but she would be expected to marry into an old Luman family and have lots of sons, just as their mother Elise had. Only Auntie Jo had broken with tradition in not marrying and living with her brother Nathanial.

It was hard for Adam to explain why he was so awful at being a Luman. He knew Nathanial thought he would grow out of it and get better but Adam wasn't so sure. He wasn't scared of death or the souls or the Hinterland – most of the souls were quite happy to step into their Lights once they knew their life in the physical world had ended. He just couldn't shake the feeling that his own life should be about more than death.

It didn't help that Adam had an extra talent – one he was careful to hide from his family. In the Luman world someone like him was called a Seer. All Lumen had a death sense, a sense that told them when a soul had died and whether it was a predicted death or unexpected. The Mortsons specialised in sudden deaths, when souls could get frightened and lost unless they were guided into their Lights quickly. But a Seer had an extra sense – what Adam thought of as his doom sense. He could sometimes feel when a soul was about to die, *before* it had actually happened – which gave him the chance to do something about it.

This meant breaking Luman law – and cheating the Fates out of souls. So far Adam had intervened in death scenes three times, most recently depriving the suicide bomber of his intended victims. So far no one suspected that *he* was involved – but if he got caught he would be put on trial by the Luman authorities and face the death penalty himself.

Adam slumped back in his chair. He was pretty sure most people his age weren't having to worry about being executed just for trying to help people. In fact, when he listened to his friends whingeing about their homework or not getting a new computer game he felt like telling them to get a grip. If that was the biggest thing they had to fret over they were doing well!

The bell on the bus pinged, jolting Adam out of his thoughts. A girl was walking past him, ready to get off. She was wearing the uniform of a nearby school and had twisted a pink-flowered bandana through her long, blonde hair. The bus hit a bump and she stumbled, almost falling into Adam's lap. 'Sorry,' she muttered without looking up, clutching on to her mobile phone and putting her headphones on.

Adam watched her step off the bus. Something about the way she walked reminded him of Melissa. He sighed. Who was he trying to kid? *Everything* reminded him of Melissa at the minute. Auntie Jo had given him a strawberry bonbon a few nights earlier and he'd fallen into a reverie, thinking how much it tasted like Melissa's lip balm. He hadn't even heard Chloe talking to him and, in the face of some crude suggestions about what he might be thinking about, had ended up pretending he was choking and subjecting himself to some 'helpful' thumps on the back from Aron. He scowled at the memory. Aron was massive and Adam's spine still felt tender.

The bus had just pulled away when, without warning, Adam's stomach clenched in agony. It was as if someone had punched him and stabbed him at the same time. He folded in two, resting his head on the seat bar, trying not to cry out. This *could not* be happening! His doom sense had been lying quiet for a week since the suicide bomb. He'd spent a whole week off mooching about in his room, bar one disastrous call-out in Italy – and now on his first day back at school his internal siren was howling in warning. He knew the signs. Someone was about to die.

The pain in his stomach was making his eyes water. He scrabbled blindly in his schoolbag for his water bottle and

12

managed a mouthful. The shock of the cold cut through the nausea and he eased upright cautiously. He felt like banging his head off the window with frustration. Why *now*? Why did he have to get a doom warning when he couldn't *do* anything?

He tried to block the premonition. He'd spent his whole life doing it – in fact, it had become second nature. He'd actually had to *try* to tune into his doom sense when he had decided to intervene and save some of the sudden deaths. The thing was there were only two occasions when the premonitions forced their way through as powerfully as this. Either lots of people were about to die – or one person who was very nearby.

He sat up straighter and tried to peer surreptitiously round the bus. Everybody *looked* pretty healthy. No one else from his school was on board but there were a few people his age wearing a variety of uniforms. The rest of the bus was full of people on their way to work, most of them in suits and no older than his parents. There *was* one older lady sitting a few seats ahead on the other side of the bus. She was coughing in sharp, phlegmy sounding barks. Adam watched her through narrowed eyes – but just as he'd decided she was the victim, the lady whipped out a packet of throat sweets and a large handkerchief and blew her nose like a bugle. He frowned, not sure whether to be relieved or disappointed. She just had a cold. And anyway, how was he going to do anything to save her on a bus full of people?

The bus paused at a zebra crossing. Adam watched the orange lights blinking and let his eyes drift past, to a side street on the left, off the main road. It was just an ordinary street, like a dozen others the bus had passed – but the stabbing pain returned with a vengeance. Adam gagged a little and turned it into a cough. He wanted to curl up in a ball on the floor and whimper but he forced himself to stare through watery eyes at the road. Hawthorn Avenue. It was a nice name but something terrible was going to happen there.

The bus moved on and as they drew level with the street Adam *willed* his doom sense to give him something more, *anything* at all. For a moment nothing happened. Then, just as they were about to pass, the light outside flickered and changed and Adam saw it, just for a split second – the white van mounting the kerb, too late, trying to avoid something – trying in vain because the girl landed hard on the tarmac, mobile phone smashing, the force tearing her blonde hair free from the pink bandana.

Adam sprang to his feet, grabbed his bag and leapt into the aisle all in one movement, almost landing on the woman in the seat opposite. He ignored her protests and ran to the front of the bus. 'I need to get off.'

The driver didn't even turn his head. 'Can't let you off till the next stop.'

Adam tried not to shout. 'I need to get off *now*!'

'Can't let you off till the next stop.' The driver might as well have been a robot for all the emotion he showed. He sounded utterly world-weary, like a man incapable of being surprised; a man who'd heard every story in the history of the world and who already knew the punchline to every joke ever told.

Adam glared at him. 'I need to get off the bus. Seriously. I have to get off!' The passengers in the front few seats were lowering

14

their newspapers and staring at him with dull irritation. His audience gave Adam an idea. He raised his voice. 'I'm going to be sick. I have some sort of bug I think. You know that winter vomiting thing?' He gave an Oscar-worthy retch and groan. It wasn't as hard as he thought it would be; the adrenalin had his stomach rolling and flipping.

The driver flinched as far back in his seat as physically possible, his deadpan expression replaced with one of complete disgust. He slammed the brake on and the door popped open. Adam was off and running before the bus had even come to a standstill.

There was no time to think about what he was going to do. Adam ran like the hounds of hell were chasing him. He could hear his heart thudding in his ears and his feet pounding on the pavement. His schoolbag was slowing him down, so he threw it over a hedge into someone's garden and kept going. He turned a corner and saw the zebra crossing in the distance. A figure was visible further up the road, moving towards him. He pelted on.

The crossing was getting closer. Adam was gasping for breath now. He hadn't run this far in ages. He had a vague sense that he probably needed to get a bit fitter if he was going to keep doing this whole saving people thing. That was the bit they never told you in comics or films – being a hero wasn't easy. Unless you'd come from another planet or been bitten by a radioactive bug you were probably going to need to hit the gym every so often.

He was close enough to see the girl now. He could also see how she was going to die. Her head was bent over her phone and she wasn't looking ahead. Worse, in the distance Adam could see a line of cars and behind them the white van. The girl was reaching the corner of Hawthorn Avenue and turning into the street. Adam tried to wave but she was too absorbed in her playlist. He gave a wheezing groan and forced his legs to go to his version of warp speed.

He tried calling her but she had her headphones on. He realised, with an awful, sickening churn, that he wasn't going to reach her in time. She couldn't see him and couldn't hear him. She was walking in a dream and the white van was almost at the end of the street.

Adam veered round the corner, just as the white van reached the other corner. The girl was almost at the kerb, ready to step into the road, lost in a daze, and the van was accelerating, the driver chatting and laughing on his mobile, and everything was too slow and too fast and there was no time to think so Adam ran straight across the road and threw himself at the girl.

And, like a real superhero, for just a second it felt like he was flying.

Chapter 2

myriad of sensations blurred together in quick succession for Adam. Wind whistled past his ears, closely followed by the long, shocking blare of a horn. His hands closed on slim shoulders in a woollen blazer and he saw the blonde-haired girl's mouth fall open in shock. A startled squeak emerged from her mouth and her breath blew hot on his cheek. There was a brief moment of imbalance as Adam and the girl tussled together, almost falling under the wheels of the van, until the momentum took them backwards onto the pavement and into a painful tangle of limbs.

Adam fell on his left arm and shoulder but managed to absorb the blonde girl's weight. She landed in a cat-like half-crouch, staggering forward, almost falling over Adam. He found himself lying on his back staring up into her face just an arm's length from his own.

She was totally unharmed. She was also hopping mad. She ripped her headphones off, swore at Adam and pulled free of his grip. 'Get off me!' She staggered to her feet and backed away from him.

Adam held his hands up in the air, wincing at the bolt of pain that shot up his left side. 'It's OK! I'm not trying to hurt you!'

The girl snorted and called him something very rude. '*You* hurt *me*? Don't come near me, creep! I do ju-jitsu!'

There was a thud of metal as the door of the white van slammed closed. The driver, a burly middle-aged man, marched over and glared down at Adam. 'What the hell are you doing, you little twerp? Are you trying to get yourself killed?' He glanced from Adam's prone form to the blonde-haired girl, noticing her angry expression. 'What's wrong, love? Did he attack you?' He pointed a stubby and vehement finger in Adam's face. 'Did you try to attack her?'

Adam blinked up at them, temporarily speechless. He hadn't expected a round of applause – after all, the van driver didn't *know* he'd almost killed the girl. Still, he hadn't expected the pair of them to join forces and beat him to a pulp either! He tried to sit up, wincing. 'Look, I wasn't attacking anybody.' He wasn't sure what was hurting him more – the bad landing or the injustice of the whole sorry situation!

The van driver gave him a disgusted look. 'They should lock people like you up.' The girl was standing beside the van man with her arms folded, shaking her head.

The unfairness of it all was threatening to make Adam blurt out something outrageous – like the truth. He swallowed hard and took a deep breath. It made his ribs hurt. 'Look, I'm really sorry. I was only messing around. I thought you were someone else.'

'Yeah, right,' the girl said with a scowl. 'Just stay away from me.' She turned and crossed the road unharmed, heading off down Hawthorn Avenue, presumably in the direction of her school.

The van driver glared at Adam. 'Just you stay down there and count to one hundred before you walk anywhere near that young lady.' He climbed back in the van and drove off slowly, as if to make the point he was keeping an eye on things.

Adam let the white van recede from view and struggled painfully to his feet. He had risked his own life to save someone else's. He didn't expect a medal. He didn't even expect thanks. He just didn't want to be called a creep for doing something good. He tried to summon up a warm glow, knowing he had saved a life but all he could feel was the warm glow of the massive bruise growing down his left arm. Sometimes doing the right thing sucked.

He scowled and limped off to reclaim his schoolbag.

No matter what else had happened, Adam always felt a lightening in his spirits as he walked up the long, stony driveway to Bonehill Charitable School. He could tell that not all of his classmates felt the same sense of good fortune as he watched them drag their feet towards the main building.

Bonehill was an old school, founded by an eccentric philanthropist more than a century ago and maintained by a trust. Places were awarded by lottery, which meant that the catchment covered a huge area and attracted students from all backgrounds. It was seen as a good school by people in the know, not that Adam's family had any clue what a 'good school' was. These things weren't important in the Luman world because no self-respecting Luman would be seen dead at school at Adam's age.

Adam didn't care. This was where he felt happiest, most at ease in his own skin. He had his friends, he was studying subjects he enjoyed and now he had Melissa as well. His heart hopped about a little thinking of her. How should he play things? She was in his form class and would be in registration. Kissing her had definitely been a step in the right direction! He didn't think he could actually call her his girlfriend just yet but if he didn't mess things up he might be able to soon enough.

Of course every silver lining had a cloud and the cloud was lurking by the front door into the main building. Mr Bulber, aka The Bulb, was standing at the top of the steps surveying his domain. A former professional wrestler turned teacher, The Bulb had somehow managed to finagle his way into the position of head teacher. His son Michael Bulber took full advantage of his father's position by terrorising the school at his leisure, earning himself the nickname 'the Beast'.

Adam scowled just thinking about his nemesis. The Beast had always been a menacing presence in school but a couple of run-ins with him outside of school had shown him that Michael Bulber had a dark side few people knew about. Typically Adam had managed to fall for the one girl the Beast held a torch for. The fact that Melissa had only been out with him a few times and couldn't stand him didn't deter the Beast in any way from pursuing her – or treating Adam as a love rival.

The Bulb shared in his son's dislike for Adam, although for different reasons – namely that Adam was clever. The Bulb didn't like clever boys. He liked boys who thought school was all about enjoying manly activities like wrestling. He especially detested geeks or anyone who liked science, computers, manga or Orc and Elf role-playing games – which placed Adam and his friends squarely at the top of his hit list.

Still, they had recently put their skills to good use. After The Bulb had cancelled a planned school trip to Japan, they had created a fake Japanese sensei who promised to teach The Bulb secret ninja wrestling moves, as long as he performed a few challenges first. They had put The Bulb in some mortifying situations – and managed to get the Japan trip reinstated in the process.

'Morning, sir,' Adam muttered as he slid past. It was hard not to smirk.

'You're late, Mortson!' The Bulb turned his cold stare on Adam, looking him up and down. 'And what's wrong with your blazer? Get yourself brushed down and get to class!' Adam scarpered towards his form room, happy to have escaped detention.

At the door, he paused, suddenly feeling nervous at the thought of seeing Melissa. There were still a few fellow stragglers in the corridor, so a full-on preen was out of the question but he *did* dust off his mucky blazer, squash his sandy hair under control and sling his bag on his unbruised shoulder in a more nonchalant manner.

He was as ready as he was ever going to be. He rolled his shoulders back, took a deep breath and strode into the classroom.

Two lessons later, Adam was slinking towards the library in a state of deep depression, all his good feelings long since evaporated. Why had he been so keen to get back here? Was he mad?

He wasn't sure what he'd expected but it hadn't been Melissa greeting him with nothing more than a cool nod. He had stared at her beseechingly across his form room while his form tutor, Mr Fenton, ranted incoherently about incomplete homework leading inexorably to failed exams, unemployment and the lunatic asylum. Melissa studiously ignored Adam throughout, chewing her lip and doodling on the back of her pencil case. He could feel his heart cracking and warm goo running down the inside of his chest towards his stomach. His internal choir was wailing gospel style, *Why, oh why, Melissa, why?* He could still taste the memory of her strawberry lip balm.

At breaktime he slouched through the library doors and mooched towards his usual table. His friends were in their usual spots, doing their usual things: Archie was sketching a scantily clad manga chick; Spike was on his laptop (no doubt hacking into the Pentagon or similar); and Dan was hovering between the two, devouring a pile of nuts and being irritating.

It was Dan who noticed him first. He grinned up through a horrible mouthful of crushed Brazil nuts. 'All right Adam? How's it going?'

Somehow Adam managed to avoid rending his own clothes and beating his chest in anguish. 'Yeah, all right.' He wasn't all right. How could they not see? How could they not see the jagged splinters of his heart bursting out through his skin?

Archie turned his sketchpad round for Adam to admire. 'Here she is. My ninja babe. This is the woman of my dreams. And now that we're going to Japan I'm actually going to get to meet her.' He leered at his picture and tucked it carefully away in his bag.

'Of course we might not have to go to Japan to see a ninja,' Dan muttered. He waggled his eyebrows and nodded at Adam meaningfully.

Adam stared at him, confused. Whatever the meaning was it was lost on him. 'Did you have a good holiday?'

Archie groaned. 'Don't ask him that. Seriously. You don't want to know.'

Dan gave him a withering look, then turned to Adam with the kind of expression normally reserved for orphans in black and white films. 'I wouldn't say it was good but it was certainly . . . eventful.'

'Don't say I didn't warn you,' Archie muttered.

'What happened?'

Dan drew in a long, shuddering breath. 'Nothing much. Except I pretty much nearly died.'

Adam blinked. Whatever he'd been expecting Dan to say it hadn't been that. 'Oh, right. Well, you know, glad you're still here.'

Dan seemed disappointed at his reaction. 'Yeah, I am! But only just!' He gave a knowing nod at Adam. 'Another thirty seconds and it would have been a whole different story!'

Archie sighed and closed his sketchpad. 'Just tell him what happened and get it over with.'

Dan scowled. 'You should be more sympathetic! I'm having an existential crisis. My mum said I'm having to come to terms with my own mortality. I have to go to counselling and act stuff out with dolls.'

Archie gave a dirty snigger. 'Yeah I'll bet you do, perv.'

Adam eyed Dan curiously. 'Your mum's some kind of

therapist, isn't she?' At Dan's nod he shuddered. It would be bad enough to have your mum psychoanalysing you all the time, but Dan's dad was a dentist. His nickname was the Dark Lord, not least because of his unhealthy interest in spy cameras. Dentist and psychotherapist. It was like the worst parental job combination in history – agony on every level.

'Just tell him what happened.' Spike spoke for the first time since Adam had sat down. He didn't even look up, frowning in concentration as he stared at his laptop screen.

'I'll tell you all right!' Dan said. 'I went to Trafalgar Square for the Septic Kisses concert the day that bomber blew himself up – and I got a photo of him just before it happened!'

Chapter 3

t was fair to say that Dan now had Adam's full attention, although probably not for the reasons he thought. 'You *what*?'

Dan nodded triumphantly. 'You heard me. I was there when that nutter blew himself up in Trafalgar Square.' He shovelled another handful of Brazil nuts into his mouth.

Adam took a slow breath in and fought to remain calm. 'Yeah, I know. But you said something about a photo? You got a photo?'

Dan swallowed hard. 'Yep. I was at the front of that gallery heading down into the square and it looked really cool with the stage and stuff, so I took a couple of photos on my phone. And then – *wham*! Massive explosion! And there was all this black smoke in the air. People were screaming and stuff.' His excitement at telling the story faded as the memories overtook him. 'It was pretty terrible really.'

'Yeah, it was,' Adam said softly. He started when the other three looked at him sharply. 'I mean, you know, the pictures. On the news. Really bad.'

'They didn't have too many pictures on the news.' It was Spike who had finally looked up from the laptop. 'Most people were videoing the concert, so they were looking the wrong way. So they've only got the CCTV footage and most of it's coming from the wrong direction. But by the time I've finished with this they'll have Dan's picture too.' He turned the laptop round towards them. 'Check this out.'

The other three leaned closer and stared at the image on the screen. Adam sucked in a breath between his teeth. The familiarity of the scene was what really jolted him. The whole square was bathed in sunlight. He could still remember how unseasonably warm the day had been and the holiday atmosphere in the crowd, everyone enjoying the weekend. Dan by a quirk of fate had been standing in exactly the right place to capture the whole scene. There was the column, at the far end of the square. There was the band bounding onto the stage, the spiky-haired lead singer waving his guitar in the air in greeting to the crowd.

And there, in the centre, between the fountains were two dark figures, alone and separate from the rest of the crowd. At the very top edge of the photo a tour guide could be seen leading a group towards the column. The group would never reach their destination. A few seconds later the bomber would detonate himself, in spite of Adam's pleas – and then all hell would break loose.

Adam closed his eyes and fought back a wave of nausea. He could still see it in slow motion – that moment when the bomber raised his hand and Adam *knew* what was going to happen. He had barely had time to step into the Hinterland and even there the force of the blast had scoured his face like hot sand. And when he had opened his eyes and seen a woman's leg lying in the physical world . . . He gulped and reached for his water bottle.

'Are you all right?' Dan was looking at him oddly.

'Yeah, I'm OK. It's just weird, you know?' Adam managed a weak smile. 'Blowing yourself up like that. Some people are mental.'

'That's not the maddest bit.' Spike's voice was low and intent as he zoomed in on the photo, focusing on the two figures. 'People keep talking about the bomber and saying they found bits of him – but no one is even mentioning this other guy. I've been digging around a bit and the police know there were two people there – but they only found the remains of one man. So who the hell is the other guy? And where's *his* body?'

Archie squinted at the screen. 'Maybe he was the bomber's friend? Or maybe he was just some tourist and that's why no one knows who he was.'

'But what happened to his body?' Spike persisted. 'Even that close to a bomb, you don't just disappear. There would be some of you left. I mean it would look more like mince than body but it would still be there.'

'Maybe it vaporised.' Adam cleared his throat and struggled on. 'You know, with the force of the bomb. Like people in nuclear bombs. They just kind of vanish.'

Spike shook his head. 'Not hot enough mate. They should have found some of him left, even if it was a good distance away. You know, a bit of foot in one of the fountains or something.'

'Shut up!' Adam said. He was on his feet without quite knowing how he'd managed to get there. His hands, resting on the table, were clenched into fists. He had seen it all – the body parts, the shredded clothing, the woman lying bleeding with her mouth moving silently. And the screams. He could still hear them in his head, the way they started slow, like whimpers and built into something loud and shrill and full of terror. 'Stop talking like that! Like it was . . . in a computer game or something!'

Spike stared at him unperturbed. 'What's your problem? They didn't find the other guy, so he must have escaped – which basically makes him a *real* ninja. Nothing wrong with tracking him down. And no one else died. If some loony wants to blow himself up, just be happy he only took himself out of action. Everyone else was OK.'

'They weren't OK,' Adam hissed. His anger was a bright, hot pulse, squashing the air out of his lungs, even though he knew it wasn't Spike's fault. 'Just because they didn't die it doesn't mean they were OK! How could you see something like that and be OK?'

Dan nodded. 'Tell me about it.' He narrowed his eyes and appraised Adam. 'Maybe you should get some counselling too.'

Adam almost snorted but managed not to. He tried to imagine sitting down and telling his whole sorry tale to some unsuspecting therapist. The *counsellor* would need counselling by the time Adam had finished . . . 'It's just mad someone doing that. And seeing the photo.'

Spike shrugged. 'You'll be able to see even more by the time I'm finished with it. I've got some software at home I can run the photo through. See if I can get the faces.'

28

Adam stared at him in horror but before he could speak someone cleared their throat behind him. 'Hi Adam.'

He turned around and froze. Melissa was standing there, the faintest hint of a smile on her face. He stared at her for what felt like a full minute until someone kicked him under the table, bringing him back to his senses. 'Ummmm . . . hey. Hi. How are you?'

'Yeah, good thanks. How was your holiday?'

Adam couldn't stop looking at her mouth. He remembered exactly what it felt like. It had haunted a couple of his dreams over the last week. His cheeks began to slow burn even thinking about those dreams . . . 'Yeah, it was good. Brilliant.'

She looked confused for a second. 'Oh right. I thought it would have been rubbish. You know with being grounded.'

Adam frantically backtracked. 'Yeah, it was crap, really rubbish. But good too. You know, because it was a holiday. Even though I was grounded. But yeah, it was good. And crap.'

She blinked but thankfully decided not to press him on the issue. 'So I have to go to the art room today but maybe we could hang out at lunchtime tomorrow?'

'That would be great,' Adam said, somehow managing to sound cooler than he actually felt.

'OK, great,' she said and smiled. She looked around Adam's friends and her smile faltered a little in the face of three pairs of shocked eyes staring at her. 'Erm . . . sorry to interrupt. See you tomorrow.'

'See you,' Adam said, beaming after her. He watched her walk away and turned back to his friends, who were still gaping. '*What?*'

'She came to find you! The fish came to find you!' Dan's eyes were like saucers.

Adam groaned. 'Stop calling her a fish!'

Dan ignored him. 'But she still likes you! Even after everything, she *still* likes you!'

Archie held out his fist and waited for Adam to bump it. 'Mate, you are totally in there. You're a legend. You threw up on her and she *still* wants to see you.'

'I mostly missed her . . .' Adam muttered, shame-faced at the memory of his not-so-romantic Valentine's night with Melissa. It had ended in him showering her feet with vomit, courtesy of Michael Bulber. With hindsight he should never have taken a *crisp* off the Beast, never mind a whole drink spiked with illicit internet substances. No wonder it had tasted so horrible.

'Yeah, I wonder what the Beast will make of you hanging out with Melissa in school,' Dan mused. 'I mean, you may have emptied the net beneath his nose but swimming about dangling bait in front of the great white is just asking for trouble.'

'Enough with the shark metaphors already,' Spike muttered. He was staring intently at the laptop once again. Adam eyed him cautiously. According to Dan, Spike had harboured a secret crush on Melissa but had never acted on it – at least not beyond lurking in the corridor outside the art room and stalking her online. That was the thing about Spike – no matter how smart he was, he always had to approach things from sideways on, sneaking in, finding access points. The problem was that approach didn't work for everything. You couldn't hack your way into someone's affections. Sometimes you just had to tackle things head on.

Like now for example. Adam tried to keep his tone casual. 'So what's this software you have for zooming in on pictures?'

Spike shrugged. 'It's the same kind of thing the police use to enhance images. I've modified it a bit though. Plus this image is better quality than CCTV, even though it's pretty far away.'

Adam frowned at the figures on the laptop. Now the initial shock had subsided he wasn't as worried. After all, the bomber and he were both blurs – plus Adam was mostly turned away from the camera. He'd been wearing giant sunglasses and had his baseball cap pulled down over his face . . . *The baseball cap!* A sudden shockwave ran through him. Dan had brought him the baseball cap back from a holiday in America – and had brought the same hat for Spike and Archie too. If Spike actually managed to zoom in on the logo . . . would the others recognise it? Adam stood up, feeling rattled, just as the bell rang for the end of break. Trying to play it cool, he shrugged. 'Well, you're wasting your time. If the police haven't managed to find anything I don't see how you're going to.'

Spike glanced up and his eyes gleamed. 'I'll take that as a challenge.'

Adam tried to smile but as he walked away he had a horrible feeling getting Spike off this project would be like parting a starving Rottweiler from a steak.

Adam could hardly keep his eyes open on the bus on the way home. His teachers, apparently incensed at a week's holiday, had cracked the whip all day and given him enough homework to keep him going until he was forty. He yawned, trying not to nod off on the shoulder of the girl beside him. Now she was out of the school grounds she had replaced all her facial piercings and if Adam slumped towards her he was likely to end up impaled.

As he trudged the short walk from the bus stop to his house, he thought about Melissa and felt a rising sense of excitement – followed almost immediately by a wave of terror. The thing was, he'd gone to see her and kissed her just after the bomb had gone off, riding high on a wave of adrenalin – the courage of the damned and all that. But what was he going to do tomorrow?

Adam sighed. Having a girlfriend was a big no-no in the Luman world. Betrothals were semi-arranged by well-meaning parents, although never against the will of the parties involved. Because of this Lumen didn't really do the whole dating thing – which meant Adam was completely clueless about the art of seduction.

His brother Luc had managed to overcome this particular hurdle – but that was just Luc. He had the gift of the gab and an easy charisma that filled Adam with a potent blend of envy and admiration. In fairness to Luc, he *had* attempted to help Adam on Valentine's night – and had also brought him safely home after Michael Bulber's stealth attack.

There was no point asking his friends for help either. None of them had girlfriends and they weren't likely to have in the short term. Archie liked girls with the kind of impossible proportions that existed only in his sketchbook (and what could kindly be described as 'niche' websites). Dan burned with hopeless passion for the elf maidens on the pages of his fantasy books and Spike was too intent on world domination to ever admit to anything as petty as actual *emotions*.

So, for now, Adam was on his own when it came to wooing Melissa. She'd told him he needed to practise kissing, so he'd taken her at face value and tried to practise on his own hand. The trouble was it tasted revolting – kind of warm and salty. Maybe he should have smeared some lip balm on it first.

He reached home and pressed his palm to the electronic scanner pad on the stone pillar beside the wrought-iron gate. The house was hidden from view behind a high iron fence, dense shrubbery and lots of old trees. The electric gates opened smoothly, then swung closed behind him on silent hinges.

Adam kicked his way up the gravel driveway, unmoved by the graceful grey stone house with its leaded windows and heavy front door, stained glass gleaming above the dark wood. Of course, what could be seen above ground was just the tip of the iceberg. Underneath the clipped lawn and ornamental trees the ground was hollowed out into vaults, crypts and a huge ballroom and dining chamber. He trudged round the side of the house, heading for the back door in the hope of a quick snack in the kitchen. Sam and Morty had been running free in the paddock but as usual heard his approach and ran to greet him, barking in welcome. They were huge – Irish wolfhounds trained as herding dogs – although it was souls they herded, not sheep.

After an energetic wrestling match he escaped from the dogs and into the kitchen. He was hungry and tired and needed some thinking time. He would throw together a quick sandwich, take it up to his room and have some chill-out time. Just some quiet thinking time, that was all he needed . . .

The kitchen door burst open and Nathanial came in, looking uncharacteristically flustered. 'Adam! Thank goodness! We were about to send out a search party. You need to go upstairs and get changed as fast as you can.'

'Why?' Adam protested.

Nathanial's face was grim. 'Because we've been Summoned.'

A few minutes later Adam was pacing up and down the tiny TV den. Auntie Jo and Adam's younger sister Chloe were sitting on the sofa half asleep. Both were smartly dressed; or at least Auntie Jo wasn't wearing a kaftan, which was pretty much as smart as she got. She didn't even look like her brother Nathanial – where he was tall and thin, Auntie Jo was short and plump. Where Nathanial was always smartly dressed, Auntie Jo looked like she had dressed in the dark and then jumped backwards through a hedge just to finish off the job. The only things they had in common were their pale complexions, dark hair and blue eyes. Adam, like Auntie Jo, hated getting dressed up. He had changed from his uniform into a suit, seething with resentment.

'Stop pacing,' Auntie Jo grumbled through a mouthful of toast. 'You're making my head hurt.'

'Last night's whisky is making your head hurt more like,' Adam muttered but he perched on the arm of the sofa beside Chloe. There had been an unexpected visitor – Alexander, Heinrich's son. Heinrich was Chief Curator – head of the Concilium, the Luman authorities. He and the other Curators had sent their sons around the globe, gathering Lumen, both male and female. Adam's heart rate had slowed down a little when he realised they weren't just looking for him. Aron and Luc had been sent to Summon the other British Lumen. Adam got to stay at home thanks to being at school – and his habit of getting nosebleeds every time he swooped. No one wanted a blood-spattered waif arriving on their doorstep.

'But why are we being Summoned?' Chloe said. 'Who are we being Summoned *by*?'

Auntie Jo yawned hugely, exposing a horrible mouthful of mushed-up toast. 'The Fates of course. Don't you remember your lessons? I didn't spend all those afternoons teaching you Luman history just so you could forget every word of it!'

Chloe scowled. 'How could I forget? Maybe if I'm lucky I can pass it on to *my* kids someday, since I can't be a Luman. What a thrill *that* will be.' Every word dripped sarcasm.

Adam felt a sneaking sympathy for Chloe and Auntie Jo. Only men could be Lumen, not women. The irony was Nathanial needed all the help he could get, especially because Adam was so rubbish as a Luman. Chloe and Auntie Jo would be *far* better Lumen than Adam – but female Lumen were expected to stay at home cooking, cleaning and having babies. Unless of course they were Auntie Jo, who remained stubbornly unmarried and instead spent her days watching zombie movies, reading online horoscopes and consuming vast quantities of toast and whisky.

Auntie Jo sighed. 'Someday Luman laws may change and you'll be able to be a Luman. Until then you need to keep the knowledge safely in your head, ready to pass on – just like I did for you.'

Chloe's mouth set in a defiant line. 'I know the paths of the Unknown Roads inside out. I should just break the law! Just swoop off and guide a soul before anyone can stop me. After all, Adam broke the law and they haven't killed *him* yet!'

Adam glared at her. 'I'm allowed to send souls into their Light. I just shouldn't have done it on my own before I've come of age.' He wasn't of course going to admit the rest, especially the bit about saving other people or deliberately not giving the soul any directions for the other side. Those bits really *would* get him killed.

Chloe shrugged. 'Anyway, I don't see why we have to drop everything when the Fates call.'

Auntie Jo rolled her eyes. 'A Luman's job is to assist the Fates, *that's* why we drop everything. And yes, *they* take orders too. But they're higher up the food chain than us and that makes them important. It's actually an honour to see the Fates, you know. Most Lumen never get to see them because they serve for such a long time.'

'So what's a Summoning?' Adam had tried to play it cool but he was just as curious as Chloe.

'Well a Summoning usually happens when one of the Fates has gone into her Light. They live a lot longer than us if they want to but they're not immortal. Sooner or later each of them will stand aside and a new Fate take their place. I don't know for sure but Atropos has been there for a long time. I wouldn't be surprised if she's the one who stood aside and needed a successor.'

Adam shivered. He didn't remember everything Auntie Jo had taught him but he did remember the role that every Fate played. Clotho was the spinner, who wove each human life into existence. Lachesis was the rod-bearer, the Fate who measured out the lifespan appointed to every human. And Atropos ... well, Atropos was the thread-cutter, keeper of the Mortal Knife – the knife which cut the thread of every human life. Of all the Fates, she was the one most to be feared. *Especially* if, like Adam, you were a rogue Luman, saving souls you shouldn't be saving.

Elise hurried in, still pushing one pearl earring into place. Adam glanced at his mother, feeling his usual discomfort in her presence. He had always been a disappointment to her but after last weekend's events she could hardly bear to look at him. Her voice was husky with cigarettes, making her French accent more distinct. 'Your brothers have returned. We must go.' She nodded her approval at Chloe, rolled her eyes at Auntie Jo's scruffy attire and frowned at Adam. 'Fix your tie! *Vite!*'

His mother was always an elegant perfectionist but today she seemed nervous. Adam gritted his teeth and followed her into the hall. Nathanial was pulling on his camel-hair coat while Aron, his eldest brother, shifted uncomfortably in his suit. He liked working out and the jacket looked tight across his burly shoulders. Luc as usual seemed completely at ease.

Nathanial glanced around and smiled. 'You all look very smart.' He was holding a small leather pouch and when he emptied it a mound of stones gleamed in his palm. 'You'll each need one of these. It's very important that you don't lose it.'

Adam took a stone and examined it curiously. It was a crystal of some sort, cloudy glass with a dull shimmer. He could hear Chloe admiring it.

Nathanial held his up. 'This is a token. We are travelling to the Realm of the Lady Fates – a great honour. It is likely that you will never enter this realm again. Only someone possessing a token from their realm can find the Fates. Have you all got your keystones?' He looked satisfied at their nods.

'Good. Let's go.'

Too late Adam remembered the one crucial item he had forgotten. He cleared his throat. 'I . . . erm . . . I need to get something.'

Six pairs of eyes of eyes swivelled towards him. His mother made an irritated sound. 'What have you forgotten?'

Adam's cheeks felt like they were on fire. He stared at the hall floor. 'I need a handkerchief.'

There was a puzzled silence, then Nathanial put a reassuring hand on his shoulder. 'It's OK, Adam. We're not guiding a soul so we won't be swooping there. You won't need to worry about a nosebleed.'

Adam blinked at his father. 'But how are we going to get there?'

Nathanial raised an eyebrow. 'We're going to walk.'

Chapter 4

he Mortsons traipsed out into the garden. Sam and Morty were back in their pen, keystones gleaming on their collars. They were working dogs but for today they were staying at home. When they realised this their tails drooped and they whined in protest.

Nathanial nodded and everyone else clasped their keystones and stepped forward into the Hinterland. Adam blinked around, trying to get his bearings. All around them lay their familiar surroundings – the garden, the house, the dogs yelping in their pen. And yet . . . everything was different. It was hard to explain how; some quality in the light made it clear they were no longer in the physical world. Adam looked at the house. If he walked towards it he could walk right through the wall.

It was always weird being in the Hinterland. Adam could still see the physical world but he was no longer there. The keystone he always wore around his neck helped him move between worlds. Once Adam came of age and got Marked like his father he wouldn't need a keystone any more but until then he relied on it to do what he had to do.

Nathanial waited until he had their total attention. 'None of you have ever entered the Realm of the Fates before and getting there can be somewhat . . . challenging. I don't want anyone to get lost.' He avoided looking at Adam but Adam's cheeks flushed all the same.

'Oh, stop being so dramatic,' Auntie Jo grumbled. 'You'll scare us all out of our wits and then we'll definitely never get there.'

Nathanial gave her a quelling stare. Adam was getting nervous. He couldn't even swoop without almost drowning in his own blood. He'd been relieved when Nathanial said they were walking but it wasn't sounding so straightforward any longer . . .

'I don't want to frighten anyone but this really is very important. We'll all be fine but you'll need to pay close attention.' Nathanial hesitated. 'You see normally in the Hinterland we see it the way we want to see it, rather than as it actually *is*. Our minds cling on to the familiar and so it appears the Hinterland is simply laid over the physical world. In fact, the Hinterland is rather different.'

'Different how?' Luc asked. He didn't seem freaked out, just interested. For the thousandth time Adam found himself envying his brother's complete lack of fear.

Nathanial smiled and half shrugged. 'It's a little difficult to explain, so you're going to have to just trust me. We're going to start walking – it doesn't matter where, or which direction we walk in; that's not important. What *is* important is that you focus your entire mind on the token I've given you. The physical world will disappear and you'll see the Hinterland as it truly is. The shock will probably jolt you back – but that's

OK. Just take a deep breath and focus on the token, until the physical world disappears again.'

'What will we see instead?' Chloe was fidgeting with her hair, twisting it round her finger the way she always did when she was nervous.

Nathanial hesitated. 'Well, my dear . . . you'll see nothing.'

There was a long pause. Adam and Luc exchanged glances. Why was their father being so *serious*? After all, he had been to the Realm of the Fates before when he was made High Luman – and *he* had lived to tell the tale!

'What I mean is the Hinterland is simply a borderland, a place between realms. When the physical world disappears there's nothing there.'

'Right. So we just walk until everything disappears,' Auntie Jo said. 'And then . . . ?'

'A doorway will appear. A door into the Realm of the Fates.'

'Well, that doesn't sound so bad,' Auntie Jo said cheerfully. 'Really brother, you should have been on the stage! You had us all frightened to death! Shall we go?'

They started walking. Adam almost relaxed – until he saw the look that passed between Nathanial and Auntie Jo. She narrowed her eyes and shook her head almost imperceptibly. Nathanial pursed his lips and nodded. Elise was walking ahead but she had one protective hand on Chloe's shoulder. Adam frowned. There was something they weren't being told . . .

They walked for several minutes, crossing roads and gardens, moving through fences and walls. 'Ignore what's around you,' Nathanial said. 'Focus on the token in your hand.'

It was Chloe who saw what they were looking for first. She

stopped with a surprised 'Oh', blinked and looked around. 'Everything disappeared! It's back now though.'

Nathanial looked pleased – but apprehensive too. He glanced at his watch. 'Good. Now, when the physical world disappears again, keep focusing on the token. A doorway will appear. Step through it and wait for us there.' He turned to his wife. 'Elise, stay with her please.'

They kept walking. Adam was just beginning to get bored when quite suddenly Chloe and Elise disappeared. He stopped in shock. Nathanial gave him a reassuring smile. 'It's OK, Adam. They've found the doorway and gone through. Keep going.'

Aron and Luc were next to go. One second they were there; the next they were gone. Auntie Jo turned to Nathanial. 'Do you want me to wait with you?'

He shook his head. 'Best not to linger. We'll see you soon.'

She hesitated, then nodded. 'OK.' She turned to Adam, unusually serious. 'Concentrate! Hold on to the token.' She turned her back on them and walked ahead. In less than a minute she was gone.

Adam stopped, feeling rattled. Nathanial forced a smile. 'See anything . . . unusual yet?'

Adam raised an eyebrow. 'Yeah, you could say that. People keep disappearing!'

Nathanial tried to sound comforting. 'You're just getting distracted by the physical world. Try closing your eyes – there's nothing to bump into here.'

Adam gritted his teeth and closed his eyes. It was hard walking along without being able to see. His *brain* knew he wasn't going to walk into anything but his body found it freaky.

He focused on the token. It was smooth but there was a ridge at one end. He tried to send his whole mind down his arm and into his fingertips, concentrating on the hard edge.

Nathanial's soft voice broke into the silence. 'Keep your eyes closed, Adam. When you open them the physical world will be gone and in its place there will be nothing. Just grey light. Don't be frightened – no harm will come to you. Now hold the token and open your eyes.'

Adam inched one eye open a crack, then both eyes popped open with surprise. The world was gone. Nathanial hadn't been joking – *there was nothing there*! There were no cars or roads or trees, just a dim blue-grey light, like dusk. No sky above him nor ground beneath his feet, just soft, cloudy light . . . It was having nothing beneath him that jolted Adam the most. He stopped and swayed, gripped by a sudden panic. Nathanial seized his arm but it was too late. The Hinterland snapped back to normal – a pale overlay on top of the physical world. They were in the middle of a road, traffic roaring past them on either side, close enough to touch if they were in the physical world.

Nathanial squeezed his bruised arm, making Adam wince. 'That's the hardest bit over. Close your eyes and try again. Trust me. I'm right beside you.'

Adam's heartbeat was returning to something like normal. He tried to shake off his fear and to his surprise it was easy because now he was getting angry. He did pretty well at school, so why was he always so rubbish at anything Luman-related? Chloe got the hang of it faster than him, even though *she* couldn't be a Luman and only came into the Hinterland to go and visit other Lumen!

43

Strangely, being angry made it easier to concentrate. He marched forward again, eyes squeezed shut, clenching his fist so tight the stone hurt his palm. When he opened his eyes he saw only Nathanial and the dim light. 'OK, I see the grey stuff again.'

'Good!' Nathanial glanced at his watch again, sounding relieved. 'Let's walk a little faster. You're going to see a doorway ahead of you. Just give it time to appear and tell me when you see it.'

Adam kept moving, wishing the door would appear so he could get this all over with. He was fed up and his father was making him nervous. Nathanial's face was calm but his body was stiff with tension. He kept glancing around, trying to look casual, but he was alert, watching for something.

Just as Adam might have stopped and snapped at Nathanial, the doorway appeared. 'I see it!' Adam blurted out, amazed. 'It's right there in front of me!'

'Excellent!' Nathanial said. His relief was palpable. 'You timed it well. Let's go.'

Light spilled through the doorway, not unlike the Light that waited for each soul after death. The thought made Adam pause. 'We're not going on to the Unknown Roads, are we?'

'No. Keep going!' Nathanial barked, looking over his shoulder and propelling Adam along by the shoulder. 'Step through!'

Before he even knew what was happening Adam was through the doorway – and staring in wonder at the scene before him.

They were standing at the top of a vast amphitheatre. High stone steps dropped away below, doubling as seats for the

44

thousands of Lumen men and their families who had gathered. Adam blinked, trying to understand what he was seeing, but it was hard. He was looking at most of the Lumen in the world.

Behind him was a long line of arches, most of them acting as doorways from the Hinterland. Families were stepping through, alone or in pairs, then waiting anxiously for relatives to arrive or peering around the auditorium for seats. There were statues everywhere, all of women, each holding a scroll, a measuring rod or a dagger. The one nearest Adam showed a beautiful, stern-faced woman holding a rod. At the base was engraved 'Lachesis XII'. At a rapid guesstimate there must have been hundreds of statues, each representing a Fate who had served and then passed through her Light into the afterlife. The Fates had been serving for thousands of years.

Adam looked down and shivered. At the bottom of the amphitheatre was a flat semi-circular stage. A high wall ran along the back with a huge arch at the centre. Even from here Adam could see the ornate carving round the top of the arch and along the three stone plinths in the centre of the stage.

A familiar voice drawled in Adam's ear, 'I thought you were lost.' Luc grinned at his father and brother and gestured below. 'We found our seats.'

They followed him down, although Nathanial was so busy being greeted by other Lumen that they soon abandoned him. Luc led the way, nodding at some of the men and flashing his most dazzling smile every time they passed a teenage girl. He whispered to Adam, 'Just think bro, your future wife is here somewhere. I reckon that's her right there.' He pointed at a sullen-faced girl who was scowling out from beneath beetle brows. Adam caught her eye and looked away hastily.

Luc seemed to know exactly where he was going and Adam wondered how – until he noticed that behind the stone seats there were standards, the kind that ancient armies carried. Each standard bore the symbol of a Luman family but Adam only recognised a few. He probably should have paid more attention to the Luman history he'd been taught as a kid but it was always so boring, learning all the different family seals and how many High Lumen had been in their line. Elise loved all that stuff but Adam couldn't care less. After all, he might be a Mortson, but it didn't seem to have made him a better Luman.

'We're way, way down near the front,' Luc said, weaving in and out between men and women calling greetings and embracing one another. 'Mother's delighted that we're going to be so close to the Fates, although some of the French Lumen are ahead of us.'

Adam rolled his eyes. Elise had a keen sense of honour and their position in the Luman hierarchy. 'I never knew there were so many of us.'

Luc's eyes were gleaming. 'I never knew there were so many girls! And some of them are hot! Maybe I should give the whole betrothal thing a go after all.'

Adam grinned. It was the first time in his life that he had seen all the Luman families gathered together in one place, although some of the women and young children were missing. Presumably a child had to be of swooping age to have learned how to get into the Hinterland. Some of the coming-of-age balls were major events but even they would only involve a few hundred people. Death never stopped and Lumen were never totally off duty. The thought made him pause. 'What's going to happen to the souls while we're here? Who's going to guide them?'

Luc raised his eyebrows. 'Think about it, stupid. If the Fates are busy talking to us . . .'

'Then they're not going to be killing anybody,' Adam murmured, finishing Luc's sentence and feeling a little queasy.

'Exactly. Just think about it. As long as we're here and the Fates are busy, not a single person in the whole world is going to die. Freaky!'

Adam nodded, his mind boggling at the idea. He wondered how long the Summoning would last. Maybe if they could drag it on for a while they could spare a whole lot of people . . .

A familiar placard caught his eyes – a flaming torch set in a black circle. It was the Mortson seal and Auntie Jo and Chloe sat beneath it, looking doleful. Elise and Aron were standing a few rows down, making stilted conversation with some of Elise's French family. Auntie Jo stood up and gave Adam an awkward hug, her face full of relief. 'You made it, then!'

Adam pulled away, half pleased and half embarrassed. 'Of course I made it. Why wouldn't I?'

'No reason,' Auntie Jo said with a rather forced grin. 'What do you think?' She gestured at the scene before them.

'It's amazing,' Adam said truthfully. It was weird enough knowing the Hinterland lay on top of the physical world but this was another realm again. 'How many of these places are there?'

Auntie Jo shrugged. 'Who knows? If you become High Luman and get your hands on *The Book of the Unknown Roads*

47

you'd probably learn more. The Hinterland and this place are entry-level stuff. There could be thousands of realms if we only knew how to get into them.'

Chloe leapt up. 'There's Uncle Paddy!' She pointed off across the amphitheatre. Her voice dropped. 'And there's Ciaron.' Her face turned crimson and she sat down again, suddenly getting very interested in something at her feet.

Adam grinned and looked across the stone rows until he spotted 'Uncle' Paddy, High Luman of Ireland. He wasn't their uncle in the strict sense, although if you looked hard enough all Lumen were related at some level. He was wiry and vibrant, older than Nathanial with a shock of silver hair and very bright blue eyes. He was talking animatedly, waving his hands around while a spellbound group stood in front of him, mouths open, until Paddy paused and delivered the punchline. There was a roar of laughter audible across the amphitheatre. Uncle Paddy had always been brilliant at telling stories.

Beside him stood a tall, young man with broad shoulders and wavy dark hair. Adam sneaked a peek at Chloe, who was making a great show of zipping up her boot. Ciaron was Paddy's oldest son and was probably destined to be the next High Luman of Ireland, unless he came to England. There was no official betrothal yet but Adam knew that Nathanial wanted Chloe to marry Ciaron and cement the bond between the families. Elise had other ideas, much preferring a match from a larger Kingdom for her only daughter. Adam felt an unexpected wave of affection for his sister. She was only a kid! If she'd been at school she would have been a third year, moaning about homework and giggling with her mates. How could anybody be thinking about her getting betrothed, even if she wouldn't actually be married off for a few years yet?

'You got here just in time.' Auntie Jo interrupted his thoughts, nodding at the front. 'The Concilium have arrived.'

Adam followed her glance and watched the thirteen members of the Concilium appear from the huge archway at the front of the amphitheatre. They trooped in a line behind Heinrich the Chief Curator, a close friend of Nathanial's. Last time Adam had seen Heinrich he'd been hiding in his father's study trying not to sneeze. The memory was uncomfortable.

The other Lumen had noticed the Concilium's arrival and were returning to their seats. Luc had bounded off to join Aron and Elise talking to some of the French Lumen, but he returned to his seat before they did and slipped in beside Adam. 'Mother's in bad form. *Grandmère* is being a right *vache*.'

Adam had to think for a second and then stifled a laugh. His grandmother was usually a cow to Elise. It was one of those things that was never discussed but Adam knew it was because of Elise's choice of husband. For some reason Nathanial simply wasn't good enough, even if he had turned out to be one of the youngest ever High Lumen. No doubt his grandmother was looking at the Curators and wishing Elise had married Darian, the newest member of the Concilium, just as she had been supposed to.

His mother slid past him, her lips compressed into a thin line. A few seconds later Nathanial joined them, having torn himself away from all the other Lumen. He looked cheerful.

A hush was falling over the amphitheatre and the light was dimming. The last voices fell silent as the Concilium sat down in the front row, leaving Heinrich alone on his feet in the centre of the stage. He smiled at the gathering and waited to let a few last-minute stragglers find a seat.

'My dear friends, how joyful I am to welcome you to the Realm of the Lady Fates. How rarely it is that so many of us can gather together!' He paused and positively beamed around the amphitheatre. 'And on such an auspicious occasion! The Lady Atropos has finally revoked her long service and stepped into her Light. Our Light is her Light.'

'Our Light is her Light,' the thousands of Lumen responded, the hushed sound sending a prickle down Adam's spine.

'And so we have a new Lady Fate to join our esteemed Clotho and Lachesis.' Heinrich paused, apparently choosing his words carefully. 'It has been customary for the Lady Fates to take the Greek names but our new Fate has chosen to take the Roman name. She will therefore be known as the Lady Morta.'

There was a shocked silence followed by a murmur of discontent. A few voices even raised in protest and the noise of the crowd rose to a subdued roar. Elise was talking excitedly in Nathanial's ear while Auntie Jo simply sat back and grinned around at the audience's discomfort. 'We're not very good at change, are we?' she whispered to Adam. 'They can't even let a woman change her own name. And poor Chloe talks about becoming a Luman . . .'

Adam shrugged. He couldn't really see what all the fuss was about. He didn't care if she called herself Princess Twinkle; he was more concerned about what she actually *did*. Atropos – or Morta – was the thread-cutter. Whenever a Luman went on a call-out it was because she had severed the thread of a human life – just as one day she would sever his own life's thread. The thought made him shiver.

Heinrich raised a hand and after a long moment the murmur of protest died away. Wisely he decided to say no more about the change of name and simply announced, 'I present to you the Lady Fates.'

Chapter 5

oly crap!' Luc whispered. 'Who the hell is *that?*'

Adam didn't even have to ask who he was talking about. As Heinrich sat down three women walked through the gigantic arch in the wall behind and each stepped up to a stone plinth.

The first woman was short and curvy with messy, blonde hair and a round, kindly face. She was wearing a smock and a long sparkly skirt. A spindle hung from the woven belt around her hips. Adam guessed she was Clotho, the spinner. She looked nice; the kind of person who would spin you a happy soul and a long life.

In contrast the second woman was thin and angular, dark hair pulled back in a bun, dressed in a grey suit which looked like it had been cut to fit with a razor. She had the twitchy energy of a hornet. Lachesis was the time-allotter. Adam could see her tapping a thin, silver measuring rod against her thigh, the symbol of her authority to measure out lifespans. She didn't look as kind as Clotho. There would be no begging or pleading with Lachesis – Adam got the feeling she would measure out every human lifespan with ruthless precision, down to the last second. No one – not him, not Chloe, not Auntie Jo – would have a moment longer in the physical world than they were meant to have.

The third woman was the cause of Luc's slobbering reverence. In spike heels, she towered over the other two, with a tousled mane of black hair and shining dark eyes. She was wearing black trousers and a corset the colour of fresh blood. She was very beautiful – more beautiful even than Elise – but something about her made a chill run down Adam's spine. There was a shimmer of something in the air around her, something dangerous.

Luc had no such reservations. His mouth was hanging open in a most un-Luc-like manner. Adam nudged him in the ribs. 'Are you all right?'

Luc blinked. 'What? Yeah, I'm OK. Better than OK.' He looked like he'd been hit by a car.

Adam smirked. This was classic Luc. In the physical world he could have his pick of any girl he wanted, so of course he decided to drool over Morta, the most fearsome of the Fates. She didn't just cut the threads – she looked like she might even enjoy it.

The small blonde woman stepped onto her podium. 'The Lady Clotho welcomes you.' She smiled, shy but warm. 'I spun your threads with care.'

The second woman stepped up. 'The Lady Lachesis welcomes you. I measured your threads with care.' She spoke with the brisk detachment of an accountant facing a never-ending sea

53

of paperwork. Maybe she couldn't see all the faces in the darkness of the amphitheatre.

Finally the third woman stepped onto her podium and stared into the crowd. Adam shivered, knowing it was insane; knowing that she couldn't see him. She tilted her head to one side and a small sigh escaped from Luc's lips. 'The Lady Morta welcomes you.' She paused, challenging her audience to protest but the amphitheatre was as still as the grave. 'I will cut your threads . . . with care.' She sounded like she was barely suppressing laughter.

Heinrich and the Concilium stood up and all the men followed. Adam made to stand up too but Elise hissed, '*Non!* Only Marked Lumen!' Adam slunk back into his seat and watched his father and all the other male Lumen who had come of age bow deeply. 'We honour you and serve you.' Their voices echoed, thunderous, rolling along the walls, leaving a great silence behind.

Heinrich faced the audience. 'My friends –'

'A moment, Chief Curator'. Morta had spoken. Heinrich turned, startled. She beckoned. After a moment's hesitation he moved towards her as a murmur rose in the amphitheatre.

'What's she doing?' Auntie Jo muttered. 'This isn't how it's supposed to be done. They're supposed to bugger off now and let us go home for dinner.'

Heinrich seemed equally surprised – not to mention uncomfortable. He faced the crowd and tried to smile. 'In . . . erm . . . a departure from the usual proceedings, the Lady Morta wishes to become acquainted with some of our noble Luman families. Specifically the British Lumen.' He hesitated. 'More specifically, our good friends the Mortson family.'

54

If Elise had seemed tense before, she positively vibrated with nervous energy now. A stunned silence had followed Heinrich's announcement, during which he had swiftly dismissed the gathering while Adam and his family blinked stupidly at one another. The other Lumen immediately began filing back up the steps, some rushing towards the arches at the top of the amphitheatre. As they hurried past the Mortsons they stared with a mixture of curiosity and pity. It was obvious that not everyone was as desperate to meet Morta as Luc was. The Fates had already returned through the huge archway, leaving the Concilium on the stage.

Elise ran a frantic but practised eye over her children, tweaking Aron's lapel, straightening Adam's tie and smoothing Chloe's hair. Her mouth was a tight line. Nathanial was just as confused as the rest of them but he was trying to look calm. 'What a pleasant surprise.'

Auntie Jo snorted and said something rude under her breath. 'What the hell's she playing at?'

'Ssssssssh!' Elise hissed. With a start Adam realised that she was afraid.

As the amphitheatre emptied, Heinrich searched for Nathanial and made a gesture towards the stage. Nathanial smoothed the lapel of his camel-hair coat and tried to smile. 'Well, this is a great honour of course. Very few Lumen ever get to meet the Fates in person.' He hesitated. 'Although it's probably better not to say too much when we go through.'

'Say nothing!' Elise whispered. Her eyes were glittering. 'Say nothing at all!'

She was starting to freak Adam out. As they descended the stairs towards the stage, Adam felt his heart thudding. His

55

palms were sweating and he tried to wipe them discreetly on his thighs. Everyone was nervous – but he was the only one who had anything to be nervous about. He was the only one who'd been running round saving people, breaking Luman law and cheating the thread-cutter out of souls.

Heinrich was waiting for them. If he was surprised by the turn of events he was hiding it well. He greeted them all with smiles. 'How lovely to see you all again – and so soon!'

Adam shifted from foot to foot. A few weeks earlier the Concilium had joined the Mortsons for dinner. Adam had spent an unfortunate half-hour hiding in a cupboard, overhearing a conversation he really shouldn't have, in which Heinrich discussed his own approaching death. He squinted sidelong at the Chief Curator, searching for any sign of ill health, but Heinrich looked perfectly well.

Nathanial arched one eyebrow. 'Indeed. And what an honour to be singled out so.' His tone was light but he gave Heinrich a searching look.

Heinrich grimaced. 'No doubt the Lady Morta will make her intentions clear.'

Nathanial nodded. Adam frowned, aware that there was subtext to what was being said but not managing to figure out what it was. He glanced around at the rest of the Curators who made up the Concilium. They were the Luman authorities who oversaw all the Lumen in the world and ensured that they followed Luman law. Being so close to them made Adam nervous – and one in particular made him sweat.

Darian, the newest Curator, was standing to one side, away from the rest of the Concilium. He had also been at the Mortsons' dinner party just a few weeks earlier – and had started an almighty row. He had accused Nathanial of having a rogue Luman on the loose in his Kingdom – a rogue who was interfering with the Fates and saving human lives. The Mortsons had reacted with fury – never suspecting that not only was Darian right but the culprit was sitting at the table with them. Adam felt a twinge of guilt all over again. It didn't help that he had found out the same night that Darian had once hoped to marry Elise – giving the French man further reason to hate Nathanial and watch for problems in his Kingdom.

Heinrich cleared his throat and made a gesture towards the archway. 'Shall we?' Adam swallowed hard, trying not to choke on his own nerves, and followed the group.

The archway led into a high-roofed tunnel. Walking through they found themselves in a small atrium with three tunnels leading off in different directions. Adam was one of the last to squeeze into the atrium, just in time to hear Morta speaking. 'Please join me.' She turned towards the tunnel on the far right when a small voice piped up from the front of the crowd. 'Please, sister, may I also join you?'

Morta turned sharply and for a fleeting second her face darkened. It was Clotho who had spoken – the spinner. Adam stared at the small blonde woman curiously. She was the one who had woven their threads – a kind of creator, even if she was just taking orders like the rest of them. She sounded timid. Morta gave her a look of barely concealed contempt, then shrugged. 'As you wish, *sister*.' She turned to Lachesis. 'And you?'

'I have no wish to join you. I bid you all good day.' Lachesis gave the group a curt nod and disappeared into the middle tunnel.

Morta stepped into her tunnel. After a moment's hesitation Clotho followed her and the rest of the group straggled along behind.

Adam fell into step beside Auntie Jo. 'They don't seem to like each other much,' he whispered.

Auntie Jo shrugged. 'Why should they? They get thrown together and left to work – but they all have different characters and do different things. It must be hard weaving the threads of life and then knowing someone is going to come along and sever them, even if they have to. I'm surprised Clotho wants to be around Morta at all.'

'But I thought they were sisters,' Adam said, confused.

Auntie Jo rolled her eyes. 'I swear I have wasted my life trying to teach you *anything* about your Luman heritage. They're not actual sisters, you idiot. It's just a title. The way Lumen say, "Our Light is your Light, brother." It doesn't mean they're literally brothers.'

'Oh, right,' Adam muttered, feeling sheepish. It was so much easier remembering chemical equations than remembering the vast and complex history and lore of the Luman world.

Auntie Jo sighed. 'Try not to say anything in here that will show your ignorance or I'll have to listen to an earful from your mother when we get home. She never believes I taught you a thing. Seems to think I spent your childhood feeding you toast and showing you zombie films.'

Adam grinned. There was more truth in that than even Elise could have dared to imagine.

They stepped out of the tunnel into a large, marble-floored hallway. A crystal chandelier hung overhead, scattering fragments of light onto the Lumen below. Velvet-covered couches were dotted around and at one end of the hallway was a long buffet table, covered with cold meats, bread, fruit and wine.

Morta turned to face them and made an expansive gesture. 'Welcome. You are my guests. Please – eat, drink and be merry. For, as someone once said, tomorrow we die.' She smiled and her dark eyes sparkled. Adam shivered.

For a long moment no one moved. Then Darian stepped towards the table and poured wine into a crystal glass. His action seemed to break some kind of spell and hesitantly the rest of the Concilium and the Mortsons moved forward. Morta clapped her hands above her head and from nowhere the sound of music filled the hall.

'Bloody drama queen,' Auntie Jo muttered – then made a beeline for the buffet.

Only Luc held back. Adam turned towards him, curious. 'What's the matter with you?' He had to admit to a certain sneaky enjoyment of Luc's discomfiture. His brother was normally poise personified.

Luc scowled. 'Nothing! Nothing's the matter!' He stalked towards the wine with furrowed brows.

Adam grinned but it was short-lived. He always felt awkward at Luman events – but this was in a whole different league. This time he was at a gathering hosted by the very Fate he had cheated out of an awful lot of souls. According to *The Book of the Unknown Roads* (the book of Luman law and wisdom) the penalty for that particular offence involved his own demise – if Morta found out.

Feeling jumpy, he sidled over towards his father, trying to look inconspicuous. Nathanial was deep in conversation with Heinrich and looked irritated at Adam's sudden appearance – but then seemed to take pity on his youngest son. 'Everything all right, Adam?'

Heinrich smiled at him. 'So, Adam, this is a great occasion! An event you will be able to tell your children and grandchildren about!'

Adam tried to return the smile, forcing himself to ignore the nervous churning he got in his stomach just thinking about the life he was supposed to live. Become a proper Luman, come of age and get Marked, get married to someone with noble Luman blood and of course produce Luman babies who would grow up to become Lumen themselves. 'Yeah, it's all pretty . . . special.'

Nathanial laughed. 'Heinrich, believe it or not Adam would rather be at school doing his GECs than here.'

Adam sighed. 'GCSEs. They're called GCSEs. For, like, the billionth time.'

'How very strange,' a woman's voice said and all three of them froze. Adam turned slowly and found himself looking up at Morta. She towered over him in her heels but was able to look Nathanial straight in the eye. 'How very strange that a young Luman from such a family should still be at school.'

Nathanial bowed his head. 'We prefer to think of it as unusual, Lady Morta.'

Morta smiled without warmth. 'Perhaps that is a better word. And is there anything else *unusual* about this boy?'

Adam stared at the ground, wracking his brain for something to say, but his mind had gone blank. Those eyes. They seemed to look right through him, turning him into a rabbit in headlights. There was some force around her that made him want to blurt out everything, just tell her he was guilty and that he was sorry and he hadn't meant to do it . . .

'He'll grow into his Luman role,' Nathanial said politely but there was an edge to his voice.

'I wonder who he takes after?' Morta said. Her voice was very soft and very poisonous. 'I was led to believe that you Mortsons are such an *old* family. So many *Keystones*! I was told your family had some talent. Well, most of your family. Not every family member has shared your aspirations for greatness.'

A glass smashed behind them, breaking the moment. Morta turned away sharply and Adam gulped in a deep breath, feeling like a weight had lifted from his chest. Auntie Jo was standing behind them, glaring at Morta with pure hatred. Adam felt a moment of confusion. All right, Auntie Jo hadn't married but she was taking Morta's words a bit personally.

'What did you just say?' Auntie Jo was looking up at Morta, unflinching. 'Is there something you'd like to say?'

'Jo.' Nathanial stepped towards his sister and curled his fingers round her arm. His voice was a mixture of comfort and warning.

'Every member of our family did their best to serve humanity. We have a long, proud history. Every one of us made sacrifices for the greater good. *Every one.*' Auntie Jo's voice was a hiss.

Morta smiled, her lip curling slightly. 'Of course. I meant no offence.' She inclined her head. 'Please do excuse me. I must attend to my other guests.'

Adam watched her walk away through saucer eyes. When he turned back towards his father he could see Nathanial was furious but trying hard to maintain his composure. 'That was unwise.'

Auntie Jo gave him a look of deepest contempt. It was shocking, as if she'd slapped him. 'I've had enough of this. I didn't come here to have our b—' She cleared her throat. 'To have our family insulted. Who does she think she is?' She was clutching the silver locket she always wore around her neck, pulling it to and fro in agitation.

Heinrich spoke up. His voice was stern but not unkind. 'She thinks she is the thread-cutter – and she is. Please remember that, Josephine.'

Auntie Jo scowled. 'She's just a monkey taking orders like the rest of us. She might pretend she's the organ grinder – but she's not.'

Nathanial sighed. He looked as depressed as Auntie Jo. 'How much longer will Lady Morta require our presence?'

Heinrich shrugged and lowered his voice. 'I'm every bit as surprised by her invitation, my friend. I hope we won't be detained much longer.'

Adam shivered. So they weren't really guests, so much as . . . captives. He looked over at their hostess. She was talking to Elise. His mother was clutching hold of Chloe and Luc with a protective hand on their arms. When Morta turned her attentions to Luc, Adam could almost see his mother willing Luc to stay silent. Unfortunately Luc was smitten. He was beaming and babbling like a lunatic. Under other circumstances it would have been funny.

Morta's voice rang out around the room, killing all conversation in an instant. 'I will speak with you all. But first, there is something I wish you to see. Come, this way.' She walked towards what appeared to be a blank wall but as they drew closer Adam could see a double door set into the stone. Morta raised her hands and the doors swung open soundlessly, revealing nothing but darkness on the other side. Morta strode forward, disappearing from view. After a moment's hesitation the Concilium followed her, with the Mortsons bringing up the rear.

Adam's heart was thumping. There was no reason to be so afraid, safe with his family and the Concilium, but there was something about Morta. Stepping into the dark with her was a bit like stepping into a dark cave, wondering if there was a wolf sleeping there . . .

The doors swung closed behind them, leaving them in pitch-darkness. Adam heard Chloe give a little gasp and Elise's comforting murmur. Then flaming torches flared into light, illuminating a long spiral staircase ascending into nothingness far above. 'Come,' Morta said and led the way up the stairs. After a moment's hesitation everyone followed. Their footsteps were strangely muffled.

They climbed for a long time. Adam could feel his calves starting to burn and he could hear Auntie Jo huffing for breath just ahead of him. The torches were dim and the constant spiral in the staircase began to make Adam's head swim. At one point he tottered backwards and panic-stricken, realised he was about to fall – until he felt Nathanial's strong hand grip his shoulder and gently right him.

At last the stairs ended – but unfortunately so did the torchlight. Adam shuffled forward blindly, afraid of crashing into someone. He heard Nathanial emerge on the stairs behind him. It was hard to know why but Adam had the sense that they were in the centre of a cavernous space. The group was totally silent. The darkness was immense and somehow profound. For a long, ludicrous moment Adam felt like crying.

'There is nothing to fear, Lumen,' Morta said softly from the blackness. 'I only wish to show you a wonder. Behold, the Tapestry of Light.'

Chapter 6

or a moment nothing happened. Then, just ahead of Adam the faintest glow appeared. He squinted, trying to see what would emerge. The glow intensified, before flaring suddenly into light all around them. A gasp and murmur rose from the crowd.

All around them the walls were alive with the light of billions of fireflies. The room was circular. The staircase had emerged at the centre of a giant sphere, a kind of globe of the world. But this globe was unlike any map Adam had ever seen before.

The lights wove a living dance, forming the outlines of countries and continents. Adam wasn't sure how he knew this because the shape and size of the countries was completely different to anything he had ever learned in geography. This map hadn't been drawn by political ambition or human pride. This was a map of human souls.

China was easy to spot. It covered a vast area – a dense, pulsating mass of lights with uninhabited zones in the west. To the north lay Russia; to the east a glittering chain of islands that could only be Japan. And further east again, across the Pacific, lay the Americas, bold and bright in places, sparsely populated in others. Adam stared mesmerised from country to country – the teeming lights of the Indian and African Kingdoms; tiny jewel-like Mediterranean islands; the vast darkness of the Poles and oceans.

Morta moved towards the lights. 'Billions of souls,' she said softly, running a caressing hand through the air in front of the wall. 'Souls at every stage of mortal life; threads growing brighter – and threads dimming.'

It was true. As Adam looked more closely he could see she was right. Some threads were writhing and burning with light while others wove through in the background, glowing softly. Some threads blazed red or gold while others were more muted shades of cool blue, soft green or lavender. And in every country on earth a handful of souls glowed with a steady white light.

'Threads dancing towards me.' Something glittered in her hand and Adam realised with a shudder that she was holding the Mortal Knife. This close he could see how long and fine the point was, a blade made for delicate, deadly accuracy. Morta moved the tip towards one of the white lights. 'See how the Luman's soul shines so very fiercely in the Tapestry. And yet one day even these threads will be cut.'

She turned towards the group and her voice was sweet but poisonous. 'All souls pass through my hands on their way to the Hinterland and their Light and . . . beyond. All souls have their time – but mine is the right to harvest some before their allotted time. My quota. Souls chosen by me, taken in their prime. You Mortsons of all Lumen understand this because you

66

guide these very souls.' She shook her head. 'Their threads still burn so bright. Death must be so unexpected for them.' She shook her head, feigning sympathy, and in one black second Adam realised that he hated her.

'*This is the law!*' Morta's voice changed and now the cavern echoed with the sudden, harsh sound. 'I may take the souls I please. It is for the Concilium to uphold the law in these matters.' She looked around the silent men standing before her. 'I trust you will all remember your duties, should anyone be so foolish as to cheat me of what is rightfully mine.'

Heinrich bowed his head but there was an edge to his voice. 'Of course, Lady Morta. Although I understand that it is within your power to limit the number of souls taken before their time. To ignore your quota and let some of these souls have their allotted time?'

Morta appeared not to hear him. She pointed to a tiny, sparkling mass to the east of a vast ocean of blackness. 'The Kingdom of Britain. Observe the white lights.' She smiled at the group. 'Those, dear Lumen, are *your* souls. Someday they too shall meet the Mortal Knife. Let us hope that is a distant day.'

Adam stared at the lights mesmerised, wondering which one was his own. He understood Morta's message only too well. She was sending a warning. She *knew* that someone was saving souls. If he kept doing it she would exact her revenge – and she would exact it on the Mortsons.

It was a subdued group that trailed down the spiral staircase in Morta's wake, back into her chamber. The 'party' dragged on, Morta chattering gaily as though nothing had happened, but there was a fresh tension in the air. Most of Adam's family seemed confused. Nathanial put on a brave face but Adam knew he understood the message. Heinrich had warned him that there was a rogue in the Kingdom interfering with the Fates. What Nathanial *didn't* realise was that the rogue was his own son.

Adam sighed, wishing he was at home. A movement caught his eye. Clotho the thread-spinner was hovering on the edge of the crowd, silent and withdrawn. Her eyes roamed over the group, studying each face in turn. When she came to Adam their eyes locked. Adam stared and she stared back, curious and unabashed, the way little kids did. For just a second her eyes widened but a moment later she turned and disappeared into the tunnel behind.

The minutes dragged by, until finally Morta seemed to have had enough of their company. She raised her hands in the air and the music stopped abruptly. The chatter of conversation died in an instant. 'Such a pleasure. Alas, I can spare you no more time.' She smiled. 'There are threads which need to be cut. Hurry home, Lumen!'

A chill ran down Adam's spine. For the whole time they had been there not one person on earth had died. He had a feeling Morta would make up for lost time.

She led the way to an alcove in the wall and pulled back a tapestry, revealing a door of ebony wood. Morta opened the door and smiled at them all. 'Farewell, Lumen. Perhaps we shall meet again someday.' She looked around the group, her eyes lingering on Luc. He tried to stare boldly back but Adam could see the uncharacteristic flush in his brother's face. Morta shook hands with each of them in turn as they left. Auntie Jo could barely contain herself but managed to touch her palm to Morta's without spitting in it first.

Adam was the last in line, Nathanial keeping him close. 'It's much easier getting home Adam but stay close to me. Once we're back in the Hinterland we can swoop as normal.'

Adam nodded, dreading returning to the weird grey light beyond Morta's realm. As he shuffled along behind the others his foot struck something and it rolled in front of him. He frowned and bent down to pick it up. It looked like a tiny black marble until he turned it over and saw the earring mount on the back. He grinned. At least Morta could lose things like anyone else. It reminded him that she was still human.

He was going to give it back to her but Nathanial had noticed his hesitation and frowned, ushering him towards the door. Not wanting to draw attention to himself, Adam shoved the earring in his pocket and managed to shake Morta's hand without making eye contact. Even the gloom of the Hinterland seemed more attractive if it meant escaping from her.

Still, passing through the doorway was scary. Stepping from a marble floor into grey nothingness made Adam's head spin. He closed his eyes, feeling sick and disorientated until he felt Nathanial's firm grip on his arm. 'It's OK, Adam. Just wait a moment. I need to speak to Heinrich and then we'll go home.'

Adam nodded and managed to ease his eyes open without falling over. The door into the Realm of the Fates had disappeared and he was back in the same dim light as before. The others had already swooped home. Nathanial and Heinrich stood a little distance away and Adam tried not to listen to their conversation, but in the deathly silence of the Hinterland it was hard not to hear even their lowered voices.

Heinrich's face was serious. 'So, a message then. It appears that our Lady Fate is paying close attention.'

Nathanial nodded, looking grim. 'Message received. I'll be watching.'

Heinrich looked relieved. 'Good. Let us think of happier matters. We have many things to celebrate.'

There was a sound in the distance. Adam paused and looked up. It was a strange hissing, rattling noise. It wasn't near but it was coming closer, the way a thunderstorm could move. He squinted into the gloom. Far off the light was changing. It looked darker.

Heinrich and Nathanial had noticed it too. 'The Fates are cautious today,' Heinrich said wryly. He embraced Nathanial. 'Best not to tarry.' He beckoned to Adam and shook his hand. 'Goodbye Adam. I look forward to seeing you all soon. My Light is your Light.'

Adam and Nathanial repeated his words and watched him disappear. The hissing sound was growing louder. Adam peered around him. 'What *is* that?'

Nathanial took his arm. 'Nothing to worry about. Come on. It's time to go home.' Adam clutched his keystone and a second later the Hinterland was gone.

Minutes later, back in the confines of his bedroom, Adam gave a sigh of relief. He had survived the encounter unscathed. Morta hadn't been joking when she said there were threads to cut – they had barely re-entered the physical world before

Mortson death senses had flared and Nathanial had swooped away to guide an unsuspecting soul into the afterlife.

Adam had lost all sense of time in the Realm of the Fates but he knew they'd been there for at least a few hours. Weirdly they returned home and found that only a few minutes had passed in the physical world. It was clear that time passed differently in the Realm of the Fates, which probably explained how the Fates lived longer than Lumen. He made a mental note to ask Auntie Jo about it – and this time he promised himself he would actually *listen* to what she told him.

His relief was slightly overshadowed by the guilt of knowing Morta was watching the Mortsons. He had an awful feeling he was pushing his luck with the whole saving people thing, including the girl earlier that day. The trouble was, how could you just stop doing it when you knew the consequences were so huge? He had the chance to keep people on earth, alive and well. It had seemed worth the risk but now that he had seen the Mortal Knife he had a feeling he needed to lie low for a while.

Adam sighed. It was time to switch his head from the life and death of people to the life and death of earthworms. Biology homework was always a riot.

Chapter 7

he following day Adam spent a nervous morning in school. Melissa had been absent at the start of registration, only to slip in towards the end. Adam's heart did its usual flip-flop at the sight of her but once again she played it cool, giving him the merest hint of a smile. It seemed she didn't want to make a big thing of meeting up with him later.

The first two periods dragged by. When the breaktime bell rang Adam could have wept with relief. His concentration was shot to hell that morning. As he headed towards the library he ran into Dan, who was mooching along looking pensive. At the sight of Adam he jerked his head in greeting. 'All right?'

Adam nodded. 'Yeah. You all right?'

Dan shrugged. 'Yeah.' He hesitated and looked around to make sure no one was listening. 'I had to go and see that counsellor last night.'

'Oh right.' Adam paused, not sure what to say. To his shame he really wanted to know what they had talked about. It wasn't any of his business but he *did* have a vested interest in knowing what Dan had said.

Luckily Dan was only too happy to tell him. 'Yeah, it was all right. She was OK. There weren't any dolls though.'

Adam grinned. 'Don't tell Archie. He'll be really disappointed.'

Dan was looking thoughtful. 'I didn't tell her about the photo. Spike said not to tell anyone about it yet until he tries to clean it up and gets a look at the faces.' He paused for a moment. 'Do you think he got away? Not the bomber, the other guy?'

Adam groaned inwardly. He picked his words with care. 'Well, he must have done, if they didn't find any bits of him.'

Dan nodded. 'I hope he did. Only – I just don't see how he could have. He was really close.'

Adam shrugged, trying to sound bored. 'Maybe he ran past the bomber. And then when the bomb went off you couldn't see him because he was behind it.'

'Maybe.' Dan didn't sound convinced. 'He must have been a really fast runner. The bomb went off about five seconds after I took that photo.'

'Look, just forget about it, will you? Stop going on about it! It's over and done with. It's like Spike said – some nutter blew himself up. Just be happy *you're* alive.' Adam's tone was sharper than he had intended.

Dan looked wounded for a second. 'I'm just saying.'

Adam felt a pang of guilt. Just because he was used to death and dismemberment didn't mean everyone else was. 'Yeah, I know mate. Sorry. It's pretty crap seeing that on your holiday.'

Dan shrugged. 'Yeah, it was.' He paused. 'Although it would be kind of cool if the other guy got away. Because he'd *have* to be a ninja then. Or have some kind of weird power. That would be amazing – if we found proof that ninjas existed.'

'I guess.'

'I like thinking about it. That there's more to the world than what you can see here.' Dan waved a hand around the bustling corridor. 'If we found ninjas were real there could be loads of other stuff real as well. Vampires and werewolves and the Loch Ness Monster. At least it wouldn't be boring.'

'There's nothing wrong with this world. Boring is good,' Adam said quietly. Sometimes he envied Dan and his friends, living safely in the 'real' world. Not knowing that the Mortal Knife was hovering over their lives like an eagle over a mouse, way up high, out of sight.

Dan didn't seem convinced but he grinned suddenly. 'So you're seeing Melissa later?'

'Yeah, probably.' It was a relief to change the subject.

Dan winked. 'Don't worry. We'll help you come up with a plan.'

Adam almost rolled his eyes but managed not to. 'Great. Can't wait.'

They had reached the library. Dan sank into his usual seat. 'Operation hook, line and sinker. That's what we'll call it.'

'Call what?' Archie mumbled from behind a graphic novel. There was no sign of Spike.

Dan pulled out a packet of dry roasted peanuts and tipped them into a pile on the table. 'Adam's plan to catch the fish and keep her.'

'*Stop calling her a fish!*' Adam hissed. He had a sudden uncomfortable image of Melissa swimming round in a fishbowl, mermaid style. He was glad no one else could see inside his head.

'Well, not throwing up on her would be a good start,' Archie sniggered. 'Sharing is caring and all that but I'm pretty sure that's a step too far.'

'What are you going to do at lunchtime?' Dan asked, his face intent.

Adam shrugged. 'Dunno. Probably just walk about a bit.' He stared at their riveted faces and scowled. 'Stop going on about it, will you? We're just going to hang out. It's fine.'

'I suppose,' Dan said, looking doubtful. 'Just try to play it cool.'

'Not possible,' Spike said from behind them. 'Better to *be* cool than to play it cool. Cool like me, for example.' He sat down, opened his laptop and turned it towards them. 'Victory is mine!'

Adam felt his jaw drop as he took in the image on the screen – followed by the bottom of his stomach. Spike hadn't been exaggerating about what he could achieve with his modified software.

They were looking at Dan's photo of the bomber and the mystery figure with him – only this time everything was magically clearer. Spike zoomed in on the figures. 'Took a while to clean it up. Had to play about with the contrast and sharpen it a good bit but it was worth it.'

Adam stared at the screen, speechless. It was like looking at a ghost – literally. He could see the bomber's face, still a little blurred on screen but burned into Adam's memory – the short brown hair and wispy goatee, thin frame and of course the huge rucksack like a turtle shell on his back. And far worse he

75

could see *himself*. The one thing saving him from immediate discovery was his 'disguise', the baseball cap and sunglasses he had worn. His face was turned slightly away from the camera but the profile of his nose and chin was clear enough, at least to him. He instinctively put his hand up to his cheek, trying to hide anything recognisable.

'There's some sort of logo on the hat. There.' Dan pointed at the screen. 'Right there.'

Spike zoomed in a little more and Adam almost choked. How the hell was he getting it so clear?! Dan had been miles away but whatever technical wizardry Spike had worked was bringing the picture way too close for comfort. 'He's probably just a tourist. It'll be some kind of I love London hat.'

Archie shook his head. 'Move your finger Dan!' He squinted at the screen. 'I think I've seen that somewhere before.' He frowned, trying to remember.

Adam felt sick. He could tell them exactly what it was. It was a dolphin wearing sunglasses. Dan had brought them all the same hat back from a holiday in America, a souvenir from some kind of water park. Adam cursed his own stupidity. He'd worn the baseball cap because it was black, ignoring the cheesy little logo. After all, what were the odds that he would be snapped wearing it by one of the few people who might recognise it – and him?

'Can you zoom in any more?' His voice was scratchy with anxiety.

Luckily Spike was too absorbed in his masterwork to notice. 'Nah. Seriously, I did well getting that much. You can see a lot more of the bomber, but this guy's facing the wrong way.' Just as Adam might have started breathing more easily Spike traced his finger along the figure's chin. 'Still, you can see his nose and his jawline. I have a couple of ideas for what I can do with that.'

Archie looked sceptical. 'I don't see how that's going to help. I mean it could be anyone.'

Spike looked smug. 'Yeah but you don't have the contacts I have.' He leaned in closer and lowered his voice. 'There's this guy I know from a hacking forum. He used to work for the CIA but they kicked him out for something. Anyway, he's one of those survivalist types, really paranoid – but he nicked a lot of their software when he was going. He reckons he has something that can analyse facial profiles and run a web search for matching photos. *Everyone* has a photo on the web somewhere. You just have to be patient. So if we're lucky it might throw something up. We might just track down our ninja.'

'A ninja's hardly going to have a photo album online, is he?' Adam was trying to sound dismissive but his voice was coming out all wrong.

Spike shrugged. 'Even ninjas make mistakes.'

Adam stood up. He could feel his heart beating at the back of his throat. 'Why are you making such a big thing about this?'

Spike scowled. 'What's your problem?'

Adam's mouth was moving and he knew it was out of control but somehow he couldn't make it stop. 'You! *You're* the problem! Snooping around on your computer all the time! Haven't you anything better to do? Why don't you give it a rest? Play football! Get a hobby or a girlfriend or something, like normal people do, instead of poking through other people's lives!'

Colour flared in Spike's cheeks but his face stayed deadly

calm. 'Oh right. So *you've* got a girlfriend now and we're all supposed to be like *you*. It was *me* "poking about" on the computer that got rid of all the videos of you throwing up on her. She wouldn't be seeing you again if the whole school was still laughing at her and the sick on her shoes.'

Archie was colouring in something in his sketchbook. His face was hidden but he was moving his pencil just a little bit too hard. 'Yeah, and she's not your *girlfriend*, is she? She just wants to hang out at lunchtime. You'll probably do something stupid today anyway.'

'Or maybe the Beast will get hold of you,' Dan added helpfully. At least he didn't seem to be taking the 'get a girlfriend' comment as personally as the other two. 'Anyway, what's wrong with knowing who the guy in the picture is? Maybe he's a ninja and he's OK – but maybe he's just normal and he's dead. He might have loads of people looking for him. His mum and all.'

Adam's mouth moved soundlessly. He had totally overreacted and now he couldn't see any way back from it. 'Yeah, well . . . Just because you *can* do something doesn't mean you should.'

'Right, unless it helps you, is that what you mean?' Spike was sneering but he was angry beneath the sneer. 'I can hack away if it helps you get a girlfriend and be Mr Normal.'

There was nothing Adam could say. Somehow he had managed to offend all his friends in one go. He knew he should probably apologise but the words just wouldn't come out. 'Whatever,' he muttered and grabbed his schoolbag just as the bell rang. He headed for the door with a sinking heart.

He basically couldn't have done anything more to encourage Spike if he'd tried.

***

The next two periods passed in a misery of anxiety. Adam tried and failed to concentrate on the history of the Weimar Republic but all he could think about was how the hell he was going to explain it if his identity was revealed. He chewed on the end of his pen, wondering if Spike was exaggerating. Could there really be such a thing as facial recognition software? And how many photos would Adam have on the internet? He hadn't done anything noteworthy enough to end up on the school website and the Mortsons had a strict ban on social media. It was possible that there wasn't a single photo of him on the internet – unless of course his friends had uploaded his photo to their pages. There was no way of asking at the minute without being even more suspicious so he would have to leave it and hope Spike was blagging it.

The one bittersweet side effect of Adam's terror was that he didn't have time to worry about meeting Melissa. The minutes seemed to drag by – but suddenly it was lunchtime. It was only as Adam made his way towards the canteen that he realised they hadn't actually arranged a meeting point. He stood in the foyer outside, shovelling his sandwich in and shifting from foot to foot. He wished he'd thought to bring some mints but at least his sandwich was ham, not tuna.

Someone tapped his left shoulder, sending a bolt of agony down his bruised arm. He turned and saw Melissa. It was hard not to just stare and stare. How did she always look so nice? She was just wearing the same uniform everyone else was but there was a kind of glow about her. He studied her face. She was wearing make-up but only a little bit. Her eyes weren't quite as disturbingly laser-like without the black stuff round them. Today he could look into them without feeling as if she knew all his secrets.

She was smiling. 'You all right?'

Adam shrugged. 'Yeah. I didn't know where to meet you but I thought you'd come here.'

She nodded and pulled a slightly squashed roll out of her blazer pocket. 'Yeah, it seemed the right place to find you.'

They looked at each other for a long, awkward moment. With a start Adam realised that she was waiting for him to do something. But what? Kiss her? Produce a bunch of flowers? Sweep her off her feet and carry her off into some overly colourful sunset? After a moment of terrible mental blankness his brain revved up a notch and managed to produce one semi-coherent sentence. 'You want to go a walk?'

'OK.' She seemed relieved that he'd finally said something. 'I can eat while we're walking.'

It got easier once they left the stifling, crowded foyer and headed out into the fresh air. It was a cold, clear day, with a hint of warmth from the lunchtime sun. Spring was coming. Adam could feel it. It lifted his spirits; made him feel more optimistic.

'So what did you do over the holidays?' Melissa was walking beside Adam, close enough that her arm brushed against his as they walked.

'Not much,' Adam said truthfully. 'I couldn't go out so I mostly just sat in my room.' That much was true. Nobody had really wanted to hang out with him at home, as if his disgrace might prove infectious. Of course if *anyone* found out the true extent of what he'd done it might well contaminate the whole family.

Melissa whistled between her teeth. 'So you were grounded the whole holiday?' At Adam's nod she grinned. 'You must have done something really bad. What was it?'

Adam snorted and managed to turn it into a cough. He tried to imagine her face if he told her the truth. *I illegally guided a soul into the afterlife while alone and underage.* And of course the rest – the bit not even his family knew. *And I didn't give the soul any directions for the Unknown Roads because I was angry that he tried to kill loads of people – people I saved, also illegally.* How would she react? He sighed. 'It wasn't really anything bad. My family are pretty strict.'

She gave him a sympathetic look. 'Yeah, my mum used to be pretty strict too but she's getting better. I think she's starting to get the message that I'm not five any more!'

Adam hesitated for a moment before asking, 'How is your mum?'

Melissa tensed. It was very slight but Adam felt the faint movement as her body stiffened and cursed himself for being so clumsy. 'She's OK,' Melissa said. 'She's waiting for an appointment. She promised she would go to the hospital and get the tests they wanted to do.' She smiled but there was something questioning in her eyes. 'Just like you said she should.'

Adam shrugged and tried to look casual. 'Well it's always a good idea to get checked out if you don't feel well.' There was no way he was admitting the disturbing premonitions he'd had before the half-term holiday – Melissa sitting by a hospital bed, holding the wasted hand of a woman who looked just like her. He tried to make a joke of it all. 'See, this is why I want to be a doctor. So I can boss people about and tell them to go to the hospital!'

Melissa smiled cautiously. 'I guess.' She hesitated. 'You know this sounds really weird but I was starting to think you were psychic or something.'

'Yeah,' Adam said. He grinned at her shocked face. 'It does sound really weird.'

She punched his arm and grinned – but then she slipped her hand into the crook of his elbow and left it there as they walked. Adam could feel her fingers burning through his blazer. He suddenly felt ten feet tall.

'Your friends looked really freaked out when I came to the library,' Melissa said.

Adam shrugged. 'They don't talk to girls much. Well, girls don't talk to them.'

Melissa raised an eyebrow. 'And you do?'

'Only my sister and my aunt,' Adam said without thinking. He stopped, horrified at his own honesty, but Melissa was smiling at him. He felt bold enough to say, 'I was glad you came to see me. I thought that . . . maybe you were annoyed at me. You know, after registration.'

Melissa's smile faded. 'No, nothing like that. I just can't be bothered with all the stupid pointing and whispering and gossiping. It was bad enough before the holidays. You know with Cryptique and the . . . video.'

'Yeah, I know,' Adam said, dying inside at the memory. He hesitated. 'You were really nice about that.'

'I like you,' Melissa said simply. She paused. 'I just don't like everyone talking about me. It was like when my dad left and everyone was sort of *looking* at me, like they were sorry for me and asking me how I was. I hated it. And here . . . everyone is always *watching* what you're doing and I just don't want it all to be this big deal. I just want things to be normal. But I do like you.'

She was looking at Adam and he looked back, feeling like his chest had gone empty and fluttery inside. 'I like you too,' he said. His voice sounded croaky. What was he supposed to do? Was he supposed to kiss her now? Why wasn't he Luc?! Luc would know what to do. Luc always knew what to do when it came to girls!

Just as he might have plucked up the courage to act, the silence was broken by squeals and shouts up ahead. A gang of first years charged out from behind a hedge, chasing a football. Adam gave them a murderous glare but they ran on blissfully unaware. Melissa rolled her eyes at them and smiled but the moment had passed. She *did* slip her hand into Adam's. He could definitely live with that for now.

They chatted about everything and nothing as they walked around. Adam relaxed and began to enjoy himself. He had forgotten how easy she was to talk to. Why had he been so nervous about hanging out with her? Admittedly their first few dates hadn't exactly gone smoothly – but she didn't seem to hold any of it against him. He liked watching her when she talked about her favourite things, like her artwork. Her eyes got very bright and she moved her hand a lot – the one that wasn't holding his.

The warning bell rang and reluctantly they walked back towards the main building. Adam looked at the daffodils pushing up in the flower beds lining the main walkway and briefly considered picking one for her – until the tiny voice of reason at the back of his head rewarded him with an image of Melissa hitting him with it and running off laughing.

Of course every ointment had its fly. They were at the bottom of the steps just about to go back into the main building, when a group of figures came round the corner and stopped dead at the sight of them. It was none other than Michael Bulber and friends.

It was the first time Adam had seen the Beast since their unfortunate run-in on Valentine's night. Was he imagining things or was there still a faint hint of bruising round the Beast's eyes, courtesy of Ripper, the bouncer at Cryptique?

The Beast jerked his head at Melissa. 'All right, Melissa?' He turned his attention to Adam, sounding almost polite. 'All right, nobhead?'

Adam glared at the Beast and his tittering gang of minions. He still couldn't believe the lengths the older boy had gone to, just to try to ruin his chances with Melissa. He wasn't really sure how you answered a greeting like 'All right, nobhead,' so he decided to say nothing.

Melissa wasn't as restrained. 'What do *you* want?'

Michael Bulber widened his eyes and hammed up an expression of the utmost innocence. 'Me? Just going inside, aren't I, like a good little boy. It's a free country. But since you're asking, I wouldn't mind taking you for a nice walk sometime. I wouldn't waste my time talking about bunnies and flowers though. Or even throwing up on you.' He did something disgusting with his tongue and his mates fell about laughing. Adam felt a brief and passionate longing to tear his throat out.

Melissa snorted. 'Yeah. Like that's going to happen.'

The Beast grinned. 'At least I'd know what I was doing with you, unlike him.'

Adam scowled, smarting inside. The truth hurt . . . He cleared his throat. 'Just leave it, will you?'

'Oooooh, just leave it, will you!' The Beast put on his most simpering voice. '*Please*, don't *hurt* me!' His mates were still laughing but as he looked at Adam the air between them seemed to snap taut. 'Maybe we should have another little chat in an alleyway sometime.'

Adam took a step towards him, anger making him reckless. 'That didn't end so well for you last time round,' he said, so softly that only Bulber could hear.

The Beast flinched and his expression became even uglier. It wasn't clear what might have happened next – if a voice hadn't boomed from the top of the steps. 'Ah, Michael, there you are! I've been looking for you.' The Bulb was standing beaming down at his son. 'Just need to have a quick word.' He turned his attentions to the others, seemingly unaware of the tension in the air. 'The rest of you, get to class!'

Melissa grinned at the Beast. 'Yeah, we'd better go. Wouldn't want to be late.' She turned to Adam and without warning stretched up and kissed him on the lips. 'See you later, Adam.' She sashayed up past The Bulb and disappeared inside.

Adam stared stupidly after her, feeling his lips tingle. His heart was swelling up, threatening to explode out of his chest cavity and cover everyone in range with warm goo. When he looked at the Beast he had the satisfaction of seeing his nemesis glaring at him. He grinned and gave him a little wave. 'See you Michael.'

The Beast's eyes burning into his back only lightened his step as he went.

Chapter 8

dam's last two classes passed by in a mixture of happy daydreams about Melissa and gloomy scenarios involving extreme violence from the Beast. The thing was, it was all very well winding him up in school – but the last time Adam had been cornered by Michael Bulber he would have been dead if he hadn't escaped into the Hinterland. Even in Cryptique it had only been Luc's presence that had saved him from a beating and forced Bulber to fall back on more subtle malice.

He couldn't risk breaking any more Luman laws. Normal people weren't allowed to know about the existence of the Hinterland, end of. Adam's disappearance from the physical world had freaked the Beast out and saved Adam from a hiding – but if he pulled a stunt like that again and the Concilium found out they would kill him anyway. His good feelings deflated a little. It seemed like *everyone* wanted to kill him these days.

He frowned, thinking about his mates. He'd been out of

order and grovelling was the only way forward. The thought of it was painful but better that than being Norman no-mates. He would swallow his pride tomorrow.

By the time he got home from school he was starving. Maybe it was being loved up, he mused as he headed towards the house, enduring his usual affectionate mauling from the dogs. All that anxiety over dating and snogging must burn extra calories or something. He couldn't help grinning when he remembered how Melissa had kissed him, so casually, in front of everyone. Like, *oh, I'm just going to kiss Adam now. I could do this every day.* Maybe she would. He hoped so...

He was just scrabbling through the fridge when Chloe hurtled into the kitchen. 'We thought you were never going to get home! Come on!'

Adam blinked, startled at her sudden arrival. Two days in a row he had arrived home, only to be pounced upon. It was unsettling.

'Come on where?'

'Into the parlour. Everyone's waiting for you!'

'Waiting for *me*? What have I done?' Adam muttered. 'I need to get something to eat.'

Chloe hissed in frustration. 'There's food in the parlour. Come on, they wouldn't tell us until you got home!'

Adam stared at her baffled. 'Wouldn't tell who what?'

But Chloe was already disappearing back into the hall, yelling, '*Come on!*'

Adam sighed. Maybe with a bit of luck they would tell him he'd been accidentally swapped at birth and he was going back to his real family now.

***

Adam walked into the parlour and stopped, discomfited to find six pairs of eyes boring into him. The parlour was a long, pleasant room with a dark mahogany table at one end. It was usually only used for parties – like when the Concilium had visited a few weeks earlier. The few chairs in the room had been pulled to one side and his family were sitting staring expectantly at him. There were two bottles of champagne in ice buckets on the table, as well as platters of sandwiches and a cake. It was the last thing Adam had expected to see.

He cleared his throat. 'What's the occasion?'

Nathanial was standing in front of the others, beaming at his youngest son. 'Sit down Adam. I wanted to wait until you got home so we could all be together.'

'Okaaaaaay,' Adam said, sidling towards the last remaining chair. It didn't *seem* like he was in more trouble. He'd half wondered if his role in cheating Morta of souls had been discovered – but he doubted they would have made a celebratory cake. Unless of course it was the last meal of the condemned prisoner . . .

Nathanial cleared his throat. 'Well, it's been an unusual twenty-four hours. Yesterday was a very special day, although you might not believe it. Very few humans will ever see what we saw in the Realm of the Fates.'

'Just as well,' Auntie Jo said. 'It would blow their minds.'

Adam nodded in silent agreement. The Tapestry of Light was beautiful and extraordinary and he would never forget seeing it. But equally he couldn't forget the long, cruel tip of the Mortal Knife dancing over the brightly coloured threads. Knowing that his own life – and the lives of everyone he loved – were at the mercy of someone like Morta was a disconcerting thought.

Nathanial nodded. 'It's just part of the responsibility we bear.'

'What was Morta going on about at the end?' Chloe asked innocently. 'She sounded like she was having a go at the Concilium. All that stuff about *her* souls and doing their *jobs*.'

Nathanial frowned. 'Nothing for you to worry about. She was merely reminding us all of our responsibilities.' He fell silent and Adam felt a twinge of guilt. His father would never in a million years suspect that *Adam* was the rogue Luman. He could hardly believe that Adam had guided the soul of the dead bomber into his Light alone but he had put that down to youthful over-enthusiasm; that Adam had something to prove because he was generally so inept at all things Luman-related. It helped that Nathanial had no idea how many people should have died that day – but of course Morta did. No wonder she was so furious at being cheated.

'Can I have a sandwich?' Auntie Jo said, eyeing the table hopefully.

'In a minute,' Nathanial said, jolted from his thoughts back to the present. 'So, to happier topics. I know none of us expected to see the Concilium again quite so soon but it did give me a welcome opportunity to discuss something with Heinrich. And I'm very pleased to tell you that he is in agreement – it's time for Aron to come of age and be Marked!'

There was a gasp of delight from Elise and Auntie Jo. Aron leapt to his feet and punched the air. 'Yessssss!' he hissed, grinning at Luc. 'Told you I'd get there before you.'

Luc shrugged. 'Of course you did. You're older than me.

89

Not exactly a surprise.' He slouched back in his chair, feigning nonchalance but his usual smirk was more of a grimace. That was the funny thing about Luc. He pretended to be casual about everything but beneath the cool exterior there was a steely – and surprising – ambition. Aron might assume he would be the next High Luman because he was the eldest son – but Adam had a feeling Luc would give him a run for his money.

Elise was on her feet embracing Aron, kissing him on both cheeks. She was proud of her steady eldest son. He might not have Luc's quicksilver charm but he worked hard and was stoic about the demands of being a Luman. Nathanial popped the champagne open and passed round crystal flutes. Auntie Jo made a beeline for the sandwiches.

Adam found himself face to face with Aron and held out his hand. 'Congratulations.'

Aron nodded and shook his hand. 'Cheers.' He hesitated. 'You'll get your turn.'

'Eventually,' Luc said, waving his glass around. 'You know, when you're about forty and you've stopped throwing up every time you guide a soul.'

Adam scowled at Luc and grabbed a piece of cake. 'Yeah, rub it in why don't you.'

Auntie Jo clipped Luc around the ear and ignored his yelp. 'So when is the big day?'

'Well, obviously we need to confirm things with the Lady Fates. We'd like as many Lumen as possible to be able to attend. There'll be a lot to organise but we're hoping in just a few weeks.'

'*Zut alors!*' Elise said, clutching her hand to her heart. 'So many things to do! The ballroom must be decorated, the linens must be washed. Candles! We must order candles!' She wobbled slightly, torn between the agonies and ecstasies of organising such an event. Adam grinned. This was his mother's dream come true – the chance to prove she was the perfect Luman wife. After all, while women couldn't guide souls their only chance to shine was as hostesses.

'Will Uncle Paddy's family be coming?' Chloe asked, looking intently at the ground.

Luc grinned. 'Will Ciaron be coming, more like. *Ouch!*' He glared at Auntie Jo, who had administered another stinging swipe to his ear. 'Stop hitting me woman!'

'Stop winding people up,' she mumbled through a mouthful of cake.

Nathanial smiled at Chloe. 'To answer your question, yes of course Patrick will be coming – as will the whole family.'

'But so will many other Lumen families,' Elise interjected, frowning slightly. 'We must have some dresses made!'

Adam grinned. Nathanial would be delighted if Chloe married Ciaron, the eldest son of Uncle Paddy, High Luman of Ireland – but his mother had much higher aspirations for her only daughter.

Nathanial raised his glass. 'Well, it's nice to end the day on such a happy note.' He nodded at Aron. 'It's not every day you find out that your eldest son will become a man. To Aron. Our Light is his Light.'

'To Aron,' Adam said in time with the others. There was something oddly touching about the moment. His family didn't often get the chance to be all together and celebrate. They were usually getting called off to deal with deaths.

As if on cue there was a collective groan as death senses flared. Nathanial sighed and closed his eyes. 'It's a car crash. A few victims by the feel of things.' He clasped his eldest son's shoulder. 'Shall we?'

Aron nodded. 'Yes Father.' He put down his glass and gave the others an awkward nod. 'Thanks for the party.'

Adam watched them leave the room together and just for once felt a twinge of envy.

Up in his room after dinner Adam tried to bury himself in his chemistry homework but he couldn't concentrate. He was supposed to balancing valencies but the letters and numbers seemed to be hopping around the page, mocking his attempts to tame them. He scowled and flung his pencil down on the desk. Normally he liked this kind of thing because in the end you could master it. Equations could be pinned down neatly, unlike all the other thoughts in his head. Not tonight though.

He mooched down to the kitchen and poured a glass of juice. The house was quiet. Elise had swept Chloe off to her personal dressmaker as soon as dinner was over. Nathanial and Aron were in the study, probably swotting for the Marking ceremony and Luc had gone out with a shifty look on his face. Only Auntie Jo was in the den, laptop balanced on her knee while she watched *Hitchhiker Horror 4*.

She glanced up as Adam came in and nodded at the screen. 'Look at her. She's driving along a road in the desert and she sees *that* guy with his thumb in the air. His eyes are looking in four directions at once, he's got a dripping holdall and he's barely got a tooth in his head – and she stops and picks him up. Who *does* that?' She shook her head ruefully at the folly of horror-movie heroines.

Adam sat down on the other end of the sofa and tried to smile but his face didn't seem to be working properly. Auntie Jo noticed of course. 'What's wrong with you?'

Adam shrugged. 'Dunno,' he said honestly. 'Can't be bothered with homework tonight.'

She snorted. 'I suppose I'll go ahead and state the obvious. You won't thank me for it but I'll say it anyway. If you give up school you won't have to bother with homework ever again.'

Adam scowled. 'I said I can't be bothered *tonight*. I'll do it in the morning.'

'I see.' Auntie Jo paused and said casually, 'So that's exciting news about Aron.'

Adam nodded. 'Yeah, it is.' The thing was, he meant it. He didn't get on that well with Aron – they were just too different – but he knew his brother was a good Luman. He wasn't inspired at saying the right thing the way some Lumen were, but like Nathanial, he was steady and reassuring. Someone like Aron would send you into the afterlife full of warm certainty that everything was going to be OK. When Adam guided souls he was pretty sure they threw themselves into their Lights just to escape from him.

'It'll be your turn some day,' Auntie Jo continued, pretending to look at something on her laptop.

Adam rolled his eyes. 'Yeah, I don't think I'll be coming of age any time soon.' He paused. 'So what will actually happen? You know, at the ceremony?'

'Don't you remember?' Auntie Jo grinned. 'I suppose you

were still a sprat the last time we went to a Marking. Well, if your mother has her way most of the Luman world will be there – or at least all the *important* families. We'll be downstairs in the Oath Chamber and the Crone will Mark Aron.'

'The Crone . . .' Adam began, then broke off. He had been to plenty of balls but only one Marking when he was younger. He had a vague memory of a veiled and shadowy figure. 'Is she the one in the cloak?'

Auntie Jo nodded. 'Tradition says we should never see her face. It's supposed to stop people lobbying her for secret Markings to get round the Concilium and the Fates. Just another way of keeping the same families top dog. After all, any Luman could get their son Marked then – and once they've come of age what would stop them from having a crack at becoming High Luman?'

Adam frowned. He'd never really thought about it before. Some of the other British Lumen were older than his father – but Nathanial had still been made High Luman. And some of the other Lumen's sons were older than Aron – but he was the first in his generation to come of age. 'But that's not fair!'

Auntie Jo raised an eyebrow. 'Since when has fairness had anything to do with who's in charge? It's just the way things have always been done. The High Luman is supposed to be picked from the whole Luman ranks – but the reality is that most High Lumen are fast-response Lumen. It was just luck that long ago the Mortsons specialised and left the other British Lumen families to guide the sick and elderly when they died quietly in their beds. And we've managed to keep things that way quite nicely ever since.'

'But what if those other Lumen are really good?' Adam persisted. After all, he was rubbish at the whole thing. Every Luman who had ever lived would be better than him! He couldn't quite bring himself to say it.

'It doesn't matter. Blood and tradition are everything.' Auntie Jo sounded weary – and bitter. 'It doesn't matter how totally unsuited someone is to being High Luman. If that's their fate, then that's their fate.'

Adam looked at her curiously. 'Yeah, but Father *is* a good High Luman.'

'I wasn't talking about your father,' Auntie Jo snapped. She sighed. 'Don't listen to me. I'm tired. All that talk at dinner about what we have to do for the ball. I'm exhausted even thinking about it!' She pulled at the silver locket round her neck, moving it from side to side the way she did when she was upset. 'Now, are you going to watch this with me or shall I just tell you tomorrow's horoscope and get it over with?'

Adam raised an eyebrow. 'Like there's any way of stopping you!'

Auntie Jo grinned and put on her horoscope voice. 'We all want to know what the stars reveal, Adam. What the future holds.'

Adam tried to smile – but when he thought about Morta and that knife he wasn't so sure that he *did* want to know the future after all . . .

Chapter 9

he next day Adam arrived at school with mixed feelings. On the one hand he was looking forward to seeing Melissa, especially if she was going to kiss him again. On the other hand Michael Bulber would be thirsting for revenge, which could only mean bad things for Adam.

Worse still, he was going to have to eat humble pie with Spike and the others. He knew he'd been out of order but the problem was he kind of meant what he'd said. Spike *was* always snooping about and sometimes it did annoy Adam. Still, Spike did have a point. Without his help Melissa would probably never have spoken to Adam again. Usually Spike was on *his* side but this time they were on opposing teams. It was just that Spike didn't know it.

In registration Adam at least got a proper smile from Melissa, which seemed like a good omen for the day. He sat surreptitiously finishing his chemistry homework while listening to their form tutor's latest rant. This one was on poor punctuality being to blame for most of the world's evils, including underfunding of the space mission. Adam felt a new pity for his form tutor, not knowing he was a thwarted astronaut turned teacher. Maybe that was why The Bulb had given him a job. After all, he was a former wrestler turned head teacher. Rumour had it that he'd paralysed an opponent in a dirty fight, hence his fall from wrestling grace.

Eager to share this new titbit with his friends he scuttled off to the library as soon as the bell for break rang. Spike was the only one there which made the whole apology thing easier, at least until he opened his mouth. 'Didn't think you'd want to sit with a snooper like me. Why don't you go off and hang out with your *girlfriend*?'

Adam sighed. 'Don't be like that. I was out of order yesterday.'

Spike was focusing intently on his laptop. 'Yeah, you were.'

It was clear he wanted more. Adam gritted his teeth. 'Look, I was a nob, OK? I was just stressing. I know that's hard for you to understand because you never seem to get stressed about anything but us lesser mortals worry about stuff.'

'Yeah, you were definitely a nob,' Spike said but he looked slightly mollified. 'And getting stressed doesn't do anything so why bother?'

Adam sat down. 'So did you get any further with the picture?'

Spike shook his head. 'Nah, still need to catch my CIA guy. The time difference is a pain. He'll be getting up soon though. I've tracked him to the Midwest somewhere so he's six or seven hours behind – but he's an early riser. He reckons he can sleep with one eye open.'

Adam snorted. He could imagine this contact all too vividly, some loony living in an underground bunker with assault weapons on the wall and booby traps under every stone, imagining it would keep him safe; not knowing Morta could simply flick the tip of her knife and he would fall down the stairs or choke to death on a piece of steak. He was Spike's kind of guy all right . . . He was saved from having to say anything more by Archie and Dan arriving. Dan bounced an almond off his head by way of greeting.

'So you're still alive,' Archie said. 'Heard you had a run-in with the Beast. You like living on the edge, don't you? Maybe you'd be better *not* having a girlfriend if it's going to get you killed.' He looked a little pleased. It was obvious he hadn't forgiven Adam either.

Adam grimaced. 'Yeah, you're probably right.'

Dan sat down and gnawed an almond, squirrelly with nervous energy. 'He'll never let you have her! The great white is unstoppable.' He shook his head, looking gloomy. 'It's unfortunate but maybe you need to find a new hunting ground. There's only room for one apex predator!'

Adam blinked. Clearly Dan had spent more time on his biology homework than Adam had. 'She doesn't even like him. I mean she definitely doesn't fancy him but she doesn't even *like* him. She thinks he's a tit.'

Archie smirked. 'Yeah, she seems to have a thing for tits.'

Adam counted to ten in his head, reminding himself that he probably deserved it. 'I don't even think he *does* like her, not really. He just wants her because he can't have her and there's nobody he likes more.'

Dan rolled an almond between his fingers, looking thoughtful. 'It's a pity there isn't someone else he likes. Someone really amazing.' He glanced up and added quickly, 'You know, because Melissa is a fantastic fish but maybe he just needs an even better fish. One he can really show off to everyone.'

Archie was looking interested now in spite of himself. 'The ultimate fish. The stuff of legends.'

Dan nodded. 'Exactly. Like those stories you see on the news because someone's caught this gigantic fish people said didn't exist. Like the Loch Ness Monster. And then a beardy guy catches a megafish and it takes ten men to get it out of the water. And then they stuff it and put it on a pub wall and it's bigger than a boat.' He stopped and looked sheepish. 'My dad made me watch a documentary about the Crestwick Carp.'

'Another fun-filled evening with the Dark Lord,' Spike muttered.

Dan was warming to his theme. 'So what we need is bait. A fish so hot that it makes Melissa look ugly. Like putting a nice little goldfish beside . . . a barracuda!'

'Eels are pretty ugly,' Archie said helpfully. 'My uncle used to drag me along eel fishing in Norfolk.' He shuddered at the memory.

'The blobfish is officially the world's ugliest fish,' Spike added, turning the laptop so they could recoil from a close-up of a gelatinous bottom-dwelling mutant.

'OK, yes, I get the point, ugly fish!' Adam said, feeling desperate. He was afraid he might actually go mad if they didn't stop talking about fish. 'So, who's going to be the good fish? The bait.'

There was a long silence. 'Hmmmm,' Dan said. 'And therein lies the problem. Not only do we have to *find* this hot fish but we also have to convince her to swim into the Beast's jaws. And she'd have to be a bit thick to do that.'

'Unless she wasn't real.' Spike glanced up at their startled faces and raised an eyebrow. 'Come on, we invented a fake sensei, a fake wrestling tournament and a whole new imaginary martial art. How hard can it be to invent an imaginary fish? Or girl for that matter.'

'I could make her!' Archie leered around the table. 'Seriously, I'd be brilliant. You have no idea how much thought I've given this.' He pulled out his sketchpad and his pen flew furiously over the pages. 'Lips . . . like this. Hair . . . like this . . . And of course the rest . . .'

There was a long pause as they contemplated the bizarre top-heavy image before them. It looked like some kind of alien with enormous breasts. Dan squinted at the picture. 'I don't think even the Beast is weird enough to find *that* attractive.'

Archie frowned. 'Whatever. I can tone it down a bit. We have a programme in the art room that can convert drawings to photo images.'

'So how's she going to know about the Beast?' Adam loved the idea of distracting his nemesis from Melissa but unfortunately Michael Bulber wasn't quite as stupid as his father.

'We could pretend she's going to come to this school. Say that she's overseas. There's a girl in my form class who just left to go and live in Australia. So we download an application form, fill it in and pretend she's legit. Then we pretend she isn't coming for a few weeks. We can just keep dragging it out.'

'But sooner or later the Beast will want to meet her.'

Dan grinned. 'Yeah, but by then he'll have gone off Melissa. It's basic psychology. He'll spend weeks comparing Melissa to the new girl and decide Wonderfish is a better catch. So Melissa will never look like a good catch again.'

Adam frowned and thought about it. Could Dan be right? Could a Wonderfish really distract Bulber from Melissa? It would certainly take the pressure off a bit if he didn't have to concentrate on impressing Melissa *and* not getting killed by the Beast. 'I suppose it might work.'

'Of course it'll work,' Spike said airily. 'Since when do my plans not work?'

Archie was squinting critically at his drawing. 'You know you're right. She needs a bit of adjustment. I'll work on some drawings this evening.'

Dan grinned. 'Operation Wonderfish is go!'

Adam rolled his eyes but he couldn't help smiling. After all, they had fooled the Bulb. Fooling Michael Bulber too was just keeping things in the family. 'OK. Let's do it.'

'So when are you going to see the fish again?' Archie was still sketching out the Wonderfish, frowning with concentration.

'At lunchtime,' Adam said, trying hard to sound nonchalant. 'I was talking to her this morning in registration.'

Dan frowned. 'You don't make it easy to keep you alive, do you? I mean until the Wonderfish is perfected Melissa is still tempting prey – which makes you prey too.'

'Don't worry. I'll be safe enough,' Adam said. 'She wants me to meet her in the art room. You know, to help her with her coursework.'

Archie snorted. 'She does know you can barely draw a stick

101

man, doesn't she?'

'I'm not going to be doing any drawing.' Adam cleared his throat and tried not to preen. 'Actually *she* wants to draw *me*.'

Spike sniggered. 'You're not my idea of a muse.'

Dan's eyes were like saucers. 'When you say she's going to *draw* you . . . it's not *that* sort of drawing, is it?' He looked around nervously checking for eavesdroppers. 'You know. The nudie stuff. *Life* drawing.' He nodded knowingly at Adam.

'No!' Adam paused. 'I mean, they don't do that in school . . . do they?'

Archie looked up from his sketchpad. 'Dunno. I've got Donnelly and he's not into that stuff at all, but Melissa's got that hippy teacher. The new one with all the tattoos. Bet she's into all sorts!'

Dan choked on an almond and scrabbled through his pocket for his inhaler. Adam could have done with a quick puff himself. He stood up as the bell for the end of break rang. 'Yeah, well, at least if the art teacher is there I won't need to worry about the Beast. And hopefully you'll have the Wonderfish ready for tomorrow.'

Spike raised an eyebrow. 'I never knew having a girlfriend was such a team effort.'

Adam had the grace to blush.

When lunchtime came, Adam sloped towards the art corridor with deep trepidation. It was a part of the school he rarely visited; he'd dropped art as soon as he possibly could. It wasn't that he didn't *like* art; he just wasn't any good at it. He often envied Archie's ability to draw anything, even if he did sometimes use it for dubious purposes.

Melissa appeared a few minutes later, looking flustered and lugging an armful of heavy, hardback books. 'Sorry. I had to go to the library first. I needed research books.' She pressed the door handle with her elbow and gestured to Adam. 'Come on in.'

Adam hesitated, feeling like he was entering the lion's den. There were a few people there already, working away with headphones in their ears. Thankfully all of them had their clothes on too. The art room always smelled the same – that weird mixture of damp clay and paint.

Melissa scurried over to the far side of the room and dropped the books on the table with a crash. 'They were killing my arms.' She rubbed the insides of her elbows and pulled a stool out from under the bench. 'Sit here, will you? I want to get the light from the windows.'

Belatedly Adam realised he could have offered to carry the books in. He'd missed a chance to shine! He perched on the edge of the stool, feeling apprehensive but trying to look cool. 'It's a nice room.'

Melissa smiled at him. 'I'm not going to bite you.'

Clearly he wasn't being as cool as he'd hoped. Adam cleared his throat. 'So . . . what is it you're doing?'

Melissa was flicking through one of the heavy books. The pages were a riot of colour. 'We have to pick some artists and create a piece based on their styles. I haven't decided on the style yet but the theme is the same whoever I use.'

'Oh right. What do you mean the theme?'

Melissa looked up at him and then quickly looked away. She seemed to be studying the book. 'What the piece is about.

103

What it has to express. So mine is on . . . passion.'

Adam stared at her for a second, then dropped his eyes to the floor, feeling his cheeks flame. Bloody *hell*! Dan was *right*! What the hell did they *get up to* up here? For a fleeting moment he found himself longing for the ether-scented air of the biology lab. 'Oh, right.'

Now Melissa seemed embarrassed. 'Look, it's a big topic. I'm just at the figuring stuff out stage. So today is just prep, if that's OK?' At Adam's nod she looked relieved. 'Great. I'm just going to take some photos to start.'

Adam froze. With Spike scouring the internet for the unknown bomber now was *not* a good time for Adam to start posing for the camera. He tried to make his question sound casual. 'What do you need photos for?'

Melissa looked amused. 'Well, you can't be here all the time, can you? I need to be able to work when you're in your other classes. Unless you're going to come and be a full-time model.'

'No, yeah, that makes sense. You don't put the photos up anywhere though, do you?'

Melissa gave him an odd look. 'Well, just on the display board here when I show the finished piece. But it's mostly going to be shots of individual body parts. No one will even know it's you.'

'That's great,' Adam said. At least his grinning mug wasn't going to end up plastered all over the internet. But his relief was short-lived. Body *parts*? Which parts exactly was she going to be taking photos of?

Melissa had disappeared into the store briefly, returning carrying a heavy camera. She came towards him, turning the lense. 'OK. So I want to get some photos of your eyes first.'

That was probably OK. He stared straight ahead as she stepped right up until only the camera was between them. The air was full of the smell of her perfume – slightly sweet and fruity. He could feel the warmth from her body close to his.

'Try not to move,' she said softly. The shutter closed and opened, closed and opened. 'You have really nice eyes.'

'Thanks,' Adam said. His eyeballs were burning from holding them open but he didn't care. He could have stayed there all day.

Melissa stepped back. 'OK, so now I want to get your lips. In the photos.' She smiled, half embarrassed.

'OK,' Adam murmured. It was weird knowing that her whole focus was on his mouth. He was usually focusing on hers.

It felt like they were there for a long time but it was only a few minutes later that Melissa finally put the camera down. 'Body parts' had thankfully turned out to mean his face and jaw and hands rather than anything Adam normally kept undercover. And even though she put the camera down Melissa stayed very close and for once Adam could read what she wanted him to do and he wanted it too. So, he kissed her.

She didn't have any lip gloss on today and somehow that was even nicer because she tasted like *her*. And kissing her properly was different from the other kisses – the short kisses in the alleyway and in front of Michael Bulber. This kiss went on and on and it was like kissing her with his whole body because this time he was able to put his arms round her and pull her in against him. And, like the time she had touched his hand in biology, he got that feeling like an electric current was running through his whole body, a tingling that ran from the back of his neck down to the base of his spine and made him want to kiss her more and more and more.

He'd worried all this time that he wouldn't know what to do and that was so stupid because of course he knew what to do. He could have stayed there forever because it was so easy and so brilliant kissing her, like the sun was shining through his whole body and lighting him up and lighting her up too.

When the bell went they ignored it, just as they ignored the bustle of other people clearing up around them. Unfortunately they couldn't ignore the arrival of Ms Havens, the art teacher. She was hard to ignore – she had bright red hair and lots of tattoos down her arms. 'Break it up, you two,' she said, not unkindly. In fact, she was smirking a little.

Melissa grinned. 'Sorry miss.'

She didn't look sorry at all. She looked happy and her happiness made the warm feeling in Adam soar, like it might burst out and shower the room with little golden lights. As they walked to the door, Melissa slipped her hand into his and whispered, 'Don't worry, she doesn't mind. She's really nice.'

'Yeah, she seems to be!' He tried to imagine kissing her in front of the Buzzard, their tiny but terrifying biology teacher. She would probably flay them alive and pin them onto one of her specimen boards.

'So I'll see you later,' Melissa said. She gave him one last kiss on the lips.

'Yeah,' Adam said, beaming. He could feel it in his cheeks. 'See you later.'

It wasn't the most inspiring thing he'd ever said. But the great thing was, Melissa didn't seem to mind.

Chapter 10

he next couple of weeks were some of the happiest that Adam had ever had and that was mostly because of Melissa. He'd always liked school and seeing his mates – but seeing her too was the best bit of every day. He still couldn't believe she'd given him another chance after their disastrous after-school dates – but for now she didn't seem to mind just seeing him at lunchtimes, usually in the art room to avoid Michael Bulber.

Operation Wonderfish had fallen at the first hurdle – namely that it required the Beast to use his school email. Still dazzled by their success with The Bulb, Adam and his friends had been confident that the son would follow in his father's idiotic footsteps. Unfortunately the Beast never seemed to log in at all.

Spike wasn't used to his plans failing and was taking it personally. 'He *has* to use his email. That's how the sixth formers get all their homework from teachers.'

Dan was shelling monkey nuts and making a mess all over their table in the library. 'Yeah, but he's the Beast. He doesn't do homework. He just terrorises other people and takes theirs.'

A gloomy silence had followed this pronouncement. It was true. That was the difference between The Bulb and his son. The Bulb might be a disgraced wrestler but now that he was a teacher he wasn't actually allowed to maim students, no matter how much he wanted to. The Beast on the other hand lived by a different set of laws and was smart enough to fly below the radar most of the time.

Spike was in vile form about the whole thing. He hadn't mentioned any more about the photo of the bomber either. Apparently his survivalist contact had gone even deeper underground, paranoid that he was being watched. Spike hadn't been able to get his hands on the facial recognition software he needed, putting his plans on hold.

So for now things were going Adam's way. He didn't mind hanging out in the art room – it was warmer than being outside and Ms Havens was pretty cool. He could chat to Melissa while she worked on her piece and then they left some time for kissing. He was feeling pretty expert these days.

All in all, things should have been perfect. There was only one blot on the horizon. Lots of people were dying.

It started gradually – an extra sudden death one day, a couple of extra the next. Adam, like all Lumen, felt his death sense flare every time a person died – but he was well practised at tuning it out. When he was in school and away from the Mortson house and Keystones it was easy to ignore. He should have noticed sooner but he was enjoying his 'normal' life too much.

The third week back at school things changed again. Exams were getting closer and Adam had to stay late on Monday for chemistry revision. Arriving home, he bumped into a flustered-looking Nathanial coming out of the back door, still smoothing down his camel-hair coat. He gave Adam a brief nod and smile and disappeared into the Hinterland.

In the kitchen Adam found his mother and Auntie Jo standing together looking worried. To his alarm Auntie Jo wasn't even waiting by the toaster – which meant that she must have actually been *talking* with Elise. Something was wrong. 'What's up?'

The two women exchanged glances. 'Nothing probably,' Auntie Jo muttered. 'It's just been a busy day. Busier than usual.'

Elise pursed her lips. '*Much* busier than usual.' She paced around the kitchen holding an unlit cigarette. The nervous *pock-pock* of her heels on the stone floor beat a tattoo in Adam's brain. 'Last week was busy too but today . . .' She stopped and frowned.

Adam shrugged. 'Well, maybe it was a bad day on the roads. There was lots of snow in Scotland. Was it mostly car accidents?'

Auntie Jo shook her head. 'They were all individual jobs. Silly things.'

'A fall down stairs, six chokings, three house fires, a scarf in machinery, two falls from scaffolding, three falls from bicycles. Plus the usual car accidents and unexpected heart problems.' Elise had been counting on her hands but quickly ran out of fingers.

Adam frowned. That *was* a lot of sudden deaths for one day. 'Where were they?'

'All over the place. A few in London. One of them was just down the road from here. The man got a bit of a shock seeing Nathanial in the Hinterland – he knew his face. Not that he can tell anyone now I suppose,' Auntie Jo mused.

Adam felt a pang of guilt. With so many deaths he should have felt *something*, especially when one of them had been close by. Thinking about it, he hadn't been having his premonitions either – and when he *had* felt the occasional twinge it had been easy to block. His happiness in school was insulating him from the Luman world, at least in the daytime. It was getting too easy to ignore his doom sense and death sense, especially when it was so risky intervening.

'It's probably just a blip,' Auntie Jo said. 'And once Aron comes of age Nathanial will have more help. Someone to help share the load.'

The problem with individual deaths was that only Lumen who had come of age could attend them alone. Luc and Aron could only assist at the minute, not work solo. A thought struck Adam. 'Will the Marking be able to go ahead? If there are lots of deaths?'

'The Fates have granted their permission. They will concentrate deaths in other parts of the globe,' Elise said. 'I imagine the new Atropos was most reluctant to put down the Mortal Knife.' Her expression could have curdled milk.

Luc came into the kitchen. 'What are we having for dinner? I'm starving.'

'Roast beef. It's in the oven,' Elise said distractedly. 'But we cannot eat until your father returns.'

As if on cue the back door opened and Nathanial came inside. He looked exhausted. 'Another job done. It was a sad one – young chap, an addict. Had an overdose. Could happen any day of the week.' He sounded like he was trying to convince himself.

'Yes, but it didn't happen any day. It happened today, along with all the others,' Auntie Jo muttered.

Chloe came into the kitchen looking pained. 'My stomach is really sore. My death sense is going mad today. What's going on?'

Elise smoothed her daughter's hair back off her face. 'Try to ignore it, darling. It's just a busy day.'

Chloe scowled. 'It's not fair. Why do we even have to get a death sense if we're not allowed to do anything with it? If I can't be a Luman I'd be better off not having one. Mine's really strong too.'

It was true. Chloe had always felt deaths especially keenly. Adam had never really thought about how annoying it must be. After all, if you couldn't actually guide souls it was just pointless – and in Chloe's case painful. Adam had another twinge of guilt that he was escaping the worst of it.

Luc smirked. 'It's so you'll know when your husband is going on a job. That way you can put his dinner in the oven to keep it warm.' He sniggered at Chloe's glare.

Aron came in the back door in running shorts, soaked with sweat after his daily gym session. He looked surprised to see them all in the kitchen. 'What's going on? Are we having dinner early?' He sniffed appreciatively. Aron loved his food.

Elise frowned and glanced at Nathanial. 'Perhaps we should, *oui*?'

'Yes, I think that would be a great idea –' Nathanial began, then stopped.

There was a collective groan. Here, surrounded by Mortson Keystones even Adam couldn't escape the sensation as his death sense flared. Nathanial closed his eyes and massaged his temples. He winced. 'It seems someone fell on a garden cane and managed to impale themselves.'

'A garden cane?' Luc said. His eyebrows were arched until they seemed to be suspended in space. '*Seriously?* How unlucky is *that?*'

'How unlucky indeed,' Nathanial murmured. His face was grey and strained. 'Elise, I think you should eat without me. I'll get something when I come back.'

'Do you want me to go with you Father?' Aron plucked at his sweaty clothes. 'I can run up and get changed.'

Nathanial shook his head. 'Don't worry Aron. I'd have to go along anyway. No point both of us missing dinner.' He gave his eldest son a weary smile. 'Come Saturday you'll be able to work alone. Enjoy your last few days of freedom.' He gave Elise a peck on the cheek and disappeared back into the garden.

There was a long moment of silence. It was Auntie Jo who summed up what they were all thinking. 'What the bloody hell is going on?'

Luc threw a sardonic glance at Aron. 'Roll on Saturday.'

'Yeah,' Aron said. He looked anything but eager.

Everyone hoped it had just been an especially bad day, that Tuesday would be better. It wasn't. If anything, the week kept getting worse. Nathanial was barely home – which meant that a task which usually fell on his shoulders fell on Adam's instead.

He'd spent a cheerful Wednesday in school messing around with his mates, followed by some quality time with Melissa. For once he'd managed to revise enough of his biology to sail through a test (being threatened by the apex predator had a way of fixing food chains in his mind). He sat on the bus grinning to himself, blithely unaware of what lay in store.

The first clue was that there was no sign of Auntie Jo when he got home. Usually she was in the den in the afternoon, watching her programmes or having a nap. The room was cold and silent, with no fire glowing or horror-movie heroine fleeing a madman. The whole house seemed too quiet.

It was almost dinner time before Chloe and Elise appeared home. They had been out for a last-minute dress fitting. The coming-of-age ball was just three days away and Elise's nerves were stretched to breaking point. It didn't help that Nathanial's calming presence was largely absent from the house.

Chloe came into the den and rolled her eyes. Adam could hear Elise ranting to herself in French out in the hall – never a good sign. 'What's up?'

Chloe closed the door and spoke in a whisper. 'Auntie Jo didn't show up for her dress fitting. Mother is furious with her.'

Adam smirked. Having a dress fitting was pretty much Auntie Jo's idea of hell on earth. 'It's not really Auntie Jo's thing though, is it? She'd probably rather go to the ball in a kaftan.'

Chloe looked distracted. 'She's always like this. You know, at this time of the year. I don't know what it is about this date but she's always weird.'

Adam stared at her in confusion. 'Like what?'

Chloe glared. 'You know, considering you're her favourite you don't really notice much, do you? Today, every single year, Auntie Jo goes nuts. She locks herself in her room and won't come out until Father talks her down. Only he's not here to do it today. He's had like another million call-outs.'

'Seriously?' This was news to Adam – the Auntie Jo bit, not

the call-out bit. The call-out thing was becoming almost normal – which was scary for the average human in the Kingdom of Britain.

'Yes! The nineteenth of March every year. I suppose you're usually at *school*.' Chloe managed to say 'school' the way other people said 'dentist'.

Adam scowled. 'Look, Auntie Jo never goes longer than two hours without a piece of toast. So she's hardly locking herself in.'

'She hasn't been downstairs all day! Mother even left some fresh bread out by the toaster before we went out and she hasn't touched it.'

Now even Adam was getting alarmed. 'And she does this *every* year?'

Before Chloe could respond Elise burst in with a loaded plate. 'Adam. Go upstairs to your aunt and tell her she must get dressed and go to Madame Gazor! Her dress is ready! I know this is a bad day but the ball is on Saturday!'

Adam took the plate of toast. It was thickly sliced and oozing butter – the ultimate lure for Auntie Jo. 'But why would she listen to me?'

Elise looked distracted. 'She'll listen. I don't know when your father will be home and Madame Gazor is . . . *capricieuse*! Temperamental! She will take the scissors to the dress if Josephine does not go for her fitting!'

Adam was doubtful of his powers of persuasion but it was nice that for once Elise expected more of him, not less of him. 'I'll see what I can do.'

A minute later he was standing outside Auntie Jo's room

holding the plate of toast, not quite sure what he was going to say. He could hear music playing faintly behind the door. After a moment's hesitation he knocked. 'Auntie Jo? It's Adam. Can I come in?'

There was a long pause. 'Go away,' Auntie Jo croaked.

Adam cleared his throat. 'The thing is . . . erm . . . well, you missed your fitting. With Madame Gazor. And Mother says you need to go and see her or she'll get a bit mental with the scissors.'

There was a loud crash and Adam jumped, almost dropping the plate. Something had just shattered against the door and Auntie Jo let loose a string of profanity that would have shamed even Spike, master of swearing as a poetic form. In between the curses Adam gathered a fairly good idea of where exactly Madame Gazor could put her scissors – and the sun didn't shine in any of the places mentioned.

He was beginning to realise how woefully unequipped he was to deal with this situation. In fact, he might have given up – but for one thing. There was a new sound from inside the room and it wasn't a sound Adam had ever heard before. Auntie Jo was crying.

Hearing that brought the world to a standstill for Adam. Auntie Jo was the one person in his family who had always cheered him on – always fought on his side. Part of him felt like running away – but there was no way he was leaving her like this. 'Auntie Jo, let me in!' He jiggled the door handle and found that the door was locked. 'Seriously, open up.' In the face of resounding silence he cleared his throat and tried to sound commanding. 'If you don't open the door I'm going to have to break it down!'

There was a snort of derision followed by a reluctant chuckle. 'I won't hold my breath here.'

Adam tried not to feel offended. At least she wasn't crying. It was time to play his trump card. 'I have some toast for you.' There was still silence but it was a watchful, listening sort of silence. 'It's really thick and there's loads of butter. It's sort of swimming about on the plate . . .'

'Oh all right,' Auntie Jo grumbled, flinging open the door. 'I'm taking the bait. Come in.' She shuffled away from the door, still in her slippers and dressing gown. After a moment's hesitation Adam followed her inside.

For someone so lazy about her personal appearance Auntie Jo's domain was scrupulously tidy. It was more of a suite than a room; there was a living area and a bathroom as well as an old four-poster bed. The room was pale and elegant and feminine. Adam felt lumbering and out of place.

The only untidy thing was the bed. The covers were messed up and the bedside table was littered with crumpled tissues and empty glasses. An almost empty whisky bottle stood amidst the debris and as Auntie Jo stumbled towards the end of the bed Adam realised with a start that she was properly drunk. For a woman who swigged from a hip flask on a daily basis she must have been drinking most of the day.

He watched her slump back on the pillows and raise her glass in a silent toast. Her eyes were red and her face was blotchy. She was clutching something Adam couldn't see in her right hand. 'Are you OK?'

Even plastered Auntie Jo was capable of sarcasm. 'Yes, I'm

fine. Great in fact. Can't you tell?' She emptied her glass and put it down a little too hard. Her right hand clenched and loosened reflexively. Adam could see flashes of something metallic glittering between her fingers.

He sat down cautiously on the end of the bed and offered the plate of toast. Auntie Jo took it without thanks and put it down beside her untouched, reaching instead for her whisky glass once again. 'How was the madhouse today then?'

Adam tried to smile. 'Do you mean this place or school?' In the face of her stony expression he sighed. 'Yeah. It was OK. Good actually.'

'I am *glad* it was good. I'm so happy that you can get away from here.' Her words were slurred but she rambled on. 'No one should be a prisoner in their own life. No one should ever feel like there's no other way out.'

Adam gaped at her, alarmed. He'd never seen her like this before. He had no idea what she was talking about but it seemed polite to say something. 'No, that would be terrible.'

'I won't let them do that to *you*.' She spoke with a hissed fervour that took Adam by surprise. 'I should have done more. I was so young and stupid!'

He stared in confusion for a moment. 'You don't have to do anything. I'm fine.'

Her shoulders heaved and she whispered. 'I didn't know. I didn't know he would do it.' It was only then that Adam realised she wasn't talking about him. Her hand opened and something silver slipped onto the bed cover beside her. Finally Adam saw what it was. The locket. The one she always wore round her neck, the one with a photo inside of a man Adam didn't know. He'd only seen inside it a few times when he was younger. Was that who the tears were for?

She was going to cry again and Adam couldn't bear it – because whatever Auntie Jo was, she was not a crier. She was his hero, he realised with a start. She'd spent his whole life making him feel better and fighting like a tiger for him to have the life he wanted. How could he make her stop being sad? 'Have some toast,' he said in desperation. 'Please don't cry!'

Maybe his fear cut through her private misery. Auntie Jo blinked at him as though she'd just noticed he was there and suddenly her eyes seemed to come into focus. She set down her whisky glass and cleared her throat. 'I'm fine, Adam. I'm just stupid today. Don't worry. Everything will be fine.' She picked up a slice of toast and took a small bite. 'See?'

Adam wasn't convinced but he could see she was making an effort. The whole situation was totally mystifying and he was frantically doggy-paddling way out of his depth. 'Yeah. Toast is good.' He hesitated. 'So . . . do you think you'll go and see Madame Gazor?'

Auntie Jo groaned. 'Bloody dresses. What have I done to deserve this?' She staggered to her feet and lurched through the door into her bathroom.

It was a few seconds before Adam realised that she had left the locket lying on the bedcover. He had never in his whole life seen Auntie Jo take it off and it wasn't an opportunity he was going to waste. A quick glance at the door showed he had at least a few seconds.

He had sometimes played with the locket when he was little, sitting on Auntie Jo's knee and opening and closing it while it dangled round her neck. It had seemed so big then; now it nestled in his palm not much larger than a coin. Holding it brought back the memory of twisting the tiny catch on the side – and when he did the locket folded open immediately.

The inside was just as he remembered. Adam felt a guilty rush of recognition. On one side was a flat piece of charcoal stone – Auntie Jo's keystone, just like his own but mounted inside the locket instead of hanging on a chain. He ignored it and looked instead at the picture facing it.

There was the man he remembered. He had dark hair and his skin was starkly pale in contrast. He was smiling a little but his eyes were sad. Adam frowned. Who was the man? He knew that at one time Auntie Jo had been betrothed, just like any other Luman girl – but no wedding had ever taken place. Why? Was this the man she had been supposed to marry? And if so what had happened to him?

There was a horrible retching sound from the bathroom and Adam cringed. At the same time there was a knock on the bedroom door. Adam just had time to snap the locket closed and fling it back on the bed as Nathanial stepped inside, still wearing his coat. He paused, taking in the sight of his son on the end of the bed and the sound of his sister being violently sick.

Adam stood and gestured towards the bathroom. 'Auntie Jo's not well.'

Nathanial frowned. 'No, apparently not.' As usual he hid his thoughts behind a benign expression but Adam felt a pang of shock. His father was so pale and drained he looked half dead. His hair was rumpled and there were grey shadows beneath his eyes.

Auntie Jo groaned and vomited again. Nathanial winced. 'Thank you, Adam. You can go now.'

Adam hesitated, feeling bad about leaving. To make things worse his death sense flared – and seeing Nathanial's jaw tighten he knew what his father was thinking. 'I can stay with her. If you need to go on a job.'

Nathanial shook his head and for a second Adam saw something black and furious bubbling beneath Nathanial's face, threatening to crack his composure. 'The job will have to wait.'

Adam stared at him in shock. Since when had Nathanial *ever* left a soul waiting? Nathanial gave him a terse smile. 'It's OK, son. They're not going anywhere. I won't be long. And come Saturday I'll have another pair of hands to help out.' He looked like a drowning man staring towards a lifeboat in the distance.

Adam nodded and escaped, half relieved and half guilty. He closed the door behind him and stood in the hall frowning.

Something was very, very wrong. He didn't know what it was. He just hoped that whatever it was Aron's coming of age was going to be enough to put it right.

Chapter 11

n Saturday morning Adam was woken early by a pounding on his door. 'Go away,' he groaned – which only served as an invitation to a bleary-eyed Chloe, who was still in her pyjamas. 'Mother says you have to get up.'

Adam squinted towards the window. 'But it's still dark!'

Chloe shrugged and yawned. 'We have to make sure everything is ready.' She disappeared back into the hall – although not before calling, 'Auntie Jo says she'll pour a jug of water over anyone who isn't downstairs in five minutes.'

Adam nestled back under his duvet. He had spent the whole evening before underground, lugging chairs from the storage chambers to the ballroom – and his back was aching. Aron and Luc had dragged heavy wooden tables backwards and forwards under Elise's critical eye until they were positioned to the millimetre in the vast underground feasting hall. Auntie Jo and Chloe had spread clean white linens on top and placed hundreds of candles on the tables and in the old iron sconces along the walls while Elise fussed with vases and cutlery. They

121

had worked until well after midnight, letting Nathanial handle all the call-outs himself. He probably hadn't been to bed at all.

No one had said anything more about Auntie Jo's misery on Wednesday. She had been sitting in the den on Thursday, paler than usual but watching her films as though nothing had happened. Adam had felt a little awkward but she was so determinedly normal he had no choice but to go along with it. If he was honest it was a relief. He knew *this* Auntie Jo – the one reading his horoscope and cracking jokes. The other one was a stranger and Adam didn't know what to say to *her*.

Now, squinting at the clock made him groan again. It wasn't even six o'clock in the morning. Adam pondered the events of the day ahead with mixed feelings. The first guests would arrive just before lunch – the Concilium and a handful of close Lumen who would help organise the huge crowd arriving for the celebrations. Aron would go through the rituals and then the Crone would Mark him. Adam had mixed feelings about seeing the Marking. He knew it would hurt.

Still, once the bloody bit was over they would have the party to look forward to. Aron would emerge into the ballroom to a cheering throng to be showered with gifts from the men and hugs from prospective mothers-in-law. They would all sit down at the heavy tables and eat food prepared by dozens of Luman daughters, eager to show off their cooking skills to their future husbands – who might be sitting right there! And finally there would be toasts, music and dancing until well into the night. At least that bit would probably be a laugh.

There was no time to indulge in further daydreams. Adam heard a heavy foot tread on the stairs and hurled himself upright. He'd been on the receiving end of one of Auntie Jo's wake-up jugs before – and she never used the hot tap.

The morning sped by in a blur of final checks and activities. Once every inch of the cellar rooms had been inspected, an almost hysterical Elise sent them all upstairs to get dressed. She flitted between her room and Chloe's while Nathanial helped Aron get ready. Adam mooched down to the kitchen and found Auntie Jo standing by the toaster. She was wearing a very unforgiving dress in an eye-watering shade of purple. At least she had left off her kaftan in honour of the occasion.

She gave a snort of laughter as Adam walked in. 'Well, it makes a change from your school uniform. Maybe we should take some photos and send them in for your friends to admire.'

Adam scowled and shifted self-consciously from foot to foot. He felt like a prat. The black tie bit was nothing unusual – but it was what he was wearing *over* his black jacket and trousers that made him really stand out. The ceremonial capes were normally stored safely away. They were made of heavy black cloth, hooded and trimmed with fur to indicate whether the wearer had come of age or not. Adam's was trimmed with black fur, showing that he was still a child in the eyes of the Luman world. Aron's would be trimmed in white fur, showing that he was able to guide souls safely into their Lights. Adam tried hard not to think about the many furry critters who had been sacrificed on the altar of Luman vanity. Elise had altered the capes so they were all the right size but Adam was still worried he was going to trip on the floor-length fabric and fall flat on his face at some crucial moment.

Elise burst into the kitchen with her blonde hair still in rollers. 'Oh for Fates' sake, Josephine! Must you spend every second of every day eating toast? I was searching for you!'

Auntie Jo shrugged unperturbed. 'Thought I'd have a bit of early lunch. We'll not be eating for hours.'

'I need some of your whisky.' She scowled at Adam's widened eyes. 'For Aron, not *pour moi.*'

Auntie Jo reached into her purple clutch bag and pulled out her hip flask. 'I'm glad he's going to have a little nip. I thought he was going to do it old school.'

Elise seized the hip flask without thanks and swept out, leaving Adam puzzled. 'I didn't think Aron liked whisky.'

Auntie Jo shrugged. 'He doesn't but it will take the edge off.' Adam's confusion must have shown because she sighed. 'Think about it. A complete stranger is about to turn up with a manual tattoo pen and etch the Mortson seal into his chest. There isn't much meat over his breastbone. Believe me, he'll be glad of a little anaesthetic beforehand.'

Adam shuddered. When she put it like that, maybe it wouldn't be such a bad thing after all if he never managed to come of age . . .

An hour later they were all ready. Adam stood in the hallway and looked at his family with a peculiar mixture of pride and embarrassment. His father and Luc were dressed almost identically to him. Aron's outfit was the same except for a strange white wrap-type shirt that exposed most of his chest, ready for the Marking. Auntie Jo had thrown a gauzy silver cape over her purple dress and Elise looked stunning in an elegant black dress with a lace cape, her blonde hair curled.

But the real surprise was Chloe. She was the last to arrive, walking carefully down the stairs in gold-heeled sandals to match her golden ballgown. Her hair was pinned up and woven through with gold threads and glittering crystals. Adam's jaw dropped as he looked at his younger sister. She looked ten years older and impossibly glamorous. He was momentarily glad none of his friends would ever meet her or he'd never hear the end of it.

She stopped beside Adam, chewing her lip. Nathanial kissed her cheek and said, 'You look beautiful, Chloe.' He looked happy and sad at the same time.

For once Luc didn't say anything funny and even Auntie Jo was looking a little shiny-eyed. 'Well, if that dress doesn't catch you a High Luman I don't know what will.'

Elise stepped over to her daughter and tapped beneath her chin. 'Head up! And smile, my darling, smile.'

Aron was flushed and nervous. 'Who's got the whisky?'

'Not too much, Aron,' Nathanial said not unkindly. 'Just a few more sips.'

Adam shuddered and found himself wishing the whole thing was over. As if on cue the front door knocker crashed, making everyone jump. Heinrich entered, smiling. He paused and took a moment to look at them each in turn. 'My dearest Mortsons. How wonderful to be with you all today.' He embraced Nathanial, kissed Elise on both cheeks and shook Aron's hand firmly. 'The Concilium waits outside. Shall we proceed?'

Aron cleared his throat. 'Let's get it over with.'

***

A few minutes later Adam was sitting on a simple wooden chair in an underground room. His family and the Concilium had walked out into the garden and through the concealed cellar doors in the lawn behind one of the yew trees. Down a torch-lit flight of stairs a passage veered off in two directions. To the right were the vaults and crypts where Keystones and dead Mortsons rested respectively. To the left were the celebration chambers they would be using later.

And straight ahead through an ornate iron door was the Oath Chamber. It was a large, oval-shaped room with a black marble floor and panelled walls carved with scenes from Luman lore and history. At the far end a high stool and small table had been placed on a raised plinth. To one side was a heavy wooden throne, covered in black velvet cushions and drapes. Two chairs faced the throne on the other side of the stool.

The rest of the chairs were some distance away, arranged in arcs facing towards the business end of the chamber. Adam was seated between Luc and Auntie Jo, with Elise and Chloe sitting nearby. The Concilium were there too, sitting in silence – apart from Heinrich. He was at the other end of the room, helping Aron onto the high wooden stool, then sitting down beside Nathanial, who was smiling reassuringly at Aron.

The cloths on the throne moved and for a moment Adam almost yelped a warning – until he realised that what he'd mistaken for some kind of malevolent supernatural cushion was actually a tiny human swathed from head to foot in heavy black fabric. The figure turned towards them and bowed but the face was obscured by a thick panel of lace. Adam sucked in a breath. He was looking at the Crone.

She nodded at Nathanial and Heinrich but ignored poor Aron completely. She turned her attention to the table. Heinrich raised an eyebrow at Elise and said, 'Shall we begin?'

Elise stood. Soft-footed and graceful, she walked the length of the chamber holding a silver dish. As she reached her eldest son she paused and simply looked at him for a long moment. Nathanial stood and joined her, taking the silver dish from her. Elise cleared her throat, raised her hands in the air and began to speak. 'These are the hands which have fed you.' She took a piece of fruit from the dish and gently placed it in Aron's mouth. 'Now they will feed you no more.'

Adam gave Auntie Jo an alarmed look. She opened one side of her mouth and whispered, 'Don't worry, he isn't going anywhere. They used to marry them off straight after the ceremony and then their new brides would take over all the cooking. It saved having two parties. They just haven't bothered changing the ceremony words.'

Elise lifted a white cloth from the dish and held it to Aron's forehead. 'These are the hands which have comforted you. Now they will comfort you no more.' There was a slight tremble in her voice but she continued, 'I brought you here as my child. Today you will leave as a man.' She kissed Aron's cheek tenderly, then turned and slipped back to her seat, her eyes shining.

Nathanial held out his hand silently and Aron reached for the keystone round his neck, pulling the thin chain over his head. Nathanial took the keystone and clasped his son's hand in his. 'I brought you here as my child. Today you will leave as a man.' He turned to the Crone and bowed his head, placing the keystone in her gloved hand. She took it without a word as Nathanial returned to his seat.

Adam swallowed hard. This was the bit he'd been dreading. He tried to tell himself that the gore would be good practice for being a doctor. The Crone turned to her table and placed the keystone in a stone mortar, then picked up her pestle and began to grind.

Adam hissed to Auntie Jo, 'Is she grinding up his keystone?'

Auntie Jo shook her head almost imperceptibly. 'Of course not. We'd be here for days. She's already been sent a chip from one of the family Keystones. This is just for show.'

Sure enough the Crone had already set the mortar down and was using a tiny gold spoon to lift a heaped spoonful of charcoal powder into a small vial. She added dark liquid from a gold jug and stirred the contents. Finally she lifted a long, thin tool from the table and stepped in front of Aron, his breastbone at her eye level.

They could tell the moment the tattoo pen touched Aron's skin. Adam flinched as he watched his brother grit his teeth, but Aron managed to sit absolutely still. Not only was a manual pen more painful than a modern electric pen but a Luman tattoo went deeper than a normal tattoo. It had to – after all, Aron would never need a keystone again. His keystone was literally becoming a part of him, being inked into his body. Being Marked would make him forever a Luman.

Being Marked also took a very long time. Adam watched the Crone's hand dart in and out with tiny, precise movements and winced. Aron's jaw was clenched and his lips were thin lines but somehow he wasn't making a sound. Adam pressed his finger against his sternum, amazed at how tender even a fingernail was, never mind the viciously sharp tattoo pen. Yet again he pondered if he could avoid getting Marked for the rest of his life. Or at least if he could become a doctor first he might be able to get his hands on some local anaesthetic . . .

He felt Luc's elbow in his ribs. 'When I come of age I'm going to get *my* tat on the back of my neck.'

Adam winced again. 'Why?'

Luc shrugged. 'Chest tattoos are OK if you live somewhere sunny but seriously – how often will you get to show it off in London? On the neck – it's an all-year-round babe magnet.'

Adam snorted. The Mortson seal – a flaming torch in a black circle – wasn't exactly the typical dolphin or Celtic armband tattoo. 'Not exactly keeping the Luman world a secret, is it?'

Luc smirked. 'Chicks love a mystery.'

Elise turned to them with the ladylike smile of a Luman hostess – and the eyes of a psychotic killer. They shut up then to avoid being flayed alive once the guests had gone home. It reminded Adam of Melissa and her laser eyes. Fleetingly, he found himself wishing she was there. What would she make of it all? The hooded cloaks, the underground chamber, the candles, the savage ritual playing out in front of them? For him it wasn't exactly normal but it wasn't scary either. If he brought Melissa down here she'd probably punch him on the nose, call the police and tell the newspapers about her near-miss with a fiendish cult in their underground lair.

The thought depressed him. His friends would probably take it better. Spike would watch the proceedings unfolding and start plotting how to become Chief Curator. Archie would be too busy sketching the whole scene to give it much thought, while Dan would be torn between the delights of finding himself in a vaguely Tolkienesque world – and worrying what his mum the psychotherapist would make of it all.

These gloomy thoughts passed the time more effectively than he realised and before he knew it the Crone was stepping away from Aron and setting down her pen. She bowed her head at him and returned to the throne. Nathanial and Heinrich helped Aron to his feet. His face was very pale and his cheeks and chest gleamed with sweat but he managed to bow to the others and say in a small voice, 'My Light is your Light.'

The Curators stood up and said in unison, 'Our Light is your Light.'

Heinrich embraced Aron, careful to avoid crushing his tender flesh in a bear hug. 'We congratulate our newest brother. Welcome, Aron Mortson, to manhood. Give no Luman cause to take away the Mark you rightfully bear.' He turned to Elise. 'We will now hear Aron's oath. We look forward to joining you shortly for the celebration.'

His easy courtesy couldn't quite hide the fact that the women and children weren't allowed to hear this part of the ceremony. Of course Elise would never do anything other than incline her head graciously and say, 'Of course, Chief Curator.' She rose to her feet and indicated that the others should follow her. Adam dutifully fell into line and trooped out of the chamber, back into the passageway.

The heavy iron door thudded closed behind them and Chloe promptly burst into tears. 'I can't believe they did that,' she wept. 'I can't believe they did that to poor Aron!' She sobbed into her hand, all her sophistication deserting her. She was once again a thirteen-year-old girl in a very expensive dress.

There was a stunned silence, then Elise swept into action. 'Stop crying, my darling! Enough! Your make-up!' A lace-edged handkerchief appeared from nowhere and dabbed up Chloe's tears before they could do any damage. Auntie Jo fussed around making comforting noises.

Even Luc seemed shaken. 'It took longer than I thought it would. It must have hurt. Like, really hurt. Hurt *a shitload*!'

Adam nodded. Inside the chamber it had all seemed vaguely normal but now they were out of the room he could see it was just one more thing to try to reconcile with his everyday life. 'Bet you're glad now that you weren't the first one to come of age?'

Luc frowned. 'Dunno. Might be better to go into it and not actually know what happens.' He tapped the side of his nose. 'Still, I'll come prepared. There's this cream you can get . . .'

His cunning plan was interrupted by Elise. Chloe was still subdued but her make-up was miraculously restored thanks to several tubes and a compact produced from Elise's lace-covered evening bag. 'We must go. Our guests will be waiting.'

Auntie Jo rubbed her hands together. 'Cheer up! Not long till we get the grub now!'

They made their way along the corridor. The Oath Chamber was well soundproofed behind the heavy door but as they made their way towards the ballroom they could hear the subdued roar of a large and excited crowd. The guests had arrived during the Marking and been led to the ballroom by trusted family and friends. The passage widened and turned a corner, revealing double wooden doors, closed against them.

Uncle Paddy was standing waiting for them, on guard duty, keeping the guests inside. 'Elise! My God woman, you get better looking every time I see you for a fact!' He grabbed her hand and raised it to his lips, then widened his eyes theatrically at Chloe. 'And who's this vision of beauty?' He pretended to stumble backwards swooning and Chloe managed a watery smile. 'You look beautiful, darling girl,' he said, kissing her cheek.

'Where's my welcome you old rogue?' Auntie Jo demanded.

Uncle Paddy shook his head, apparently overcome with sorrow. 'Ah, Josephine, don't remind me! Don't remind me of what I've missed out on! If you'd only been born a few years sooner I'd have thrown myself at your feet and let you walk over me until you agreed to be my bride!'

Auntie Jo snorted. 'You wouldn't have lived to your advanced age with me walking all over you.' She grinned and they embraced with real affection. 'It's good to see you Paddy.'

'Well Luc, Adam.' Uncle Paddy nodded at them. 'How was the Marking? Did he stay quiet like a man or sing like a woman?'

Luc grinned. 'He never made a sound.'

Uncle Paddy threw his hands in the air triumphantly. 'Of course he didn't! That's the Mortson blood in him! He's made of stern stuff is young Aron! Just like you two!' He winked at Adam, who smiled hesitantly. He wasn't sure he deserved the credit Uncle Paddy was giving him.

Paddy turned to Elise, dropping the patter, suddenly business-like. 'Your guests are inside, enjoying some refreshments. You've done a lovely job on the place.'

Elise smiled. 'Thank you, Patrick. It's kind of you to say so.'

'The family are all looking forward to seeing you.' He winked at Chloe. 'I can tell you that one young man in particular is looking forward to seeing a certain girl in a golden dress.'

Chloe's cheeks flushed. Elise kept smiling but her eyes were steely. 'Yes, Chloe is looking forward to seeing *all* our guests this evening. Shall we go inside?'

'Of course,' Paddy said, gallant as ever. As he opened the door and announced their arrival Adam shot an angry look at his mother. If Chloe had to get betrothed at all, why didn't Elise just let her get betrothed to Ciaron instead of casting about searching for someone more important? All right, Uncle Paddy wasn't technically their uncle but the families were close; certainly much closer than the Mortsons were with Elise's family. Most of their French relatives were too busy looking down their noses to be friendly.

They were greeted by polite applause and there was no more chance to ponder the mystery of snooty relatives before a swarm of people pressed forward to greet them. Adam's hand was shaken and his cheeks kissed until both were burning. The room was bursting. Hundreds of people had turned up to see the newest Marked Luman and they were dressed for a party. Elise fell into step as the perfect hostess, greeting all her guests graciously, admiring the height of sons and the dresses on daughters.

Luc was watching the whole spectacle with sardonic pleasure. 'So, time to suss out the talent. Do you want me to find Monobrow for you? You know, the babe we spotted at the Summoning? I thought she looked just right for your future wife . . .'

Adam scowled and tried to stay close to Elise. They had only managed to greet a quarter of the guests before a trumpet blew behind them. The double doors were open again and Heinrich and the Concilium were entering. The room fell silent. Heinrich spread his arms. 'My dear friends. Allow me to present to you our newest Luman brother. I give you . . . Aron Mortson, Marked Luman!'

A sheepish-looking Aron entered with a beaming Nathanial. He looked much better, in spite of the raw black mark on his chest. There was an almost hysterical roar of approval from the crowd.

Luc grinned. 'Let's get this party started!'

Chapter 12

wo hours later Adam was sitting at a long bench with Luc and Auntie Jo. The air was rich with the scent of dishes from every part of the globe. Adam stared at the mountain of food on his plate, wondering where to start.

At least he'd been able to take off his heavy ceremonial cloak. After his rapturous welcome, Aron had to greet the guests, receiving gifts from the men and kisses from the women. At this point the girls and women had vanished to lay out the food for the feast ahead while Aron was being fêted by the crowd. Finally, flushed with adrenalin and embarrassment he had led the formal procession of Marked Lumen into the feasting hall.

All the unmarried girls stood behind a long bench, platters and bowls of food on display in front of them while their mothers fluttered about behind. It was all a bit surreal; girls in beautiful dresses and heels standing serving soufflés and samosas. The trouble was that being a Luman wife meant being a hostess, so looking good wasn't enough – you had to be able to cook and entertain your guests too. Adam imagined Melissa standing beside him and died a little inside. She'd think she'd stepped into some kind of awful costume drama.

Food had been heaped on his plate until it wouldn't hold any more and only then had Adam made his escape to the table. Luc had somehow managed to carry three plates back with him, which Auntie Jo was taking full advantage of. None of the girls had wanted to give her any food – after all, she wasn't exactly a prospective husband. Adam picked through the mess of dishes on his plate without appetite. It was all so cringeworthy. He glanced up at the far end, where Aron was sitting in the place of honour with his father and the Concilium. Elise's seat was empty; no doubt she was checking on Chloe's progress and pretending that she hadn't helped her daughter with the elaborate concoction Chloe was serving.

Auntie Jo scraped the last morsel from her plate and burped discreetly. 'Lovely. Some of those girls should be professionals. Their talents are wasted at home.'

Luc raised an eyebrow. 'You know, since you're not married, shouldn't *you* be up there? You should be catching a husband.'

Auntie Jo smiled. 'Funnily enough, I was always better at eating the food than cooking it. Your mother on the other hand is a fabulous chef and barely eats a thing. Oh, the cruel irony of it all!'

'But you must have done this when you were younger? You know, when you were a teenager.'

Auntie Jo's smile faded a little. 'That was a million years ago. Back when dinosaurs walked the earth and all that. Anyway, you'll all have to marry good cooks and then at least I'll be well fed when I come and visit.'

Adam tried to imagine Auntie Jo at Chloe's age and felt a pang of curiosity. After all, once upon a time she must have seemed like any other Luman daughter, not the quirky character she was now. What had she been like? Had she been pretty? He thought about the locket round Auntie Jo's neck and the picture inside. There was something familiar about the young man in the photo. Had Adam met him before? He must have been Auntie Jo's intended husband but for some reason they hadn't ended up betrothed. Maybe he had ended up marrying someone else. Could he be one of the Lumen here this evening?

His musings were interrupted by Chloe's arrival. She looked hot and bothered but pleased too as she slid onto the bench beside Auntie Jo. 'I thought I was never going to sit down. My feet are killing me.' She gave her gold sandals a baleful glance.

Luc smirked. 'Don't get too comfy. You're going to have to dance soon.'

Chloe swore under her breath. 'Don't remind me. One of the Chinese Lumen made me promise him the first dance. I tried to get out of it but he's like some kind of *stalker*.'

Auntie Jo raised an eyebrow. 'The Chinese Lumen are big players. Your mother will be delighted.'

Chloe scowled. 'I don't want to live in China. I want to stay somewhere close to Britain.'

Auntie Jo shrugged. 'Britain is a small Kingdom. There are more souls in a small Chinese Kingdom than most of Europe put together. You'd be top of the pile if you married a Chinese Luman.'

'Yeah, and it doesn't matter where you are when you can swoop anyway,' Luc said logically. 'I mean, it's not like it would take you long to come home for a visit. As long as you were allowed to.'

Adam looked at the sudden tightness in Chloe's face and felt sorry for her. She was thirteen years old. She shouldn't be worrying about having to move to the other side of the world. Their world was mad. Totally mad! 'Maybe you'll still get betrothed to Ciaron,' he said, trying to sound encouraging.

Luc shook his head. 'Mother will never allow it. Trust me, she wants you to be Luman royalty. Ireland's tiny. She'll want you somewhere like India or America at the very least.'

Chloe scowled. 'Yeah, well, Father likes Ciaron. And it's up to him anyway, not Mother.'

Auntie Jo was forking up the last mouthfuls from Adam's plate. 'Don't worry about all that tonight Chloe. Just try and enjoy yourself.'

'Have you even managed to talk to Ciaron yet?' Adam asked innocently.

'How am I supposed to talk to him when I have to sit with *you* lot?' Chloe snapped. She looked close to tears. 'I'll talk to him later.' She stood up abruptly, almost tripping over her long skirts. 'I *hate* these shoes!'

They watched her retreat in silence. Auntie Jo sighed. 'Welcome to the wonderful world of Luman womanhood,' she muttered and emptied her wine glass.

Chloe's abrupt departure left them all feeling subdued – and in Adam's case guilty. He was rubbish at being a Luman and resented every call-out – but at least he had some control over where he would live and work. Chloe would probably be a far better Luman than him – but just because she was a girl she didn't get that choice. What would it be like, knowing you had to leave your home and marry a virtual stranger?

Of course, Adam realised with a sudden chill, he would be able to stay in Britain but he would still have to marry a stranger when the time came. Male Lumen generally got betrothed when they were slightly older than female Lumen – but by the time Adam was Aron's age he'd be seriously expected to have a future bride in mind. How was he going to break that to Melissa if things worked out between them? He gulped at the thought of explaining *that* under her laser-eyed scrutiny . . .

He was glad when they were finally able to leave the tables and make their way into the packed ballroom. The room looked amazing. The sprung wooden floor glowed beneath the crystal chandeliers and hundreds of candles burned along the walls. A stage had been erected at one end for the band to play. All of the band members were male Lumen from minor families. By playing at balls they could get their families invited to events they would otherwise be excluded from – and give their children a chance at raising their status.

Adam felt a sudden, passionate dislike for the Luman world. The whole thing was sick. Here he was, swanning around, being eyed by girls who didn't know him just because his father was High Luman and they had loads of Keystones. Did his potential admirers even know that he couldn't guide a soul without throwing up? Or were they just as suckered in by the Mortson name as everyone else?

Luc of course was in his element. 'Babes everywhere. I don't even know where to start.'

Adam snorted. 'Yeah, but this isn't like Cryptique. You can't just cop off with someone and get away with it. You'll end up betrothed before you even know what's happening.'

Luc gave an airy shrug. 'Well, on the bright side, if it's not like Cryptique I don't need to worry about you throwing up on someone's feet. Anyway, trust me. I know how to keep the mothers on side.'

'It's the fathers you need to worry about,' Adam muttered. It was fair to say that Lumen took their daughters' prospects seriously. In his book it didn't make sense to annoy someone who could send your soul straight into the afterlife.

Auntie Jo was standing on tiptoe peering towards the stage. 'Well, your parents are ready to start the dancing. I wonder who Aron's going to choose for his first dance.'

Adam stared curiously at the front of the ballroom. As hosts his parents would lead the dancing, joined by the Concilium – but tradition decreed that the newest Marked Luman would be one of the first on the floor. Every guest would be watching feverishly to see who he would choose as a partner. After all, this could be the first step on the road to betrothal.

An elbow hit him in the ribs. 'It's Monobrow!' Luc whispered ecstatically, pointing across the room. 'She came! You're all set for romance, bro!' He nodded towards the girl from the Summoning.

Adam looked at her with a mixture of horror and guilt. She was wearing a bright orange dress the size of a car and had her hair piled up in curls beneath some kind of tiara – but nothing could really distract attention away from that unfortunate eyebrow.

The Lumen on the stage were picking up their instruments and the band leader raised an eyebrow at Elise, who nodded discreetly. As the first notes swelled out Nathanial bowed formally to his wife and took her hand, leading her into a waltz. The married members of the Concilium offered their hands to their own wives – but all eyes were on a furiously blushing Aron. After a moment's hesitation he approached a pretty Indian Luman in a sari and jewelled sandals. She stood rooted to the spot for a moment, shrinking beneath the envious or amused gaze of the crowd, but managed to take Aron's hand and follow him onto the dance floor.

There was only one unmarried member of the Concilium and he was looking around the ballroom with an expression of unbridled resentment. He seemed to be searching for someone. At the same moment Auntie Jo cursed loudly enough to make several Lumen look around in surprise. 'Oh, he wouldn't dare! The little snake! I refuse!'

Adam and Luc watched with a mixture of horror and delight as Darian approached Auntie Jo. His expression would have curdled milk – but protocol was protocol. Auntie Jo was unmarried and the sister of their host – and technically available. The fact that they hated the sight of one another was entirely beside the point. In fairness, the last time they had met Auntie Jo had revealed to the whole room that he had unsuccessfully wooed Elise. Clearly the memory was still etched into his psyche. As he reached them he gave a bow so stiff his spine almost snapped. 'May I have the . . . *honour* . . . of this dance?'

Auntie Jo had frozen. She was usually the master of the pithy comeback but for once she'd been blindsided. She revved furiously in neutral for a moment, then sighed heavily, realising she was trapped. Even Auntie Jo wouldn't humiliate a Curator at a Marking ball. 'Erm, yeah. All right.'

Adam sniggered and tried to turn it into a cough. It wasn't the most gracious acceptance. He watched Darian grit his teeth and whirl Auntie Jo into the centre of the dance floor. At the front of the room Nathanial was dancing with Elise. She was smiling up at him. For a moment Adam could almost imagine them at ball like this one twenty years earlier, both of them only a little older than he was now. He felt a curdling mixture of embarrassment and affection.

Luc rubbed his hands together. 'Time to go a-hunting. Don't wait too long or you'll be left with the dregs . . .' He darted off sideways, his eye clearly set on someone – and a moment later re-emerged with a blonde Californian beauty.

Left alone Adam gulped and risked a cautious peek around. Everywhere he looked there were girls hoping for a dance, watched beadily by parents. A few of the nearest girls eyed him hungrily. He felt like a worm at the centre of a flock of very hungry chickens.

There was a delicate cough beside him. '*Bonsoir*, Adam,' a sweet voice intoned. He turned and found himself looking at a pretty girl with blonde hair and brown eyes. Her hair was piled into an elaborate mop of curls and she was wearing a dress that resembled a dessert; a frothing mixture of white net and satin. 'Don't tell me you don't remember me?'

Adam stared blankly at her for a second, then felt his jaw drop with sudden recognition. 'Marianne! Wow, you look . . . different!' He cleared his throat, feeling desperately awkward. He knew Marianne was some kind of cousin a few times removed – but the last time he'd seen her she'd been a snot-nosed kid having a tantrum at their French grandmother's house. Somehow she had morphed into a porcelain doll.

There were no tears or howls of wrath tonight. Marianne seemed perfectly composed. 'But of course! It has been too long, dear Adam. You look *très beau*. Very handsome. And what lovely music.' She smiled expectantly.

It took Adam a minute to realise what she wanted. 'Oh yeah. Erm . . . do you want to dance?'

Marianne's eyes widened to saucer size. 'Why yes, how lovely!' She managed to sound surprised even though it had blatantly been her plan all along.

There was a moment of fumbling awkwardness as Adam wrestled her into a dancing stance. Happily his lessons with Madame Gauche-Pieds hadn't been wasted all those years ago. Marianne was a good dancer but the whole thing felt so contrived. It had been much more fun dancing with Melissa in Cryptique – even if Michael Bulber had managed to bring the evening to an unromantic conclusion. At least Melissa had wanted him there because she knew him, not just because his surname was Mortson.

Time had a funny way of moving faster when there was music on, Adam realised a while later. He was on to his fourth dance partner; he'd never been so popular with the ladies. Marianne had been reluctant to let him go and had made him swear they would dance again before the night was over.

At least dancing meant he got a good view of everything. Auntie Jo had escaped Darian's clutches (or vice versa) and was being squired around the floor by the ever-gallant Heinrich.

143

Darian was circling Elise, ignoring his partner completely, clearly lying in wait for an opportunity to pounce on the object of his devotion. It was a slightly gross realisation for Adam that someone fancied his mother that much. Luc was dancing with a succession of model types while Aron seemed to keep returning to the pretty Indian girl he'd first danced with.

And at last Chloe had managed to pair up with Ciaron. Adam watched him sourly without knowing why. Ciaron was just too sickeningly perfect. He was tall and broad-shouldered with wavy dark hair and the heroic good looks of some mythological Irish king. He could just imagine Ciaron guiding people onto the Unknown Roads with that lilting accent . . . He probably managed to make the directions sound like poetry.

Still, at least Chloe looked happy. She was chatting animatedly, her cheeks flushed. And Ciaron was listening to her, nodding and grinning with those perfect white teeth. Elise had spotted them too and was frowning slightly as she danced with Rashid, an Indian Luman who was one of the youngest Curators. Adam smirked. She was trapped for now and Chloe could enjoy her dance without interruption.

But after another few dances Adam was getting restless. The ballroom was heaving and the air was hot. There were no windows in the underground room and Adam began to feel stifled. The music was so loud it was hard to make conversation with his dance partner without putting his mouth right against her ear – and he didn't want her to get the wrong idea. The only girl he really wanted here was the one person he would never be allowed to bring into his world – and that was Melissa.

The dance ended. His dance partner's disappointed face only

piqued his resentment. Worse still he could see that Darian had finally managed to get his hands on Elise and was pulling her in much closer than was considered polite. Adam frowned, hoping that the ceremonial swords didn't end up coming out to play.

The final nail in the coffin was hearing a French accent calling his name. 'Adam! My dance! It is time for our next dance, *oui*?' Marianne was fighting her way towards him. For someone so dainty she was moving like a rhino through the reeds, barging through the gathered Lumen. Even thinking about another dance and her not-so-subtle hints was making Adam feel light-headed.

He needed air. Pretending not to see her (and feeling only a tiny bit guilty), Adam turned on his heel and fled.

It took a few minutes to weave and dodge through the crowds but finally Adam found himself outside the Oath Chamber. The air was cooler here but he had a desperate urge to be above ground for a while. The corridor behind him was empty and he darted up the stairs and through the cellar doors, emerging on the lawn in the shadow of the yew trees.

There was a terrifying growl – followed, thankfully, by a happy yelp of recognition. Sam and Morty bounded towards him, their tails wagging madly. They had been left above ground on sentry duty and they were happy to see him, sniffing at his pockets for treats. Adam petted them roughly, basking in their simple, undemanding affection. They didn't care that he wasn't smooth with the ladies, or that he was a rubbish Luman. They just adored him. It was nice to have some true fans.

He set off across the grass, round the side of the house

towards the kitchen door, planning to get them something tasty from the fridge. Just as he reached the back door Morty stopped and went still. He gave a low growl and stared into the darkness towards the paddock.

Adam hesitated, his hand on the kitchen door handle. He shouldn't have left the party – but maybe he wasn't the only one who'd needed some fresh air. Was Marianne *that* desperate to claim her dance? He squinted into the darkness, wondering whether to make a run for it or go back and accept his fate gracefully.

Morty growled again and this time Sam joined him. The weird thing was that neither dog set off in pursuit of whatever was bothering them. Sam's growl tailed off into a whine – and with a start Adam realised that they were afraid.

There was a sudden, soft crunch of footsteps on the gravel drive up ahead of him. A shadow passed along the hedge; a dark figure, cloaked in black. Morty gave a small yelp of terror and both dogs turned on their heels and fled back towards the front of the house.

Adam stood rigid with shock. The wolfhounds weren't just family pets; they were working dogs, trained to herd souls in the Hinterland. They weren't easily spooked – but something was scaring them so badly they had abandoned him in the darkness. For a moment he hesitated, wondering if he should return to the party and get some back-up – but then he was going to have to explain why he was above ground in the first place and listen to Elise's lecture on good manners. He'd rather face whatever unknown terror was waiting in the darkness.

Still, it would have been nice to have some company. 'Thanks a lot,' he muttered over his shoulder at the dogs, who were no doubt hunkered down somewhere safe by now.

He moved stealthily along the hedge, trying to walk lightly on the gravel, listening for any sounds – but the figure had disappeared into the paddock and their footsteps were muffled on the long grass. As he reached the end of the hedge, he hesitated. Who was there? It might be a Luman – but then why would they be sneaking about above ground? His immediate distrustful thought was that Darian was up to no good – but there was no way Darian would miss out on his dance with Elise.

He moved across the grass in silence, wishing he had his ceremonial cloak on. His white shirt was like a beacon in the darkness. He paused between the yews, listening for any sound but all he could hear was the hiss of the night breeze through the leaves and grass.

The last thing he expected was the voice right behind him.

Chapter 13

have waited for you, Adam Mortson.'

Adam spun round and backed away in one stumbling motion, frightened and furious at getting caught. He'd turned from hunter to prey in the blink of an eye. He squinted into the darkness, searching for a shadow. 'Who's there? Show yourself!'

There was the faintest trace of movement in front of him. 'Do not be afraid. I mean you no ill will.'

Adam frowned. Hearing the voice again . . . he was sure he'd heard it before. It was a woman's voice, soft and pleasant – although still pretty freaky in the dark. 'Who are you? How do you know me?'

His eyes were adjusting to the light now and this time he saw a definite movement; an arm rising through the air. At the same time the faintest hint of a glow appeared, illuminating a hand. The glow spread, casting a pale light on a figure in front of him – small, hooded in a black cloak, just the tips of her blonde hair shimmering beneath the heavy fabric.

Adam stared, for once speechless. He was having trouble

believing what he was seeing – or rather who he was seeing. 'You're . . . I know you. You're that Fate!'

The woman smiled, just as she had at the Summoning – shyly. 'Yes. I am Clotho, the spinner.'

Adam wanted to shake his head until his eyes rattled and the world made sense again. 'But . . . you're here.'

Clotho nodded. 'I am but I cannot linger long. We must speak, Adam Mortson. Not here and not now.' She pulled her other hand from her cloak, fast enough to make Adam flinch back instinctively – but when he looked again she was offering him a small green glass bead. 'You must come to my realm. We can talk in safety there.'

Adam hesitated before he took the glass. She must be mad, coming here in the middle of a coming of age ball with so many Lumen gathered together. What would she have done if he hadn't come above ground? Would she have gone down into the ballroom? It would have caused a stampede. 'How did you know you would find me here? Outside, I mean.'

Clotho looked uneasy. 'I am tarrying too long, Adam Mortson. Come to my realm. I will answer your questions there.'

Adam shook his head. 'No. I'm not going anywhere. How did you find me?' A thought occurred to him. 'Did you do something to me? Did you *make me* come up into the garden?'

Clotho sighed. 'I did not force you to speak with me. I merely . . . influenced you.'

Adam stared at her. For some reason her words were making him feel a little bit sick. 'I thought I was doing it myself,' he said slowly. 'You shouldn't have done that.'

For a second Clotho looked stricken. 'Forgive me. My time is short. You are in danger. There was no other way.'

Adam felt his heart leap. 'What do you mean I'm in danger?' He backed away a little, his mind racing. *She knew!* She knew about the bomber and the bus girl and the homeless man and the car driver! She knew that he had saved them and now she had come to kill him! 'I'm not going anywhere with you!'

Clotho was breathing quickly. She hunched over a little, clutching at her chest. 'I wish to help you, Adam Mortson. I will do what I can to protect you.' She put her other hand on her stomach and groaned softly.

Adam frowned. She didn't look like a threat; she looked sick. If anyone was in danger right now it seemed to be her. 'Are you all right?'

Clotho straightened up although it seemed to take a lot of effort. 'I dare not linger. Let me help you. Come to me, in my realm. I will do all I can to save you. Save your family.' Her voice was getting weaker and the light around her was fading.

Adam blinked at her, confused and alarmed. 'But when? When will I come?'

'Soon.' The word was a whisper as the last of her light disappeared. 'Come soon.'

Adam squinted into the darkness but his night vision was gone. And by the time he could see anything Clotho was gone too.

Adam's head was swimming. How was he going to go back to the party? He'd only had a glass of champagne to toast Aron, otherwise he might have wondered whether this was all some kind of drunken dream.

150

As he crossed the lawn he struggled to get his thoughts in order. Clotho had taken a big chance coming here tonight and she seemed to want to help him. But who was out to get him? And why? It must be because he'd been interfering with the Fates – but if that was the case, why hadn't Clotho just killed him there and then?

His dark thoughts were interrupted by a shadow moving on the lawn. Adam's heart sank. Who else was lying in wait for him? But as he inched closer he recognised the figure draped in shimmering cloth.

Chloe jumped – then relaxed. 'Oh, it's you. Don't tell on me!'

'I won't.' Adam eyed her curiously. 'What are you doing up here?'

'Same thing as you, I expect,' Chloe said. 'Taking a break.' She was holding something dangling from her fingers. After a moment's squinting Adam recognised the dull glimmer of her gold sandals.

'I thought you'd be downstairs dancing with Ciaron.'

Chloe scowled. 'I can only dance so long. You try waltzing all night in high heels.'

Adam winced at the thought. He was enough of a liability on the dance floor in flat shoes. 'It's good, isn't it? The party.'

Chloe shrugged. 'I guess. So good we're both hiding up here.'

Adam stared at her. Chloe was holding the hem of her dress off the ground. In the faint light from the stairwell below Adam could just see her bare toes wiggling in the grass. Her feet must have been freezing.

'I thought you liked all this stuff. Dresses and dancing and meeting Lumen.'

'It's not like I have much choice, is it? So it doesn't matter if I like it or not, I still have to do it.' Chloe looked at Adam and something in his expression made her laugh a little bitterly. 'You don't get it, do you Adam? You spend all your time running away, pretending you're not a Luman – but that's all I've ever wanted to be.'

Adam frowned. 'You only think that. You've never been on a job. You don't know what it's like.'

'And I never will, will I?' Chloe snapped. 'What's so hard about it? It's just swooping. And telling people where they have to go on the Unknown Roads. It's not rocket science.'

She made it sound so easy – and for most Lumen it was. Their father and brothers just got the job done. They didn't mess things up or complicate things by worrying about saving people. That's why they were good Lumen and he wasn't. That's why Chloe would be a good Luman too, Adam realised. She had something he didn't: a kind of detachment. In the end she just accepted the rules the way everyone else did. 'It's not as easy as you think,' he said at last. 'You make it sound simple but it's not.'

Chloe sighed. 'Of course it's simple, Adam. Just not for you.' She shook her head, frustrated. 'Funny, isn't it? You're the one who doesn't want to be a Luman – but I'm the one standing here dressed up like a doll. *You* should be the one worrying about dancing and getting betrothed.'

Adam stared at her. He never really talked to Chloe properly. She was just his little sister. Somehow in the last few months she had started growing up and he hadn't even noticed. It was weird how you could live in the same house as someone and still

152

feel like you didn't really know them at all. He tried to make a joke of things. 'Well, I'm not very good at dancing either.'

'I guess not,' Chloe said. 'Don't tell anyone I'm up here. I just need a break. I'll be down in a minute.' Before he could say anything she was walking away into the darkness, swinging her sandals just a little too hard.

The party was deemed a great success by everyone who mattered. After the last guests left, a buoyant Elise led the way back to the house, her face triumphant. Nathanial had a calm glow of satisfaction – tempered by the fact that his death sense flared within just a few minutes. Clearly Morta had been itching to get back to work. Aron volunteered to do the job on his own as a newly qualified Luman but was told to enjoy one last night in bed to get over the shock of the Marking. Luc and Auntie Jo had enjoyed the ladies and the food respectively and even the dogs went to their pens happy, having recovered from their scare.

Only Adam and Chloe seemed to have had any reservations about the whole evening. For Adam this was no shock; he was used to feeling like the odd one out in his family. Still, it had never occurred to him that Chloe might feel the same way. Of course she made the occasional pointed remark about becoming a Luman – although not in front of Elise – but Adam had always assumed she was happy to set off along the well-trodden path of betrothal, marriage and running a Luman home. Now he wasn't so sure.

He spent Sunday helping with the great clear-up while Aron did his first solo jobs and Nathanial slept off the exhaustion of the prior weeks. Some of the Lumen wives and daughters

153

had returned to help – including Aron's dance partner from the previous night. Thankfully there was no sign of Marianne. Adam didn't have time to think about dodging her – he was too busy worrying about when and how he was going to go and see Clotho. Last time he had been in the Realm of the Fates he had never really felt in *danger* but he couldn't forget his father's tension or the creeping sense of menace in the Hinterland – the feeling that they weren't alone. It wasn't souls freaking him out but something else. He needed information and he knew who would help him.

He picked his moment carefully, when Auntie Jo had sidled off to the kitchen for a break. Adam muttered something about getting them all more silver polish and scarpered. When he opened the back door into the kitchen he found Auntie Jo at the table, with her hip flask angled over a steaming cup of coffee. 'You caught me,' she said with a guilty grin and took a swig from the flask. 'I needed a break from all the competitive polishing.'

Adam grinned and sat down opposite her. 'Yeah, Chloe's stuck there with them. Mother doesn't seem to care too much what Luc and I do. We've put away all the chairs.'

'Oh well, a Luman girl needs to know how to get a high shine on silver cutlery. It's an essential life skill.' Auntie Jo rolled her eyes.

Adam studied her and tried once again to imagine Auntie Jo as a teenager. It was impossible – seeing her younger and slimmer with tidy clothes and tidy hair and plans to get betrothed – but he'd seen the locket. The man inside was still a mystery. The whole *thing* was a mystery and awkward and thus avoided by everyone. Even now Adam found himself pretending Auntie Jo's drunken tears had never happened. Presumably no one would mention it or even think about it again until the following year. Hopefully Nathanial would be at home next time.

Auntie Jo raised an eyebrow and Adam realised he was still staring at her. He cleared his throat and said quickly, 'Chloe didn't seem to enjoy it much last night.'

Auntie Jo sighed. 'Of course she didn't enjoy it Adam. It's a glorified cattle market. Why would she enjoy it? Your sister isn't stupid you know.'

'I know.' Adam hesitated, seeing his opportunity – then took the plunge. 'I know she can't be a Luman but maybe she could do something else. You know, like become . . . a Fate.'

Auntie Jo choked on her coffee. After she recovered she gave him a long look. 'I wouldn't wish that on her either,' she said quietly. 'The Fates make their own sacrifices. No family, no friends, seeing all the people you love walking the Unknown Roads long before you can ever follow . . .' She shivered, tailing off.

'Are there other people there too? In the Realm of the Fates?'

'Not living there. They don't need helpers. They have their work to do and they get on with it.'

'But who made all the food and stuff?' Adam remembered the buffet table. Somehow he couldn't imagine Morta wearing an apron and washing grapes.

'Things work differently there,' was all Auntie Jo said.

Adam realised he was going to have to be direct. 'It's just that when we going there . . . you and Father seemed a bit nervous. So I thought there might be someone else living there. In the Hinterland.'

Auntie Jo gave him a beady look. 'Sometimes you actually notice more than we give you credit for.' She shrugged. 'I suppose it doesn't matter now. You'll probably never go to the Realm of the Fates again or not until you're much older.' She lowered her voice even though they were alone. 'The way Lumen normally see the Hinterland protects them and protects the Hinterland itself. You see it as an overlay on the physical world. But when you see the Hinterland as it really is then a kind of clock starts. The Hinterland is guarded, to stop people just roaming about.'

'By what?' Adam felt a mixture of triumph and terror. So there *had* been something there, watching them. No wonder the normally cool Nathanial had seemed rattled.

Auntie Jo hesitated. 'Nothing you need to worry about.' As Adam opened his mouth to protest she raised a quelling hand. 'I don't know Adam. Lumen don't hang about long enough to meet the Hunter who guards the Hinterland. Trust me, you don't want to see it. That's why very young children are kept out of the Hinterland. Ironically they find it easier to see the Hinterland as it truly is. Their minds haven't started to close to other possibilities. They don't cling to the physical world the way older Lumen do. And as soon as one person in a group sees the true Hinterland, the Hunter becomes aware of their presence. It's like a timer starts. There was an awful tragedy a long time ago, where a little one must have seen the true Hinterland and not told anyone. A whole Luman family were taken.'

Adam stared at her in horror. 'When you say *taken* – what

does that even mean? Where did they go? And what *is* the Hunter?'

'Nobody knows, Adam. And it doesn't matter.' Auntie Jo cleared her throat and reached for a restorative swig of whisky. 'You'll probably never need to worry about it again. You did well getting there. Put it from your mind.'

Adam wanted to ask more. Auntie Jo's tantalising hints had left him more confused, not less so. Unfortunately there was no way of pushing for more information without arousing Auntie Jo's suspicions – which would lead to the kind of grilling that made secret police look like nosey neighbours.

One thing was for sure. Adam had been right to be nervous on his last visit to the Realm of the Fates – and this time he'd be on his own.

Chapter 14

he following morning Adam's thoughts were a whirl as he made his way to school. The bus ride passed in a blur of hazy scenarios where he fought his way through the Hinterland, dodging a monstrous enemy. He had spent most of Sunday evening lurking near his father's study, hoping to get in and get his hands on *The Book of the Unknown Roads* but an exhausted Nathanial had spent the evening working while Aron did his first evening of solo call-outs. With no further information on the unseen menace in the Hinterland, Adam had considered a range of possible weapons, from rowan branches to ceremonial swords liberated from the vaults beneath the house. The problem was rowan branches were hard to fit in a schoolbag and Adam had never used a ceremonial sword for much more than dance practice. Without becoming an actual ninja in the next eight hours he would be more of a danger to himself than his unknown enemies.

He managed a brief chat with Melissa at the end of registration and promised to meet her in the art room at lunchtime for another posing session. If he was honest this was for the purely selfish reason that he hoped he'd be rewarded with a snog at the end. After all, knowing what lay ahead of him after school . . . it could well be the last kiss for the condemned man.

At break he had only just walked into the library when an excited Dan squawked his name and waved him over to their table. Archie and Spike were staring at the laptop screen intently. For a long, panic-stricken moment Adam wondered if his face had been successfully identified and whether he should leg it.

'We did it! We finally got the Beast to take the bait!' Dan hissed, spraying the table and his friends with semi-chewed pumpkin seeds. His eyes were gleaming crazily with a mixture of excitement and terror. 'He thinks the Wonderfish is for real!'

Adam moved behind Archie and Spike and studied the screen for confirmation. 'So he finally logged in to his email?'

'Yeah,' Spike murmured. 'He got a text telling him that he'd won a prize and the claim link was in his email. Unfortunately it had expired but the Wonderfish was waiting by way of consolation.'

'She's like the best thing I've ever drawn,' Archie said, his face reverent. 'Seriously. She's the perfect woman, or as close as she can be without being a ninja. I thought even the Beast wouldn't believe that bit. I had to rub out the nunchucks.'

'Probably wise,' Adam muttered studying the 'photo'. Archie had managed to convert his modified drawing to what looked like a slightly blurred photograph. The picture still freaked him out, mainly because it looked a lot like Chloe. The thought of Archie dreaming about a girl who looked just like his little sister was a bit close to home for Adam's taste. 'So did the Beast like the look of her?' (That idea was even worse.)

For the first time Spike grinned. 'Oh yes. In fact, he decided to return the favour. Sent a few pictures of his own. I'm downloading them now.'

There was a ping from the laptop and a slide show of photos popped up. The first was innocuous enough: a close-up of the Beast showing his 'hard' face. Dan whimpered and took a step back from the computer on instinct. The second showed the Beast shirtless in a pose reminiscent of an angry bodybuilder, muscles popping and teeth clenched. And the next one . . .

'Bloody hell!' Spike said, stunned out of his usual maddening composure. 'I did *not* want to see that!'

Adam contemplated sticking his head in a bucket of boiling water, in the hope of erasing the image of the Beast's naked buttocks from his cringing brain. 'He doesn't hold back, does he?'

Dan held up one scrawny arm and wistfully clenched his right bicep. 'If I was that massive I'd be taking photos of myself too.'

Archie held up his hand. 'OK, let's just stop there. Thinking about your arms is bad enough but your arse is a step too far. The Beast is hooked on the Wonderfish. What happens next?'

There was a long pause as three pairs of eyes swivelled towards Adam. He hesitated, not sure what to say. The thing was, he'd been hanging out with Melissa in the art room and thus hadn't seen the Beast around. The art block, like the library, had teachers mad enough to challenge the Beast, so he tended to stay away from them. While he was leaving them alone it seemed unwise to rock the boat. 'Well, maybe we can just keep emailing him. You can do some more pictures. Of Chl— of the Wonderfish.'

Archie leered horribly. 'It would be my pleasure to keep drawing the Wonderfish. Maybe her next pictures can be the bikini shots.'

Dan shuddered. 'Yeah but what if the Beast sends his version of the bikini shot? He might go full frontal next time.'

This was an unwelcome image and led to a roar of disgust and an angry 'Ssssshhhhhh!' from Mrs Nostel, the school librarian. She brandished a box of herbal tea in their direction.

'Sorry,' Adam hissed. He turned back to Spike. 'Maybe let's just string him along for a while. At least then if I want to go for a walk with Melissa at lunchtime I won't need to worry about the Beast jumping me.'

'You can always go out with her after school, you know,' Spike said. 'I mean it's a bit naff always hanging out in school.'

'Yeah, but he's still grounded, aren't you?' Dan sounded sympathetic.

Archie shook his head. 'Seriously what did you actually *do*? I mean, you didn't actually kill anyone, did you?'

Pretty much the opposite, Adam thought. 'My parents are just really strict.'

Dan nodded violently. 'Yeah, I bet they're like my parents. Always going on about doing my homework and studying and stuff, even though the exams are miles away!'

Adam almost laughed out loud at the thought of anyone in his house giving a monkey's uncle about homework but managed to mutter, 'Yeah, *really* strict, totally obsessed with work.' It was true, they *were* obsessed with work – just not the school kind.

161

Spike sighed. 'Well, until they lighten up I guess it's up to us to keep the Beast off your back.'

Archie grinned. 'As long as the Beast keeps some clothes on *his* back I can live with that.'

Adam managed a pleasant lunchtime in the art room with Melissa. She did insist on doing some work as her deadline loomed closer but there were still some happy minutes left devoted to hanging out and kissing her. It was tricky getting the balance right. Kissing was brilliant but he actually liked talking to Melissa. He kept meaning to give her a call in the evening after school but it was hard to find a moment when no one was snooping about and listening. He was already in enough trouble; if Elise thought he had a girlfriend as well she would whip him out of school before his feet could even touch the ground.

He still hadn't seen what Melissa's artwork looked like and after the Beast's nude photos he was starting to get worried. The theme of the piece was passion. He didn't want to get big-headed, but there was plenty of passion when they kissed. In fact, there was a bit more passion than was really comfortable given where they were. What if Melissa was making her artwork really true to life? Adam knew there was going to be a big display of all the work in a couple of weeks. Some special guest was supposed to be coming in too. He didn't want to have his naked flesh revealed to the whole school. His mates would never let him live it down.

But all day, no matter how much fun he was having, gnawing at the back of his mind was the knowledge that Clotho was

162

waiting. He'd come to the conclusion that the only way he could get there was by going straight after school. Because time moved differently in the Realm of the Fates he should have time to get there and back and still catch his bus home before any of his family noticed. It was a foolproof plan. All he had to do was get through the Hinterland without getting beheaded, eaten or torn limb from limb by whatever unknown guard was lurking out there in the gloom. With a name like 'the Hunter' he didn't get the impression it would snuggle him to death.

As the final bell rang at the end of school Adam felt a queasy sense of disbelief. He was going to do this. He was actually going to do it. He slipped into the boys' toilets and pushed his cubicle door closed, leaving it unlocked. There was no better place for him to step into the Hinterland unseen. He waited till the last stragglers stopped spraying each other with water and ran out into the corridor, hollering and laughing. He studied the small crystal Clotho had given him. It wasn't unlike the one they had used to go to the Summoning but it was green instead of clear, with a hint of gold gleaming at the centre.

Stepping into the Hinterland was easy with his keystone. He began walking. It felt strange moving through the school unseen; through walls and windows and even through the staffroom just because he could (he'd always known Mr Burns and Miss Oakes were friendly but he hadn't realised just *how* friendly . . .). He imagined unleashing this particular ability on Archie and decided the girls in the PE changing rooms would never be safe again. That was the thing about being a Luman – there were so many ways to abuse the abilities that they had. No wonder their world had to be kept secret. If someone like

163

Spike could get his hands on a keystone and figure out how to use it he really *would* end up ruling the world.

As Adam left the school building behind and set off across the playing fields it was tempting to keep seeing the Hinterland as usual; the invisible world on top of the physical world. The trouble was this wasn't getting him any closer to the Realm of the Fates. Now that it was time to see the true Hinterland properly Adam realised there was every chance he wouldn't be able to get there at all. Last time he had relied on Nathanial to help him stay focused – and that was before he knew something was out there waiting to pick him off. How could he deliberately lose sight of the physical world, knowing that as soon as he did so he would become prey?

Adam forced himself to stop. He put his hand in his pocket and pulled out the stone, admiring the veins of gold as they caught the light. Clotho wouldn't have given him the stone if she didn't think he could get to her realm. He had to do this.

Remembering Nathanial's advice from last time, he closed his eyes and continued walking, concentrating all his attention on the stone in the palm of his hand. *Forget the physical world,* he thought. *This is the Hinterland, place of souls. This is a place with its own rules.* Clotho's stone felt different from the last one. It was cooler and smoother. He let it nestle there like a seed taking root and growing . . . and when he opened his eyes the physical world was gone.

The shock of his success momentarily jarred him back – but he snapped his eyes closed and focused once more. Opening them and seeing the endless, grey twilight, Adam stopped and felt a rare thrill of elation. *He'd done it!* He'd done it all by himself! So he might not be High Luman just yet, but maybe he wasn't quite as incompetent as he'd thought.

He walked on, with just a hint of a swagger in his step. This was *easy*! After all his worrying Adam began to enjoy himself. He started jogging, loving the lightness in his body that came from being in the Hinterland. It was so weird, running across nothing but grey light. He was conscious that whatever was out there was aware of him now. Presumably the Hunter knew he was there. He paused, thinking. No one seemed to know exactly what it was – or at least no one had lived to tell the tale. He allowed himself to imagine, just for a minute, that *he* was going to get a glimpse before escaping to safety at Clotho's. Maybe for once he would do what others hadn't done and live up to the Mortson name. He could see it now: his own scrawling handwriting in *The Book of the Unknown Roads*, giving the first ever description of the Hunter.

It was tempting. Adam peered into the pearlescent light, searching for the elusive guard. The Hinterland seemed endless and unchanging – but far, far off he thought he saw something and a thrill between terror and excitement shot from the top of his neck to the base of his spine. It was a shadow, nothing more, but as he squinted he was sure he could see *something*. This was amazing! How would he be able to go home and not brag about this?

Usually in the Hinterland Adam could still hear the sounds of the physical world and even feel a faint trace of the wind (it always seemed to be able to cross the veil between worlds) but just as the sights of the physical world vanished in the true Hinterland, so did the sounds too. The only sound Adam could hear was the thrum of his own blood – and something else. He was sure he'd heard it the last time too, a soft rattling hiss, when Nathanial and Heinrich were talking after the Summoning. They hadn't wanted to hang about – and anything that made a High Luman and Chief Curator cautious was probably worth giving a wide berth.

Reluctantly Adam decided not to push his luck. If it came to it he could always tell Luc that he'd seen it (he didn't have to let on that it was miles away). Anyway, he wouldn't be telling anyone about this trip for a long time, if ever. Adam turned his back on the distant shadow and started walking again. He let his eyes dance through the dim light ahead, waiting for the golden edge of the doorway to appear.

Only it didn't. Adam stopped and frowned. Was there something he didn't know? He'd been with Nathanial and he was pretty sure there were no magic words; his father had been talking to *him* not muttering incantations. He wasn't doing anything *wrong*. He just needed to keep walking and keep thinking about the doorway.

The thing was it was hard to think about the doorway when you were thinking about something else – namely the monster that was coming to get you. The sound was getting louder, loud enough to hear over the thud of his own heartbeat. Adam turned and looked behind him, any trace of cockiness vanishing without a trace. There *was* something there now, that was for sure. It gave him the sense of a storm approaching, massive and unyielding, rushing closer, and some primitive instinct made him want to run, even though he knew it would overtake him.

That's what it wants. He realised this quite suddenly – that this Hunter, whatever it was, relied on speed and terror like any other predator. If he ran he would be running in blind panic and whatever it was would engulf him. It was getting closer now and was very hard to ignore – still far away but like watching the swift approach of a tornado. There was the same sense of a great swirling, dark, consuming energy. The dim grey light that seemed to permeate the Hinterland was fading, becoming something deeper and more opaque.

Deliberately now Adam turned his back on it once again. It was hard when every nerve cell in his body was screaming that he should run and hide and lie down and cry and maybe it would leave him alone. He clenched his fist around the stone, feeling the smooth, hard coolness of it beneath his fingertips. The doorway was out there. He knew it was. He was going to find it and go through it.

He walked, steady and deliberate, holding the stone in front of him like a talisman and all the time behind him the hissing, rattling was turning to a dull roar. He could feel something now, as though a thousand tiny hands were plucking at the fine hairs on the back of his neck and the fear was enough to make him forget about everything else – apart from the stone. He clutched the stone and sent out one thought: *Clotho. The doorway. Help me.*

And there, ahead of him, was a thin gold line, racing like fire against the deepening gloom. It rippled out and curved and cut through the darkness until there was the outline of the door. The roaring sound behind him was deafening and something else came out of it: an awful, howling scream of rage.

There was no more time. Adam ran.

Chapter 15

dam had no time to worry about what was waiting on the other side of the doorway. As his fingers grasped the handle he had a second to wonder where he would emerge on the other side: the amphitheatre? Morta's den? The Tapestry room? He could feel the louring presence of the Hunter close behind, blocking his capacity for rational thought. He shoved the door open and threw himself inside.

'Hello, Adam Mortson,' Clotho said. She was standing a couple of metres away from him, holding a teapot, and didn't seem at all surprised by his sudden entrance.

Adam turned without greeting her, desperate to close the door behind him and keep the Hunter at bay – only to find it closed already. There was just smooth wall and polished wood, where seconds earlier there had been the grey light of the Hinterland.

'You are safe, Adam. Sit down and be at rest. Let me take your coat.'

Adam peeled off his school blazer and blinked around him,

feeling like someone in a particularly vivid dream. Whatever he'd expected it hadn't been this.

He was in what looked like a cottage from a fairy story. The room was a small parlour, with a chintz-covered sofa and armchair. One half of the sofa was occupied by an enormous cat the colour of charcoal. The floor was polished wood, covered with tasselled rugs in places. A walnut piano gleamed darkly in one corner, reflecting the mellow light from two lamps and the cheerful flames licking wood in the fireplace. A bookcase filled a whole wall, crammed with a mixture of leather-bound classics and some fairly heavy-looking medical books. A few of the titles seemed to be about genetics. The doorway he had come through was gone but there was a normal wooden door on the other side of the room. The window beside it revealed a damp green landscape beyond. Raindrops pelted against the window – raindrops that definitely hadn't been falling on Adam in the Hinterland.

'I love the rain,' Clotho said softly. 'It always makes me feel so cosy sitting by the fire, listening to it falling.' As if in response to her words there was a sudden howling gust of wind outside and a fresh spatter of drops hit the glass.

Adam sank gingerly onto the other end of the chintz sofa, keeping a careful eye on the cat. Its ears twitched and it opened one piercing green eye, before deciding Adam was no threat and going back to sleep.

Clotho was fetching brightly patterned plates and cups. 'I should not have worried about you getting here. With Mortson blood you were never going to be in peril!' She smiled at him.

Adam thought about the huge, engulfing presence of the Hunter racing up behind him. 'I wouldn't bet on that,' he muttered. He cleared his throat. 'Would you like a hand with anything?'

'No need. Everything is ready now.' Clotho placed a tray on a low walnut table and poured out the tea. She seemed shy all of a sudden, handing him a cup and saucer without making eye contact. It was only when she sat down again that she sneaked a peek in his direction. 'I rarely have visitors.'

Adam resisted the urge to snort. Having to dodge a monster probably put most people off knocking on the door and dropping in for a cuppa. 'Your house is very nice.' He hesitated, looking through the window at the darkening landscape outside. 'Where are we exactly?'

Clotho smiled but there was a hint of sadness. 'The Hinterland is a barren place. We each make our own landscape.' She leaned in conspiratorially. 'Lachesis always keeps hers the same – a sort of apartment block. I change mine around a lot. Sometimes I like the countryside and sometimes I like the sea. I find the waves very soothing.'

'I see,' Adam said, even though he didn't. He didn't understand any of this. What did she want with him? The fact he wasn't dead yet was encouraging. 'I thought I was going to come out in the amphitheatre. You know, where we were the last time?'

'I did not give you the token for the amphitheatre. That is only a meeting place. I gave you something of mine, so it would lead you to my own realm.' She paused with an expectant look on her face and after a moment Adam realised that she

170

wanted her token back. He scrabbled through his pocket and pulled the stone out, wiping trouser fluff off it before handing it over. 'I realise this is strange for you. I mean you no harm, be sure of that. It is wonderful to spend time with someone so young and so mortal. Now, would you like some cake?' She lifted a silver dome from a plate. 'I made it myself from scratch. I used to like baking in my old life so I thought I would do things properly.'

Adam blinked at the sudden change of direction. He eyed the sad-looking sponge with dismay. It was the only thing in the room that didn't look as if it had fallen from the pages of a fairy story. Still, he didn't want to hurt her feelings, so he nodded meekly. Her face lit up and she cut him a generous chunk. It landed on the patterned plate with a heavy splat, oozing cream and jam. She watched him expectantly as he chomped through a half-cooked mouthful. He managed to swallow it and smile. 'Very nice.' He decided to try and distract her. 'It was very kind of you to invite me but . . . you said you had something to tell me. Something about me being in danger.'

Clotho sighed and leaned back in her armchair, nursing her cup and saucer. 'I should not have returned to the physical realm but it *was* exciting. I wish I could have come down to see the ball. It's many, many years since I've danced at a ball.' Her face was wistful.

Adam studied her. What did she mean many, many years? She didn't look much older than Elise but there was something about the way she said it that made it sound like a long time. 'Have you been a Fate for long?'

'Oh, a few hundred years now I expect,' Clotho said dreamily.

171

'After the first century the months and years all start to merge together.'

Adam stared at her speechless. A few *centuries*? How could she be so casual about it? She was the oldest creature he'd ever come across. How on earth was she still alive? Of course she wasn't technically on the earth – she was in the Hinterland.

As if reading his mind she said, 'Time moves differently here, Adam. Or maybe we are outside time. I have never really understood. Atropos was always better at that kind of thing.'

'You mean Morta?' Adam said carefully.

Clotho's face tightened. 'No, not the newcomer. The last thread-cutter. We were friends, good friends.' She paused. 'She really *was* a sister to me. I miss her.'

'What happened to her?'

Clotho shrugged. 'What happens to all of us in the end. She grew weary. It was time to stop. She was here a hundred years before I came along, so I think she had earned her retirement.' She gave Adam a wry smile. 'Sometimes I can understand the appeal of a nice long rest!' She sprang to her feet with a sudden burst of energy, taking Adam by surprise. 'Would you like to see my work? What I do?'

Adam nodded, his head whirling. All right, Auntie Jo had said the Fates stayed in their roles for a long time but he hadn't realised just how long. Clotho still looked like she had years ahead of her. She moved calmly around the room, setting things right and retrieving his blazer. Adam shrugged it on and only hesitated a moment when she opened the cottage door and ushered him out into the rain.

He found himself outside a thatched cottage, perched on

top of a hill. A sea of grass lay below them, sweeping down to a dark mass of forest at the bottom. The forest seemed to circle the entire base of the hill. It was like standing on an atoll in the centre of an ocean. Adam tried to see what lay beyond the forest but it blurred and faded into the falling dusk.

Clotho raised her hand and the rain ceased in a moment. A split second later sunlight – or something very like it – bathed the countryside. 'Rain isn't so nice outside.' She led him along a stony path, running behind the house.

Adam stopped in surprise as they came to a vast wooden barn. 'What is this?'

Clotho smiled. 'This is where I make things.' She unlatched a huge wooden door and stepped inside. Adam followed, peering into the gloom. 'Let there be light,' Clotho said softly and from nowhere a warm, golden glow filled the air around. He was looking at the world's biggest sewing room.

It was staggering. Inside the barn there were endless aisles of wooden shelves, stacked with spools and spools of thread. Some threads were fine and some were thick; some were pastel coloured while others almost burned with their own brightness in the dim light. One thing was for sure – the barn was deceptive. From the outside it looked big but inside it looked like this place went on forever.

Clotho reached into her skirts and her silver spindle appeared. She led Adam down one of the endless aisles, through the towering rows of shelves. Adam had never seen so many colours and types of thread. It was like the biggest sewing supplier in the world. He was fascinated by the sheer variety. He couldn't help stopping to look at some of the colours – then hurried to catch up with Clotho.

What felt like hours later they emerged near the back of the barn in front of a series of vast pieces of spinning equipment. Some looked like they had been borrowed from a folk museum; others like they had been liberated from a high-tech factory churning out millions of metres of thread a day.

Clotho gestured at the machinery. 'I spend most of my time here. This is where I make my souls. And when they are made Lachesis measures them for the Tapestry of Lights.'

Adam felt a vague disquiet that something as individual as a soul could be mass produced. 'How many do you have to make every day?'

'A few hundred thousand most days,' Clotho said. She smiled at Adam's stunned expression. 'Remember, time moves differently here. A day in your world is a long, long time here. The first Fates spun every single soul by hand but with modern medicine there are so many mortals born that it is no longer possible. I still spin as many as I can with my spindle.'

'But can't you have a helper?'

Clotho shrugged. 'There are no helpers. We are what we are. This is just how things are done.'

There it was again, that phrase – the favourite phrase in the Luman world. *This is just how things are done*. This was why only men were Lumen; why Chloe would marry a stranger and be sent to the far side of the world; why Morta could murder as many souls as she liked just because she had a quota. Adam thought about his father's exhaustion and tried not to scowl. Was he the only one to ever think about changing *anything*? For all their swooping and keystones and balls, most of the Lumen he knew were like sheep, blindly following orders. 'I see.'

Clotho was studying him. 'You are different from most of our kind, Adam Mortson. I have watched you for some time now.'

A prickling sense of danger slid down Adam's spine. 'I'm not very interesting to watch.' He tried to make a joke of it. 'Now if you saw what my brother Luc gets up to you'd find him much more entertaining.'

'Oh, but you *are* interesting. The things you do . . .' Clotho tailed off and tilted her head to one side, birdlike. 'The thoughts you must think to act as you do. To put yourself in so much danger for strangers.'

Adam stared at her, feeling sick. His mind was a black hole. There was nothing helpful in there right now; no smart comeback or brilliant explanation. How much did she know? He hadn't planned for this. Stupidly he'd assumed that bringing him here meant she wouldn't hurt him. Now he realised that it didn't mean *anything*. He was just one soul, breaking laws that had been there for thousands of years, and Clotho could make a billion more souls in his place. Maybe he was a curiosity. She was probably going to kill him now.

But as Clotho looked at him her eyes were shining. 'I know why you save them,' she said and her voice was barely above a whisper. 'You see them as I see them. Every thread is precious. I weave this knowledge into as many threads as I can, as many souls as I can. The knowledge that every single human soul is precious.'

Adam's heart was thumping. So she *did* know what he was doing – and yet somehow she didn't seem angry. 'I just want to help people,' he said slowly. 'I don't want to break the laws or get anyone into trouble. It's just . . . I know when some of

175

them are going to die. Not all the time but – sometimes I can stop it. I want to give them longer.'

Clotho nodded but her face was sad. 'She knows.'

His heart kicked up a gear. He didn't have to ask who Clotho was talking about. 'Right.'

'As they are mine to spin they are hers to sever.' There was a bitterness creeping into her voice that Adam hadn't heard before. 'Atropos took as wisely and carefully as she could, bound though she was by the actions of mortals. Her successor has not yet learned wisdom. Maybe it will come in time.' Clotho didn't sound convinced.

Adam hardly dared to ask the question but there would never be another chance. 'Who made Morta a Fate? And you?'

Clotho looked at him for a long moment. 'We are *all* threads, Adam. Even the Lady Fates.' She fell silent and Adam thought she wouldn't say anything more but she sighed and shook her head. 'We all have our freedom, within limits. Morta knows that someone is cheating her of souls and when she finds you she will kill you. She is free to do this, as I am free to try and save you. I have warned you but I can do no more. You are free to act as you choose but there are consequences. Tread carefully, precious soul.'

Warmth filled Adam. When she called him 'precious soul' she meant it. All his life he'd felt like a failure, as if he was walking a tightrope, one step from disaster. Every other Mortson seemed to know their place in the world but he never had. He had been a disappointment to everyone – but not to Clotho. She was looking at him with something like love. It wasn't favouritism; he had a feeling that she looked at every soul that way.

176

As if she was reading his thoughts, Clotho smiled. 'All of you passed through my hands on your way into your mortal life. All of you are known by me and valued by me, however short or long your thread is. Always remember that. Protect the other souls if you choose, but protect yourself too.' Her face changed, growing weary. 'I am glad to have spoken with you, Adam Mortson but now there is work to do. Other souls must pass through my hands, just as you once did.' Her eyes left him and roamed over the nearest spools of thread. 'They are waiting,' she whispered and moved soundlessly to the shelves. 'This one will be short and strong, bright and brittle.' Even as she spoke she was gathering threads: a dark red, a fine gold, a thin black knotted cord. 'You must leave me now.'

Adam nodded even though she didn't see. Her attention was gone, absorbed in her work as she twisted threads together, dropped her spindle and began to spin. For a moment he hesitated, wondering if he should ask for directions, then decided against it. How could you interrupt the creation of a soul? Imagine the harm that could do. For a moment he thought about the evil humans could sometimes be capable of. Was there just a mistake in their thread? Maybe – but Adam wasn't convinced. After all, as Clotho had said, every human had free will, just as the Fates did. How you used it, *that* was the important thing.

He took a last look at Clotho and slipped away.

Minutes later he was on the verge of regretting his decision. He had assumed the stacks would follow straight lines and lead him eventually back to the point where they had come into the barn – but in fact the stacks were bisected at intervals by other shelves of threads. It was hard not to get distracted and sneak a peek. Some of the threads were beautiful and as he veered off to have a look he would spot others and then others and before he knew what was happening he was in the middle of a great maze of shelves. He wandered fruitlessly, trying to find something familiar but the shelves went on as far as the eye could see.

Adam stopped, unwilling to admit to feeling a pang of fear. He supposed he could call out to Clotho but would she even hear him? He had an awful feeling he could wander here forever, just as a soul could wander lost on the Unknown Roads. He stared around him, trying to get his bearings; trying to come up with some kind of plan that would get him out of there. In the end he admitted defeat and just started walking.

After what felt like a long time, just as real panic might have set in, Adam squinted ahead and realised he could finally glimpse a wall at the far end of the row. He took off at a run, hoping there would be a corridor of some kind and not just a dead end. To his indescribable relief a path followed the line of the wall in both directions. Now all he had to do was follow the wall along until he reached the doorway.

He didn't walk for long before he found what he was looking for. The path ahead was cut off by a bookshelf and just before it was a plain, wooden door set into the wall. He opened it, expecting to see the light outside – only to find pitch-darkness ahead. Adam stopped, frustrated. Where was the door he had come in? This place seemed to go on forever. He could go back the way he came and hope to find another way outside – but what if there wasn't one? Or what if he got lost again? He gritted his teeth. A doorway of any kind had to be better than no doorway at all.

He stepped inside and stubbed his foot on a stair. There were no lights. Bending down and searching with his fingers, Adam could feel the edges of the bottom few steps, rising straight ahead into the darkness. His spirits sank but he began to climb, almost on his hands and knees, hoping that another doorway would reveal itself. The door into the barn closed behind him, plunging him into utter blackness. It reminded him of the stairway last time he had been in the Realm of the Fates but that had been a spiral staircase. This one rose straight up.

Thankfully it was much shorter too. Adam had been tentatively climbing for only a minute when he raised his foot and brought it down into thin air. He almost toppled backwards down the stairs but managed to throw himself forward into the darkness instead, landing painfully on his hands and knees. There was something horribly familiar about it all. He had the same sensation of being a tiny speck at the centre of somewhere huge and cavernous.

He could guess where he was. The trouble was, last time he'd been here Morta had been the one to light the place up. Still, he'd seen Clotho in action – calling for light, bringing rain to a standstill with a raised hand. In this realm things could be manipulated with words and intention. The question was, were the Fates the only ones who could do this? He cleared his throat as quietly as possible and whispered, 'Let there be light.'

For a long moment nothing happened and Adam felt a jolt of terror, alone in the dark in this forbidden place. Then, just as before, a faint glow crept into the air around him and points of brilliant light appeared on the walls, racing along like sparks on petrol, spreading out and illuminating everything – a vast, globe appearing all around him with Adam the axis at the centre of the wheel. He was standing once again before the Tapestry of Lights.

He knew he shouldn't be here but seeing the Tapestry so close and on his own sent a thrill through Adam. Every soul in the world glowed in the wall before him. His eyes darted from country to country, thinking about all the people he knew. Threads blazed red and gold and green and white, like a rainbow of fireflies. He stepped away from the stairwell and searched until he found the tiny knots of Britain and Ireland, high up out of reach, perched alone on the edge of the vast darkness of the Atlantic. Up close the lights seemed magnified. The threads were no ordinary pieces of cotton or wool. They were alive and moving, a great swirling river of lights weaving together in a kind of harmonic dance.

Adam wasn't sure how long he stood there for. It was mesmerising, letting his eyes roam endlessly over the Tapestry, knowing that his own light glowed there somewhere. Absorbed in what he was seeing something jarred him back to the present with a faint sense of irritation. It took a moment for his mind to register the sounds behind him and when it did it sent alarm bells ringing in Adam's head.

Voices. He could hear voices. Someone was coming.

Chapter 16

here was no time for panic or even thought. Adam took the instinctive path of every hunted animal and fled towards the darkness – but there was nowhere to hide. The chamber was empty of furniture and decoration so even if he was able to will something into existence all it would do was draw attention to him. He ran towards the wall in the black space of the Atlantic where only the occasional tiny pinpricks of light shone and threw himself flat on the ground. *I need to hide*, he thought fiercely. *Make the shadows darker, blacker. Make me invisible.* There was no way of knowing if he had succeeded in changing anything.

The voices were close now. In Adam's eagerness to see the Tapestry he had completely failed to notice that his stairwell wasn't the only one still there. A few seconds later Morta's familiar face appeared. She rose up from her stairwell and stalked into the chamber looking beautiful and furious and deadly, the Mortal Knife gleaming at her side. Adam willed himself into the floor and felt himself sinking down into the shadows. *Not*

too far, he thought hastily. He didn't want to suffocate.

Morta was talking in short, angry bursts. A figure rose up behind her – a man – and as he turned Adam felt a cold shock of recognition. He was looking at Darian. Adam frowned from the shadows, some of his fear displaced by anger. There was something a bit too convenient about all this. Adam knew that the Frenchman hated Nathanial, blaming him in some way for thwarting his plans to marry Elise. It didn't help that Darian was a Seer like Adam and one of the few people who could know that souls were being saved. Finding him here with Morta was more than a coincidence, Adam was sure of it.

Morta was close now; close enough for Adam's senses to scream in warning. Fortunately her focus was on the wall where Adam had been standing just a minute earlier, staring at the Kingdom of Britain. Her eyes were furious but her voice was calm. 'I have taken many extra souls and yet you tell me there have been no more souls saved?'

Darian moved smoothly behind her. 'The last I know of was three weeks ago in our physical time. But I cannot always be in Britain. My duties with the Concilium force me to travel frequently. Soon I will be able to return.' He hesitated.

Morta's attention was on the lights ahead of her but she seemed to sense the Luman's anxiety. 'Speak freely.'

Darian grimaced. 'Your freedom with the Mortal Knife has caused . . . concern. We Curators have been called to session frequently. If you were to relax your efforts somewhat I could return to Britain for longer. My absence would not be noted. I could gather information. Find the rogue and bring him to you.'

'The son is the rogue.' Just as Adam's heart might have

exploded in his chest Morta continued. 'The second son. The boy Luc. I am certain of it.'

Darian looked at her curiously. 'What makes you think this?'

'He is in love with danger, as I was once.' Morta smiled, almost fondly, and studied the glowing map of Britain. The tip of the Mortal Knife glinted as she turned it over between her fingers. 'Such a bright light. Such a great shame to cut it off and yet . . .' She shrugged. 'I shall take my time and enjoy it.'

'I must prove it.' Darian's voice was low and urgent. 'There must be evidence I can bring before the Concilium. Do nothing yet Morta. Be patient.'

Adam could tell straight away that Darian had said the wrong thing. Morta pulled back from him and her face became cold. 'Be patient? You tell *me* to be patient? Believe me, *mortal*, no woman survives in the Luman world without understanding *patience*.'

Darian's face was calm but his voice betrayed him. 'I only wish to do things properly. The Kingdom of Britain is in disarray. The rogue alone is not to blame. The High Luman must bear his share of the blame.'

'Perhaps you have been mistaken Darian. Perhaps there is no rogue, robbing me of souls. Perhaps you wish to use me for your own purposes.' Morta stepped closer to Darian and slid the tip of her blade towards his belt. She moved her hand and the knife trailed up his torso, caressing his neck and coming to a standstill under his chin, tilting the Frenchman's head back. 'What game are you playing with me, Luman?'

Darian stared straight ahead and didn't flinch. 'I would never be so foolish, my Lady Fate.'

'No.' Morta studied him for a moment, then tapped the flat of her blade against his cheek. 'It would be foolish indeed.' She bent her head and kissed the hollow of his throat, then turned back to the wall. Behind her Adam watched Darian relax. Morta stared at the Tapestry of Light for a long time. 'A little longer. I shall give you a little longer. And then I shall bring such a wave of deaths that the rogue will have no choice but to intervene. And you will be waiting to expose him.'

She turned and strode back to the stairwell without even looking at Darian. The Frenchman watched her and Adam saw the spasm of fear and hatred that crossed his face – but a moment later he followed her, impassive once more. Leaving Adam alone.

It took Adam a few minutes to find his courage and leave the shadows. His mind was racing. All the extra deaths in the Kingdom of Britain – they weren't an accident. They were there to try and draw him out. All he had wanted to do was save some lives. Now because of him more people than ever were dying.

He felt hot and sick with guilt – then forced himself to stop and think. This wasn't just about him – it was about Morta and Darian. After all, Clotho said the old Atropos had chosen wisely and spared as many souls as she could. Morta on the other hand seemed to delight in the deaths. He thought of the caressing way she held the Mortal Knife and shivered. Who in their right mind would give someone like Morta that kind of power? He knew the Fates were only another link in the chain. There were higher powers than them. Somebody somewhere had appointed Morta – and they had made a mistake.

As for Darian . . . Adam felt a fresh wave of rage. Darian didn't care about the law or the Fates. All Darian cared about was Elise and getting back at Nathanial. Without meaning to Adam had given him the opening he needed.

Worst of all – they thought it was *Luc*! Adam could understand why. Luc was cool and in control and a little bit devilish. Maybe this was why girls liked him so much – even Morta. It was also why Adam felt invisible beside him and for once this might be a good thing. But how could he stand by and let Luc get killed for something he didn't do? What if Morta lured Luc to see her, just as Clotho had persuaded Adam back into the Realm of the Fates? Luc was just arrogant enough to believe that a Fate wanted to meet him for a date, not that she wanted to kill him!

His thoughts were whirling. He had to get out of there. But how? Stealthily he slipped back towards the stairwells and began to creep down the stairs. Halfway down he paused. There was no point just going back into Clotho's weaving room; he could wander there forever. He needed another doorway, one that would take him back into the Hinterland. He'd been scared of the Hunter before but Morta was turning out to be much more terrifying.

As he descended the stairs Adam tried to visualise what he needed. *A different doorway. A doorway that will take me away from here and back to my world.* He pictured it almost fiercely: pale wood, a plain metal handle and beyond he pictured the endless grey light of the Hinterland. *I want to go home.*

And at the bottom of the stairs instead of one door into the barn there were two. He looked at the new doorway with a mixture of fascination and relief. A world where you could just imagine things into existence. He could get used to this.

He eased the door open and crept back into the Hinterland. Thankfully there was no sign of the Hunter. Adam didn't hang about out of curiosity. He'd seen as much of the Hunter as he ever wanted to. He clutched his keystone and swooped home, hoping no one would be in the garden. At least he knew Morta hadn't been cutting any threads when he left. She'd probably been plotting with Darian or kissing him or cutting him into little pieces with her knife. Adam had a feeling she would enjoy any of those activities equally. Whatever she was doing at that moment, hopefully she wasn't killing anyone.

The garden was empty and Adam scurried off into the paddock, dabbing his nose and trying to kill time. His hours in the Hinterland had only been a moment in the physical world and he didn't want to arrive home too early. No point raising suspicions. Now that he was safely back he felt weak and shaky. It was a relief to be on firm ground again.

Darian was more of a threat than Adam had ever imagined. Before he'd thought Darian was simply snooping about, trying to make a good impression on the Concilium. After all, Darian was one of the youngest Curators in Luman history. Now Adam realised that he had underestimated Darian's hatred of Nathanial. The question was, what was Darian hoping to achieve? Elise and Nathanial were lawfully married. Divorce was incredibly rare in the Luman world. Even if Nathanial lost his position as High Luman, Elise would still be married to him. The only thing that would separate them was death . . .

Adam froze. Was it possible? Was this why Darian was so

desperate for proof of the rogue Luman's wrong-doing? After all, Adam had sneaked a peek at *The Book of the Unknown Roads* and the penalty for interfering with the Fates had been all too clear – the death penalty. Was Darian hoping to implicate Nathanial too, hoping that he would share in the rogue Luman's fate and face execution? A coldness stole over Adam that had nothing to do with the spring air. It made a twisted kind of sense. With Nathanial dead and the family in disgrace and stripped of their Keystones, Elise would have no choice but to marry whoever would have her.

Even so, the whole thing was mad! This was his *mother* they were talking about! Yes, she was beautiful, but she was hardly some supermodel or rock star! Darian was a Curator. He could marry *anyone*. Some of the most powerful Luman families in the world would gladly hand over their daughters for betrothal. Why the obsession with Elise?

Adam frowned. There was a back story here and there was only one person who could fill him in. Unfortunately even Auntie Jo was going to get suspicious if he grilled her two nights in a row. He had never exactly been a keen student of Luman history and gossip. She was going to be curious about why he was suddenly so interested in the Luman world.

Luck, however, was on his side. When he finally risked going into the kitchen Aron and Luc were missing but everyone else was there – and so was Uncle Paddy. Better yet, there were two bottles of Irish whisky on the table, one of them half empty. Auntie Jo was sitting beside Uncle Paddy with a brimming glass, already looking merry. Hopefully she would be feeling talkative later on. 'You nearly missed our visitor Adam!'

'Yeah, I was at school,' Adam said, not quite meeting anyone's eye. 'Hi Uncle Paddy.'

'How are you Adam?' Uncle Paddy was grinning at him. 'I love your duds.'

Adam grinned in spite of himself. 'Thanks. What's for dinner?' This was usually the first question he asked when he got home so he reckoned he was just playing it cool and acting normal.

Elise was standing at the counter mixing something in a bowl. 'Cassoulet.' She stirred in short, angry bursts.

Uncle Paddy winked at Adam. 'Don't they always say the girls can't resist a man in uniform? Is that what this school business is about? Come on, you can tell me. We're all friends here.'

'No girl worth knowing will be impressed by a school uniform. A coming-of-age shirt is a different matter.' Elise's smile would have frozen lava. 'Will you be joining us Patrick?'

'Stay if you can Patrick,' Nathanial said quietly. He was sitting at the table nursing a small glass of whisky. He looked shattered. 'I can't promise I'll be joining you all for dinner but I'd like to catch up afterwards.'

Uncle Paddy stood up and shook his head. His face was sympathetic. 'I won't keep you Nathanial. Here's hoping you get to eat a meal in peace.'

'Are there loads of sudden deaths in Ireland too?' Adam asked on impulse – then bitterly regretted the question when everyone turned and looked at him.

Luckily Uncle Paddy didn't seem to find it strange. 'No Adam. If anything we're quieter than usual. Our new Lady Fate seems to be keeping that knife of hers busy in the Kingdom of Britain.' The way he said 'lady' implied the exact opposite. He clapped Nathanial's shoulder. 'I'll send Ciaron over to help out any time you want. Just say the word.'

'I'm sure that won't be necessary Patrick,' Elise said. 'Now that Aron is Marked we have extra hands.'

Uncle Paddy shrugged. 'Well, the offer's there.'

'Thank you Patrick,' Nathanial said. 'And Ciaron is always welcome here, any time he wants.'

'He'll be glad to see you all. Especially one young lady not too far away.' Uncle Paddy winked at Chloe.

Elise pursed her lips and stirred harder.

It was late before Adam managed to corner Auntie Jo. To everyone's surprise there had only been one call-out that evening. For the first time in several weeks Nathanial had eaten at the kitchen table with the whole family. There had been fervent speculation as to why Morta was allowing them a quiet night. Adam had eaten in guilty silence, thinking about the conversation he had overheard. It seemed Darian had been granted his wish. Fewer deaths in Britain meant lighter duties for the Concilium – and more time for him to snoop about and catch the rogue. Adam was going to have to tread carefully.

Although he hadn't forgotten Darian's words. *No souls have been saved for three weeks*. It was true. Adam hadn't saved anyone since the girl on the bus on his first day back at school. Thinking about it made him feel sick and guilty – but what choice had he had? His doom sense had been quieter than usual, probably because he had been so happy most of the time. Even during the last week when Morta had wielded the Mortal Knife freely he had only felt some of the deaths as they happened and none before. And knowing now that Darian and

189

Morta were working together – what else could he do but be *glad* he hadn't walked into their trap?

Nathanial had gone to bed early, trying to catch up on some sleep while things were quiet and Elise was playing the piano in the music room. All four Mortson offspring were gathered in the den with Auntie Jo, watching her latest find: *Zombie Lovechild's Revenge*. Adam waited impatiently for the others to drift off one by one. Auntie Jo drank steadily as the film reached a spectacularly gory conclusion. She was yawning by the time Luc read a text message and slipped out of the room. Adam felt a momentary twinge of alarm, then realised that Morta probably wouldn't have to resort to using a mobile if she wanted to contact Luc.

Finally it was just the two of them. Auntie Jo slumped back in the sofa. 'I need to go to bed but I can't face walking up the stairs. Do you want to carry me?'

Adam grinned. 'Maybe if Aron and Luc were here too . . .'

'Cheeky brat,' Auntie Jo grumbled, then ruined the effect by grinning back. She sloshed the last of her drink round in her glass. 'So what's up? I get the feeling you're lurking with intent.'

Adam grimaced. He hadn't been as subtle as he'd thought. He wasn't sure of the best way to bring the conversation round. Better to stick to the present before he began delving into the past. 'Why was Uncle Paddy here?'

Auntie Jo shrugged. 'A social visit, I suppose. Things have been quiet in Ireland recently, at least for the fast-response Lumen. The "Troubles" have calmed down, so that helps. Plus that witch has been keeping her knife busy here. I think this is the first evening your father has been at home for a week.'

This wasn't really taking the conversation where Adam wanted it to go. 'I thought he might be here to talk about Chloe. You know, her and Ciaron getting betrothed.'

Auntie Jo yawned like a cat. 'He wouldn't talk about that in front of the family. He would have a quiet word with your father. They *were* in the study for a while before they came into the kitchen. These things are delicate matters, you know. There's a lot of pride at stake.'

Bingo, Adam thought. This was his way in. He kept his voice as casual as possible. 'Yeah, I guess Father is pretty conscious of that stuff. You know, with Mother marrying him instead of Darian.' He held his breath, praying she would take the bait.

Luckily the whisky was working its dark magic. Auntie Jo sighed and rested her head on the back of the sofa. 'Yes, I think one betrothal scandal in the family was enough.'

Scandal? This could get interesting, Adam thought. 'So how did they meet? Father and Mother?'

Auntie Jo shrugged. 'The same way anyone meets. At a ball.' She smiled and her face softened, suddenly becoming much younger. 'I used to love a good ball. It got us out of the house. And that one was a humdinger! Ironically it was Darian's Marking ball in Paris. Your mother was there and I have to admit she looked amazing, but she was a proud little madam – worse then than she is now, if you can believe it. Everyone expected she would be betrothed to Darian. They both have High Lumen in the family so they seemed like a sure thing.'

She fell silent. Adam tried to prompt her to go on. 'Well,

maybe they were too close? You know, the families? Like maybe they were too closely related. All that genetic stuff.'

Auntie Jo gave another enormous yawn. 'I doubt genetics had anything to do with it. The whole Luman world is related in degrees. After all, Mortson was a French name. We're related to Darian on *both* sides of the family if you go back far enough. Funnily enough, that's why we got excited when you were younger and we thought you might be a Seer too. There were a few Seers in Darian's line.'

Adam brushed away a guilty pang. It was better for everyone if they thought he had grown out of being a Seer and his little talent remained a secret. 'So why didn't Mother and Darian get together then?'

Auntie Jo raised an eyebrow. 'Because she fell for your father of course. And boy did she fall!' She sniggered suddenly and dropped her hand, making a whistling sound and letting her palm splat onto the sofa. 'She was supposed to be working the room that night but she couldn't stop dancing with Nathanial. You saw them the other night – they've always danced well together. Your grandmother came and told her off but she ignored her. She was besotted.' She paused for a moment. 'You know, Elise and I have never been close but I will say one thing for her. I have never for a moment doubted that she loves your father with everything that is in her. She loves you too, all of you. She isn't always good at showing it – but she would throw herself in a fire for any of you, without even blinking.'

There was a long silence after these words. For some reason Adam's throat had tightened and he had to swallow hard to make it go back to normal. 'So they got married and lived happily ever after?'

Auntie Jo grimaced and took another swig from her glass. 'Well, yes and no. There was a lot of opposition to the betrothal, especially from Darian's family. After all, he had practically been raised with Elise so it had seemed like a sure thing. I always felt sorry for him you know. I don't like the man but I do pity him. It was supposed to be his big night – and then an upstart from Britain came and ruined all his plans. And he had loved your mother all his life. He thought they belonged together.'

Adam stared at her, bewildered but trying not to show it. After all, the Mortsons were hardly *upstarts*. They had plenty of High Lumen in their line too and Nathanial was one of the youngest men ever to become High Luman. 'But the wedding went ahead.'

'After a fashion. It probably wasn't the wedding your mother had dreamed of.' Auntie Jo smiled but there was something else there – a sadness. 'And now here we all are.'

There was no way Adam was letting her finish there. 'What do you mean? Did something happen?'

Auntie Jo yawned again. 'I'm not supposed to be telling you this Adam.'

Her eyes were closing and her words were slurring. Adam knew he was taking advantage of her drinking but he had to get to the bottom of this. Nathanial's life might depend on it. *All* their lives might depend on it. He stayed silent, willing her to go on.

At last Auntie Jo sighed. 'I suppose you'll read about it in the history books eventually. The wedding was cancelled.'

'Why?'

'Because our family was tainted with scandal and the Luman world turned its back on us. More than one wedding was cancelled that year.' There was no mistaking the anger now in Auntie Jo's voice – or the bitterness.

Adam's head was full of questions after that statement but he knew he was almost out of time. 'So how did Mother and Father end up married?'

'They eloped. We never knew which of the Curators performed the Ceremony and they always refused to say. I've always suspected it was Heinrich. He had just joined the Concilium. He's always been a romantic at heart.'

Adam's jaw was hanging open. He snapped it shut. This was too bizarre! Heinrich, Chief Curator, performing an unauthorised betrothal and wedding? His *parents* running off like something out of *Shakespeare*? All these people pretending to be respectable and telling him he had to be a good boy and get betrothed and come of age and be a good Luman . . . and yet when they were younger they were all running about like *crazies*?! He shook his head, struggling to reconcile his picture of his parents as he knew them (the perfect Luman family) with the romantic figures from Auntie Jo's story.

'A happy ending,' Auntie Jo said and gave a strange laugh. 'Everyone loves a happy ending.' She staggered to her feet. 'I need to go to bed now. Goodnight Adam.'

Adam opened his mouth to ask her more – but it was too late. She had gone. His head was whirling with scenes from the past. At least now he could understand why Darian hated Nathanial so much – although in some ways it would have made more sense to hate Elise. Maybe love wasn't rational. Maybe

Darian couldn't bring himself to hate Elise for hurting him. Maybe he still believed even now that someday they could be together. If his plan to hunt down the rogue succeeded he might have his wish fulfilled.

Adam sighed and followed Auntie Jo upstairs. It was only in his room that he thought of all the questions he should have asked. What was the scandal that had tainted the family enough to end a betrothal? And from what Auntie Jo had said, more than one betrothal had ended over it. The question was: whose?

Adam tried to sleep but seeing his aunt's sadness, he had a horrible feeling he knew the answer to that question.

Chapter 17

or the first night in an age not a single Mortson was disturbed from their slumber by a call-out. Ironically the only one with a restless night was Adam. His dreams had been haunted by a mishmash of images from the past and the present.

He was at a ball, whirling Melissa round a dance floor, worrying that her school uniform made her look out of place. Darian stalked past with a blood-stained knife, hunting one of the dogs, while Auntie Jo sat on a throne in a white dress gorging herself on wedding cake.

It was a relief to wake up and throw himself into the shower. Dressing in his bedroom, Adam stared at his reflection. Somehow no matter what else was going on in his life his school uniform acted like an anchor, pinning him in place. *I still live in the real world. The Luman world is only one bit of it*, he thought almost fiercely, his blue eyes wild and bloodshot in the mirror. *I can keep living in the REAL world if I just try hard enough.*

He crept downstairs, hoping for a peaceful slice of toast and a chance to look through his biology notes in preparation for the Buzzard's latest test – only to be intercepted on the stairs by a bedraggled-looking Auntie Jo. Adam stopped and stared. He hadn't expected to see Auntie Jo this side of dinner time after the whisky she had put away the night before. Obviously he wasn't the only one who'd had a restless night.

She held her hand up before he could say a thing. 'You know why I'm waiting for you. I was indiscreet last night. I talked about things that shouldn't have been mentioned and I want you to forget about them. Certainly don't repeat a word of what I said.' She waited for him to nod in agreement and frowned. 'Good. You were rather devious last night Adam. You knew I'd drunk a little more than I should have. I found myself wondering why you were so interested in betrothals and the past. Then I realised why you were suddenly so keen.'

Adam's heart accelerated slightly. *What does she know?* Had Auntie Jo managed to put two and two together? Had she somehow figured out that he had returned to the Realm of the Fates? Did she suspect Darian of some kind of mischief making? What was he going to do? Deny everything or come clean and blurt the whole truth out?

Auntie Jo smiled, then winced and clutched her head as though she were trying to hold it in place. 'You needn't look so frightened. It's perfectly normal at your age to be thinking about these things.'

Now Adam was confused. 'Yeah, I guess. Only . . . what things do you mean?'

Auntie Jo snorted. 'It's fine if you're not ready to tell us who she is. Just rest assured, whatever might have happened in the past the Mortson name is as proud as ever. Whoever she is, she'll be lucky to have you. When you're ready just have a quick word with your father and he'll start arranging a meeting. Of course it's unusual for a younger brother to go down this road before an older, Marked brother – but not totally unheard of. You'll be fine. Forget everything I said last night.' She closed her eyes and rubbed her temples. 'Now, if you'll excuse me I'm going to go back to bed and die quietly.'

Adam blinked and stared at her bedroom door as it swung closed, his brain trying to process what he'd just heard. Finally a slow grin spread across his face. *She thinks I've picked a wife!* He put a hand over his mouth, trying to hold back a snort of laughter as he scuttled downstairs to the kitchen. This was perfect. For a moment he'd thought she'd figured out the truth or at least part of it. Now he was off the hook.

He was still chuckling as he headed for the bus stop. He'd got away with his interrogation and now he had a cast-iron excuse for snooping into family history. Adam had a feeling it was going to be a good day.

It wasn't just a good day; it was an awesome week. For once everything seemed to be going Adam's way. As he wandered the corridors at school there was just a hint of a swagger in his step. It was like somebody somewhere was watching out for him.

The number of sudden deaths had plummeted to lower levels than ever before. Nathanial and Aron spent a day catching up on sleep, then spent the rest of the week bemused but happy. There was something about Nathanial's presence at home that cast an aura of calm across the whole household. Adam had never realised before how much they all relied on his father to soothe frayed tempers and keep the peace. Auntie Jo even cut back on the whisky for a few days, possibly because of the legendary hangover she'd had after Uncle Paddy's visit.

Nathanial's presence at home had another bonus effect: making it harder for Luc to slip off unobserved. Adam had worried about going to school and leaving his brother unguarded, even though for now he should be safe. If Morta was waiting for the rogue to strike she would be waiting a long time. Adam was determined not to do anything stupid for the time being which meant Luc was probably safe enough – but it helped having more people at home to look out for any unusual visitors. Tall, gorgeous, crazy, knife-wielding brunettes were at the top of the list . . .

As a bonus, Melissa had almost finished her coursework. Adam still hadn't seen it but Melissa bubbled with excitement every time she talked about it. Ms Havens loved it and thought it could be entered for competitions after it had been submitted for moderation. She'd even hinted that the mystery guest – some kind of artist – would love it too. The visit was scheduled for the art show at the end of the following week.

Adam was torn between bursting with pride and nervous terror. What if he was butt naked in the picture? What if it ended up winning something and getting plastered all over the news for his family to see? And even worse: what if it was a true likeness and ended up on the web for Spike's facial recognition software to find and identify? Thinking about this gave him a sweaty half-hour of panic until he reasoned that a painting didn't exactly count as evidence of being present at a crime scene. He took some deep, calming breaths and pushed such negative thoughts from his mind. Things were going his way. He might as well enjoy it while it lasted.

His friends were in a good mood too. On Friday they got a rare chance to hang out in class time. Their whole year group was dragged off timetable and called to the assembly hall for a careers guidance session. Their form teachers had cunningly failed to mention this, knowing that some people wouldn't have bothered getting out of bed that morning.

Adam spent a hurried ten minutes with Melissa in a dark corner of the art store before scuttling off to join his friends in the assembly hall, still wiping lipgloss off with the back of his hand. Since he'd started going out with Melissa his lips had never felt so supple – a combination of friction and her various pots of goop getting transferred onto him. He was still grinning when he joined Dan and Archie. 'Where's Spike? Don't tell me he managed to get out of this?'

Dan was rooting through a plastic bag of yoghurt-coated nuts and dried fruit, picking out the raisins so he could flick them at people during dull moments. 'He had a breaktime detention. Something about pointing out that Mr Rooney had added twelve and fifteen together and got thirty.'

Adam rolled his eyes. Rooney was a joke. He glanced round the hall, waiting to see Melissa sneak in late so he could grin at her, when to his dismay he saw a familiar figure. 'Oh no. It's Mrs Gollum. She's taking us today.'

There was a collective groan and a chorus of muttered complaints, quickly picked up by other tables. Mrs Goldrum was sent out from the Careers Service into local schools.

Unfortunately for her she resembled Gollum from the *Lord of the Rings* films, earning her the nickname Bride of Gollum – or Mrs Gollum for short. She was painfully thin with straggling hair, greyish skin and large sweat patches beneath her arms. Before and after any talk she could be found in her car in the car park chain-smoking hand-rolled cigarettes. She was pretty well-intentioned but she was possibly the most boring speaker ever to tread the polished floors of the various schools in her area.

Mrs Gollum had all the authority of a tadpole so it was no surprise when The Bulb stalked into the assembly hall, looking very much like a man who wanted to wrestle someone to the floor and gouge their eyes out. 'Settle down!' he bellowed and quiet was miraculously restored, broken only by a few nervous titters. Having paraded through the school in high heels a few weeks earlier, The Bulb was a man with a mission: to restore terror into the hearts of everyone he came across. 'Mrs Goldrum will be speaking to you for a few minutes and then you have to fill out the forms she's left on your tables. Not a sound!'

Adam heard as far as 'Thank you, Mr Bulber' before tuning out every word Mrs Gollum was saying. Judging by the vacant expressions of everyone around him he wasn't alone in this. Only Archie was staring at her with an expression of profound concentration which baffled Adam until his friend picked up his pencil and started sketching on the back of his Career Assessment Test. A minute later he slid it across the table and Adam only just gulped back a snort of laughter at the sight of Mrs Gollum hunched on a rock with a fish in one hand and her careers manual in the other.

Eventually movement rippled through the hall Mexican-wave style. The talk was over and they were free to answer the questions on the sheets in front of them. If Adam had hoped these would be exciting he was going to be disappointed. He studied them and imagined writing honest answers:

1. *Are you cool under pressure?*
Not when guiding the dead or dodging giant tornado-shaped predators in the Hinterland.
2. *Are you creative?*
Creative with the truth.
3. *Are you a risk-taker?*
You could say that . . .

Dan gave a heavy sigh. 'You know school is so crap that I spend my whole life waiting to get out of here so I can get a job, some money, an amazing flat and a fast car. And then they give you a sheet like this and try to make you think the *rest* of your life is going to be this boring too.'

Archie yawned and added the words *My preciousssssss* to Mrs Gollum's careers manual. 'I already know what I want to do. I want to draw cool stuff and get paid loads of money for it. Does that mean I can go back to art?'

Adam grinned, then realised Mrs Gollum was bearing down on them. 'Just tick some boxes,' he hissed. Conscious of The Bulb's louring presence in the hall, Dan and Archie did some rapid scribbling.

Mrs Gollum appeared, wafting in a gentle cloud of violet perfume and stale cigarette smoke. 'Now, boys, how are we getting on here?' She took their sheets and pored over them, frowning slightly. 'Now, which of you is Dan? Ah, now Daniel, your answers are rather inconsistent. You see, *here* you have ticked that you are good with your hands but *here* you have ticked that you are clumsy. Which is it dear? What do you want to do when you leave school?'

'Be a dentist,' Dan answered stolidly.

'*Dark Lord & Son Dentistry. Your pain is our gain,*' Archie muttered, sniggering to himself. His expression changed to one of alarm as he realised Mrs Gollum was about to turn over the page and discover her less than flattering portrait. 'No miss! Don't look at that! Look at my sheet! What should I do?'

Mrs Gollum was delighted to be asked for an opinion. She beamed at Archie and scrutinised his questionnaire. Her smile faded a little as she took in his answers. 'Well, I have to say these are a rather . . . unusual set of skills.' She shuddered and handed back the sheet.

Archie shrugged. 'I'll find my niche.'

Mrs Gollum was reading Adam's sheet now with an expression of profound relief. 'Well, this one seems much better. You want to be a doctor. Excellent, Adam!' Her brow furrowed. 'Although it does say here that you don't do well with blood.'

'My own blood, that is. I'm fine with other people's,' Adam said without thinking. 'Most of the time anyway.'

Mrs Gollum blinked. 'Do you see a lot of people bleeding, Adam?' She hesitated, chewing on the end of her pen. 'Do you *enjoy* seeing people bleed?' As Adam struggled to find some way of explaining what he meant she gave a very forced smile and said, 'Not to worry, dear,' before scribbling something on her clipboard. She seemed to be underlining it a lot.

It was at that moment that Spike finally made an appearance. 'Sorry I'm late.'

Mrs Gollum frowned. 'Well you've missed out on the careers questionnaire now.'

Spike appeared unruffled. 'Don't worry. I know what I'm going to do.'

'Really? And what's that?'

'I'm going to be Batman.'

A long silence followed this pronouncement. Mrs Gollum frowned. 'I mean a proper job dear. Let's not be silly.'

There was a collective hiss of indrawn breaths around the table before everyone looked at Spike. Adam winced. Spike made a point of not being bothered by name-calling – but calling him stupid, silly or anything similar was like a red rag to a bull.

Sure enough, Spike's eyes had narrowed to slits. His mouth was a tight, twisted line in his face. Adam braced himself, feeling sorry for Mrs Gollum. She didn't *mean* to be an idiot, she just couldn't help it. Now Spike was going to give her a verbal flaying that would leave her in pieces and Spike in big trouble.

However, after a pregnant pause Spike surprised them all. He closed his eyes and breathed deeply in through his nose and out through his mouth. He repeated this several times while the rest of them watched him in bemusement, not excluding Mrs Gollum. At last his eyes snapped open and he gave the teacher a level gaze. 'It's not silly miss. It's an excellent idea. Being Batman.'

Mrs Gollum seemed to be torn between irritation and fascination. Maybe she thought she had another dangerous lunatic on her hands. She stood with her pen poised over her clipboard, quivering with nervous tension. 'But dear, he's not real, is he? It's not a real job. We'd all like to be a superhero sometimes but alas, most of us end up doing something rather more prosaic, don't we?' She gave a titter of laughter.

Spike's expression was one of superhuman calm. 'He isn't a superhero, or at least not in the conventional sense. There were no radioactive bites or space rocks involved. I prefer to think of him as a self-made man.'

Mrs Gollum cleared her throat. 'I'm not really sure what you mean –'

'Batman was just really rich and then he used his money to become Batman. It's basic economics. He had the money to invent cool stuff and learn his ninja moves. So, I'm going to be a hacker first to get the money and then I'm going to use it to become Batman. Only not Batman obviously because he's old school. Maybe Eagleman or Cobraman.'

'You could be Porcupine Man,' Dan said helpfully. 'You know, going with the Spike thing? Spiky? Porcupines?'

'Yeah, don't be Cobraman. Too much Lycra. I can sketch you a few costume ideas,' Archie said with a totally deadpan expression.

Adam bit his lip to stop himself grinning. Mrs Gollum was looking from face to face, uncertain how best to proceed. Eventually she decided to cut and run. 'Well, there are some very interesting ideas at this table boys. You all seem to have your future careers in hand. I don't think you need me any further.'

They didn't laugh until she was a safe distance away. Dan grinned at Spike. 'That was brilliant. I wish I'd said that. Anyway, what does *she* know? Why would you have to be good with your *hands* to be a *dentist*?'

Adam raised an eyebrow but said nothing, fervently praying that he would never have to let Dan anywhere near his teeth. He turned his attention to Spike. 'You didn't flip when she said you were silly. I'm impressed.'

Spike shrugged. 'I meditated. It's what Batman would do. Mindfulness. Zen. I've been reading up on all that stuff. If it's good enough for Batman it's good enough for me.'

Archie snorted. 'Yeah, whatever. Where were you? How come you got out of the first bit?'

Spike smirked. 'I was busy. I had more interesting things to do.'

'Did the Beast make contact?' Dan was twitching with a mixture of eagerness and terror. 'Is he still searching for the Wonderfish?'

'Yeah, he's still invested.' Spike narrowed his eyes. 'So I sent some gushy emails – I weally, weally wuvs you I do blah blah blah – and then I told him no more naked-ass pictures. I mean I thought about getting a few extras and plastering them round the toilets but he's such a freak he'd probably be happy about it.'

'Well he is pretty buff,' Dan said wistfully. His eyes widened as the other three turned and stared. 'What? He is! He's still a psycho but he must go to the gym every night. If I looked like that I wouldn't bother wearing clothes. Well, maybe some pants. But that's all.'

Spike shuddered. 'Forget about the Beast. He's a footnote. The real reason I was late was because of something much more important.' He waited till he had their complete attention, then lowered his voice dramatically. 'I was making contact with my source. My CIA guy.'

'I thought he'd vanished?' Archie stopped drawing and put down his pen, a sign that he was giving this his complete attention.

Spike rolled his eyes. 'Yeah, he'd gone to ground for a couple of weeks. He reckoned something was coming to get him. As in, something from the *stars*. I'm pretty careful myself but this guy has turned paranoia into an art form.'

Dan flicked a yoghurt raisin at a neighbouring table and grinned at the hissed chorus of rage from the girls sitting there. 'He sounds like one of those tinfoil-hat types. I saw a programme about them. They're all like, "Help! They're coming to take me back to the mothership! Save me!" I mean, seriously, if you think a tinfoil hat stops aliens stealing your thoughts, the real question is: why would the aliens want *you*?'

Adam was watching Spike and holding his breath, desperate to hear what he said next. He tried to sound only casually interested. 'And what did he say? I mean, apart from the alien stuff?'

Spike whipped out his portable hard drive. 'Oh, nothing much. Only that he's sending me his facial recognition software tonight.' He grinned at them. 'And luckily I'll have a whole weekend to play around with it. By Sunday night I'll have it crawling the internet for our mystery bomber and his mate.'

Adam stared at him, hoping that the colour wasn't draining from his face. 'Do you think you'll find anything?'

'Dunno. It'll probably take a while. I'm going to put in a few faces I know to test it out. Then I'll let it loose on the web. See what it comes up with.'

Dan looked sceptical. 'I know you're going to be Porcupine Man one day but seriously, why do you think you're going to have more luck than the police?'

Spike smiled coldly. 'Because unlike the police I don't quit. Batman always gets his guy – and I will too.'

Adam swallowed hard. Things had gone his way all week. Somehow he felt like his luck was running out.

Chapter 18

ver the weekend Adam should have been relaxing. He knew his classmates would be having long lie-ins, demanding breakfast, playing computer games and hanging out with friends. He tried to imagine what it would be like if this was his life. Instead he was on guard duty, watching over one of the most slippery characters in London – namely his brother Luc.

Adam didn't believe that Morta would strike just yet. Yes, she may have had Luc in her sights and Adam was going to have to come up with some way of distracting her. For now though the sudden deaths were staying low, which meant she was giving Darian time to snoop. Adam still felt a pang of guilt at not saving people but it was way too dangerous. It was bad enough risking the wrath of the Concilium on his own, never mind risking his whole family because a Curator had a grudge against his father.

Still, Adam couldn't help worrying that Luc would do something stupid. It didn't help that his brother was still besotted with the Fate. Saturday was wet and cold and Luc obviously had nothing better to do than stay at home for the afternoon. Nathanial and Aron were taking it in turns to do the handful of call-outs, leaving Luc free to mooch into the den, where Auntie Jo and Adam were watching *Zombies vs Hitchhikers*. Auntie Jo was already getting stuck into the whisky. Adam and Luc exchanged glances. It was an early start even by her standards. 'Having a private party, are you?' Luc said from beneath a raised eyebrow.

Auntie Jo scowled and paused her film. 'It's cold outside. It's just a little nip to keep me warm. *Uisce beatha*, as Paddy says.'

'Yeah but I don't think he means the "water of life" stuff literally. You don't actually have to drink it like water.' Luc yawned and mimicked Uncle Paddy's accent. 'So, what's the craic?'

Auntie Jo looked irritated. 'It's not like you to be moping about at home on a slow day. I thought you'd be off enjoying your freedom now that the call-outs are back to normal.'

'I thought I'd hang out here and liven the place up,' Luc said.

'Are you going out tonight?' Adam tried to sound casual and disinterested.

Luc shook his head through another yawn. 'Dunno yet. Need to see what's happening.'

It all sounded like a promisingly quiet evening – but of course by early evening Luc's mobile was on fire and after dinner Adam caught him slipping out of the back door. 'Where are you going?' His voice sounded shrill in his own ears.

'Out.'

Adam was desperate to know more. 'Yeah, but where? What are you doing? Are you going to Flip Street? Or meeting someone?'

210

Luc stared at him, bemused. 'What, are you like my minder now? I'm going out. That's all you need to know.'

'You could take me,' Adam blurted out, trying to stall him. 'I can just run up and get changed.'

'Yes, Adam, what a brilliant idea. Why don't I take you out, bribe a particularly stupid and violent bouncer into letting you in with me and then watch you throw up all over the girl you're trying to cop off with. That sounds like a great night out.'

Adam scowled. Dragging up the painful memories of Cryptique was just low. He tried another tack. 'Yeah, there's probably some girl you're meeting. I don't want to cramp your style.'

He was waiting for a crushing Luc-comeback but to his surprise Luc shook his head. 'Nah. No girl. I've lost interest.'

Alarm bells were going off in Adam's head. 'Why?'

'I don't want a girl. I want a *woman*. And not just any woman. I want someone like *her*.'

Adam's heart sank. He didn't *need* to ask who Luc was talking about but he checked anyway. 'You don't mean Morta, do you?' At Luc's nod he groaned and shook his head. 'What is it with you?! You're mental! She's a Fate! She's not just some woman in Cryptique.'

Luc shrugged. 'I reckon she likes a bit of a challenge.' He gave a filthy leer. 'Must get pretty lonely up there all by herself. I could help her pass the time.'

She's not as lonely as you think, Adam thought. Aloud he said, 'Look, she's a nutter. She's been killing people for fun! You heard Heinrich – she doesn't *have* to take every single soul to meet her quota but she does it for *fun*!'

Luc sighed. 'I know. She's a real psycho. A smokin' hot psycho!' He grinned and opened the door, slipping out into the garden.

'Don't go near her if she calls you! Seriously, find someone else!' Adam hissed at the retreating figure. He had a sinking feeling there was nothing he could do to save his brother from himself.

It was a relief to get back to school on Monday, although Adam still had a guilty feeling that he should be at home on Luc duty. In the end though, what could he actually *do*? Without telling Luc the whole story, there was no way of explaining the danger he was in. Telling the truth was impossible; the consequences were too huge. Luc wasn't a snitch over the small stuff, but this was putting the whole family in jeopardy. Besides, trying to keep tabs on Luc was like herding cats. All he could do was hope that Morta stuck to her deal with Darian.

Melissa had finally finished her art coursework. Adam offered to meet her in the art room as usual but she shook her head. 'To be honest, I could do with a break from the smell of paint. Can we go for a walk?'

Adam hesitated. After an exhausting weekend trying to keep Luc out of trouble the last thing he wanted was a face-off with the Beast. Still, they couldn't hide in the art room forever. All he could do was nod and try and look enthusiastic. It was a cool, cloudy day, which at least gave him an excuse to put his arm round Melissa's shoulders. She snuggled in closer as they walked and for a moment Adam thought his heart might explode in his chest. The novelty of having a girlfriend hadn't worn off yet, especially someone as cool as Melissa.

Melissa seemed quieter than usual and it didn't take long to find out why. 'So my mum got an appointment, at the hospital. She's going there next week.'

'Oh, right,' Adam said. He wanted to say something encouraging but he couldn't forget the premonitions he'd had, back before half-term. He'd never had his doom sense flare for anyone, unless they were just about to die. He'd never even met Melissa's mum before but somehow he just *knew* she was the woman in his dreams. She looked like Melissa.

'I'm going to go with her. My aunt couldn't get off work. There's no way I'm letting her go on her own.'

'She'll be glad you're there,' Adam said quietly. He glanced sidelong at her. He didn't know where Melissa's dad was – she rarely mentioned him. He just knew that she was really close to her mum. What was it going to do to her if something was wrong? As in, *really* wrong?

'She's a bit scared.' Melissa's voice was trembling a little. 'She doesn't show it. Well, she tries not to but I know she's scared.'

'She'll be fine.' He was lying. He was pretty sure she *wasn't* fine at all – but whatever was wrong with her, maybe it could be fixed. He hoped so. He couldn't bear seeing Melissa so sad. He tried to change the subject. 'At least you won't miss the art show. Your mum will be really excited about that.'

It worked. Melissa brightened up and started talking about her artwork. Her voice was brittle with something between nerves and excitement. 'Everyone is going to get out of class on Friday to see our pieces. It's not usually displayed at this time of year but Ms Havens has a friend from art college coming. She won't tell us who it is yet – but she has a gallery and she's going to display some of our work if she likes it. Ms Havens thinks I have a really good chance of getting something in. How amazing would that be?'

'Pretty amazing,' Adam said, grinning at her. His grin faded slightly as they entered the main building. It was buzzing with people – and if he was feeling generous, 'people' included the Beast and his friends.

Melissa seemed blissfully unaware that anything might be wrong. She waved at some of her friends and darted over to talk to them. The Beast had clocked Adam's presence and had fallen quiet, his group staring menacingly in Adam's direction. Adam took a surreptitious peek around the foyer, hoping to see a teacher, but there was no one useful on the scene. The problem was the Beast loved an audience. An opportunity like this would be almost irresistible. When you ruled with terror, a public act of vengeance was worth ten times more than a private one.

Adam tried not to look worried. He'd escaped from the Beast once before by disappearing into the Hinterland. It was totally forbidden but under the circumstances (dark alley and certain death as an alternative), Adam had decided that breaking Luman law was the lesser of two evils. Now, in the packed foyer, there was no prospect of escaping, short of turning tale and running. That probably wasn't going to impress Melissa much. But what was the alternative? Stay here and face a public beating?

Adam walked on, excruciatingly aware of the Beast's eyes on him. Weasel, the Beast's most loyal minion, was practically salivating with excitement. He was thin and spotty and vicious

– and he was eyeing Adam with barely concealed glee. 'Look at him, Michael! Look at that little prick. He came in with Melissa!'

There was a long silence. Adam slowed and turned to meet the Beast's gaze. Whatever was going to happen was going to happen. It was going to be public and horrible and humiliating, but he wasn't actually going to die, which was something to be thankful for. He might get a mouthful of Michael Bulber's fist but at least he wasn't dodging Morta's knife.

And then, just as he was bracing himself, the miracle happened. Michael Bulber sneered at Adam and said loudly, 'Who cares, lads. Let him have her. Sloppy seconds. Why would I want *her* when I've got *this* waiting for me?' He held up his mobile phone for them to admire a photo – a photo Adam recognised immediately. 'She's coming here soon and she's gagging for me. She's Italian. She's called Bellissima, Bella for short. Bellissima Pesce.'

Adam's eyes widened and he only just stopped himself from guffawing. Laughter would be fatal. His Italian was limited to a few phrases but if he'd heard correctly, Spike had called their mythical babe 'Beautiful Fish.' He bit the inside of his lip and tried to look deeply jealous until he was safely past. Weasel's disappointed face was a picture. Spike was a genius. The Beast had bought the Wonderfish thing hook, line and sinker. He couldn't wait to tell his friends. Adam's thoughts were racing at a hundred miles an hour but that didn't matter. The Wonderfish had saved him.

A moment later Melissa hurried up to join him. 'Sorry! I was talking to Ellen.' She glanced back over her shoulder at where Bulber was laughing and jostling with his friends. 'What happened? Did he give you a hard time? What did he say?'

Adam gave her a beatific smile and threw his arm round her shoulders. 'He didn't say anything. We won't have to worry about him for a while. He's got other fish to fry now.'

Adam was still on a high when he went to chemistry revision after school. As he looked round the lab he had the most surreal feeling. This time last week he had been on his way to meet Clotho in her realm – and narrowly dodging the Hunter and Morta. Now a week later his only imminent danger was dying of boredom. His life was always a juggling act but sometimes it was weird even by his standards.

A few more reluctant souls wandered in before the class started, and among them was Spike. Adam was surprised to see him but he nodded at the empty stool beside him. Spike slouched over and flung his laptop on the bench. He didn't normally bother with revision classes, so it was a surprise seeing him there. His memory was like a high-definition camera; he read things once and they got etched into his brain forever. Adam wished *his* memory was like that. It would have made it much easier getting through tests, especially when you couldn't revise because you were guiding souls in a war zone.

Spike hopped onto the stool and answered the question before it was asked. 'It was either this or detention. At least here I can get on with some work. In detention they just make everyone copy out those worksheets about eight million times.'

'They make *you* copy out the sheets because you've already filled them in before. You should have done more of the Batman

216

breathing stuff.' Adam grinned. Spike was the smartest person he knew but he wasn't very good at doing what he was told. Adam could never decide whether Spike was going to rule the world or end up locked up in a prison cell with clear walls . . .

Spike grunted in reply and opened his laptop. He never looked particularly healthy but even by his standards he was looking corpse-like. His skin had a grey hue and the shadows under his eyes stretched halfway down his cheeks. He was studying the screen with a disgusted expression. 'I spent all weekend working on my face recognition programme and I finally got it running overnight. It's trawling the web and getting hits but they were all really random in the tests I did with people I know. Sometimes it's the person I'm looking for. Sometimes it's a family member. Sometimes it's nobody.' He shook his head. 'I need to refine it.'

Adam peered at the screen. The programme was searching busily through the billions of pictures on the internet, but Adam was pretty sure he was safe. He had always been careful to avoid school photos, and family photos were kept in leather-bound albums. The Luman world wasn't exactly up to date with technology but even the Concilium had realised that with new, digital cameras there was a danger in sharing photos online. Just occasionally a soul would leave its body – only to be returned to it after swift medical treatment. Most of the time the only thing the soul remembered was their Light and a warm, hazy sense that someone was there taking care of them. It wouldn't do for them to spot their guide leering out of an online photo site. Of course the one thing he couldn't control was police surveillance, like CCTV images. There were thousands of cameras all over London. Still, surely even Spike wouldn't start wading through that kind of footage?

As if reading his mind Spike scowled at the screen. 'I tried getting more of the CCTV footage, to see if Baseball Cap had ever looked straight into a camera, but he kept his face down most of the time. Trust Dan to only get him from the side. A face on picture would have made it easy. Baseball Cap was really careful. S'pose he would be, if he's a ninja. '

Lucky, not careful, Adam thought. *And definitely not a ninja.* When he thought of the CCTV cameras he must have walked past that day . . . He could have been caught like a rat – and all because Dan was in the wrong place at the wrong time.

The revision class started. Adam made a valiant attempt to master the basics of valencies even though his thoughts were all over the place. Spike's laptop was super-booted to the nth degree but it was whirring and chugging under the strain of his search. It was a constant distraction. Spike didn't even pretend to be listening to what was going on in the class, giving all his attention to the photos flickering across the screen, checking them and the percentage match against the picture of Baseball Cap hovering on the far side of the screen.

Adam couldn't quite shake the feeling that he was looking at a ghost, seeing himself standing there. It made him want to laugh or shriek, knowing that he was sitting right beside the person who was trying to hunt him down. Like something out of a nightmare, he watched the endless parade of images flutter across the laptop screen, freeze for a few seconds, then disappear beneath a new image. Still, as the pictures marched onwards he made a conscious effort to relax. The thing was, every picture was totally different to the last. There were men, women and children of every race and colour in an infinite variety of poses. Some were in corporate headshots; others were brandishing barbecue tongs or grinning over birthday cakes. Some were black and white photos dredged from historical archives, all because one person at the centre of the group had a jawline or a cheekbone reminiscent of his own. He stifled a grin but tried to sound sympathetic. 'Look, it was always a long shot. Even the police haven't been able to find the guy.'

Spike was squinting at each face in turn, as if he could match them by sheer force of will. Occasionally he pressed pause and scrolled back a few frames, as though he was scared of having missed something. He was muttering under his breath. 'The parameters are too wide. I need to tighten them up.' Frustrated, he slammed his hand down on the bench, making everyone in the room jump awake.

'Sebastian! What on earth are you doing?' Their teacher Mrs Suresh was glaring across at them. It took Adam a minute to realise who she was talking to; he couldn't remember the last time his friend had been called anything other than Spike.

It took Spike a minute to realise too, not least because he hated being called Sebastian. Still, after previous encounters, Mrs Suresh was one of the few teachers he was slightly in awe of so he settled for replying, 'Nothing,' through gritted teeth.

Mrs Suresh wasn't mollified. 'Since you're obviously not listening to a word I'm saying you can run a message for me. No, leave your computer where it is! Believe me, you'll be back before the end of the session.'

Spike was scowling – but even he wasn't going to risk

after-school chemistry every day for the rest of the year. He stomped up to the desk with a pained sigh and took the envelope from the teacher's hand.

Mrs Suresh continued as though nothing had happened and the class slumped back into sleepy incomprehension. Adam's eyes were closing and he forced them open. He watched the screen on Spike's laptop, hoping for some kind of entertainment, but the hypnotic slide of photos only made things worse. His eyelids were drooping and his eyes drifted over the images, one after the other, after the other, after the other until –

Adam jolted upright. He stared stupidly at the screen, unable to believe what he was seeing. The image was already moving on and he panicked. He had to get it back! He lunged for the keyboard, then forced himself to stop. He needed to be careful. If he disrupted the programme Spike would want to know why – and if Adam had seen what he *thought* he'd just seen then Spike needed to never, ever know that photo existed.

Hardly daring to breathe, he hovered over the mouse pad until the programme controls appeared, then pressed pause. A smiling couple grinned out of a wedding photo, champagne glasses raised in a toast. In the time it had taken him to come to his senses the photo had changed several times. He needed to go back. He clicked the arrow key, and the image changed to a smiling Jewish boy at a bar mitzvah. He pressed again, trying to tell himself he'd been dreaming, that it wasn't possible, that no one would be stupid enough to –

And then, as the photo burst back onto the screen, he stopped telling himself anything and simply stared.

Chapter 19

everal hours later, Adam was still in shock. He lay on his bed chewing his lip, trying to ignore the sick, churning feeling in his stomach. It wasn't like he was easily freaked out – his life wasn't exactly normal – but it had always made a kind of sense because of who he was. He was a Mortson and the Mortsons were Lumen. He might not like it – but he'd always known who he was because of his family. They had each other, even if they weren't the typical suburban family.

Just recently though he'd been starting to feel like there were more secrets than he'd ever imagined. It was like lots of tiny pieces in a jigsaw were coming together and falling into place – but frustratingly he still couldn't see the whole picture. It had started with Morta's sneers at the Summoning. Then there was Auntie Jo's day of drunken sobbing and then her confession that his parents had been forced to elope, even though Nathanial was a Mortson. And why did the French side of the family largely shun them even now? Family and connections were everything in the Luman world. He had never thought about it before but now it was beginning to hit him: there was something in his family's past that didn't add up – and the photograph provided him with his first solid piece of evidence.

When he first saw the picture appear on Spike's laptop screen Adam had almost thrown up with sheer terror. He couldn't believe what he was seeing. But after the initial shock a kind of survival instinct had kicked in and left him with just one thought: get rid of the photo. Get rid of the evidence – but not without getting a copy himself first.

He had been expecting Spike to walk back in at any second. As he plugged his memory stick into Spike's laptop he could *see* his hands shaking and feel the awful, giddy rush of his heart beating. He dragged the photo onto the memory stick and was just about to delete it when another thought had occurred to him. It was all very well having the photo but where had it *come* from? What was the source? And how had it ended up on the web in the first place?

Fear and his need to know had fought frantically. In the end Adam's curiosity forced him to gamble that he had just a little more time. He clicked on the photo and let it link him to the source page. He had wanted to solve the mystery there and then but there wasn't time. He took a screen shot and dragged it onto the stick, then pulled it out. He was just deleting the picture when the lab door opened and a scowling Spike returned. He presented Mrs Suresh with an envelope and a filthy look – but it didn't stop him noticing that Adam was hovering over the computer.

'What are you doing?'

Adam had breathed in slowly, hoping his voice wouldn't betray him. He'd managed to close the page – but not to delete it from the browser history. 'Nothing. I just thought I recognised someone.' He pointed at the picture of the boy at his bar mitzvah, trying to sound disinterested. 'I just thought I knew his face but I don't.'

Spike snorted. 'Yeah. That would be a pretty big coincidence.'

Yeah, wouldn't it just, Adam had thought bitterly. Last week he'd been feeling like everything was going his way. This week the tide was turning on him.

The last twenty minutes of the revision class had passed in a daze and he almost screamed with relief when he finally got out of the lab. But Adam hadn't been able to go straight home. Instead he made his excuses to Spike, checked the coast was clear and scurried into the library. Only the sixth formers were supposed to stay after school but the few who were there were too busy with their own stuff to notice Adam slip in and quietly boot up the computer and printer. Half an hour later he'd been on the bus home, his mind a blur.

And now here he was, lying on his bed and looking at the source of his misery and confusion. He'd recognised the faces immediately – or two of them anyway. His father and Auntie Jo were recognisably themselves, albeit much younger versions. His father looked like he was barely out of his teens. Seeing Auntie Jo was a shock. Whenever the photo had been taken she hadn't been wearing a kaftan but some kind of summery dress with her dark hair pulled back off her face. She wasn't thin but she was much slimmer and her eyes were sparkling above a wicked smile. She was pretty. It felt weird seeing her because something about her – a kind of playfulness – reminded Adam of Melissa. His aunt was in the middle of the photo, Nathanial's arm slung round her shoulders. On the other side she clasped the arm of the unknown man; the man Adam had always wondered about and whose face he was poring over now. The man in the locket.

His hair was dark, although not as dark as Nathanial's. He had a pale, thin face and very blue eyes. His pose was relaxed and like the others he was smiling – but there was a hint of something else around his mouth, something sad. His eyes were watchful and haunted. He looked like a man trying very hard to be happy and not quite succeeding.

In contrast Nathanial looked happier than Adam had ever seen him. There was no trace of the tiredness in his face or the careworn stoop Adam sometimes saw in his shoulders when he thought no one was watching. He stared straight into the camera, grinning broadly. Strangely, his pose reminded Adam of Luc; the same hint of barely suppressed swagger. It was eerie. A few months earlier Nathanial had confessed that he had dreamed of being a race car driver. At the time Adam had scoffed at the thought of his kindly, conscientious father doing anything so dangerous – but it didn't seem as ridiculous an idea for *this* Nathanial.

And as for Auntie Jo . . . she was glowing. Something about being beside Nathanial and the mystery man made her light up like a torch. She wore his picture in the locket around her neck. He must be the man she was once supposed to marry. But who *was* he?

Or, to be more accurate, who had he once been? Adam moved the photo printout to one side and looked at the second page, feeling sombre. This was the reason the photo was on the web in the first place, in defiance of the ban on online photos. He studied the screenshot, knowing he was intruding on something he had never been supposed to see.

The picture was from an online memorial website. The post was simple and anonymous – the photograph and a few lines of text – but Adam could guess who had written it by the date. It had been posted a couple of weeks earlier on the 19th of March – the day Auntie Jo had been sobbing in her room, drunk and miserable enough to throw caution to the winds and ignore their laws.

My grief is darkness but Lucian: you were our light. You were real; you existed. We do not forget. For now we must not speak your name – but we are not ashamed. We may not understand but we love you still. Some day we will meet again because our Light is your Light.

Adam stared at the printout for a long time, trying to will it to reveal its secrets. Who was Lucian? What had happened to him? Obviously he had died and walked through his Light onto the Unknown Roads. But why? He was young and Lumen rarely took ill or died young – their keystones seemed to protect them. In the photo he looked only a few years older than Nathanial.

And why would his life – or death – be a cause for shame? When a Luman died he would be guided into his Light with a family Keystone, passing through onto the Unknown Roads and returning briefly to hand over a freshly 'charged' Keystone and pass on any wisdom that could be added to *The Book of the Unknown Roads*. Guiding a dead Luman was an honour and a source of pride; a last chance to say thank you after a life of service. The Mortsons were an old family and if Auntie Jo had been betrothed to this man then he must have been from a good family too. None of it made any sense.

There was a knock on the bedroom door. Adam scrambled to hide the papers under his duvet as Chloe walked in. She gave him a knowing look. 'Don't worry. I won't even ask. Every time I have to go into Luc or Aron's room *they* hide stuff too. You lot are disgusting.'

Adam scowled, unable to deny anything in case she demanded to see what he *did* have. 'What do you want?'

'Dinner will be ready in ten minutes. It's late tonight because Father had a call-out.' From her sing-song tone Chloe had obviously delivered the message to everyone else.

'How many call-outs were there today?'

Chloe shrugged. 'Just a few. Nothing out of the ordinary. Luc went along because Aron wanted a day off.'

Adam relaxed back into the pillows, feeling a twinge of guilty relief. With everything else going on he'd forgotten about Luc's fatal attraction for Morta. At least if he was going on call-outs he wasn't off doing anything stupid. Chloe was almost out of the door when Adam called her back. 'So what did *you* do all day?'

Chloe turned and gave him a withering look. 'What's it to you?'

Adam wasn't sure why he'd asked. It had been an impulsive question and one he was already regretting because Chloe's expression could have curdled milk. Still, now that he thought about it, Chloe might be the way to find out more about the mystery man. She spent most of her time hanging out with Elise and Auntie Jo. Surely they must *talk* about stuff? Chloe, he realised with a start, was an untapped mine of information. After all, she was the one who had told him about Auntie Jo's annual bout of melancholy. What other secrets did she know? 'I'm just interested.'

Chloe sighed. 'Well, Adam, let me think about it. Today I practised the piano while Mother picked every note apart. *Then* I made watercress and anchovy soup, which was as disgusting as it sounds, and *then* I had some tapestry practice and finished embroidering a handkerchief for Father. And then I went out with Mother and watched her terrorise the butcher until he found her the exact piece of meat she wanted because it had to be *perfect*.' She rolled her eyes but her shoulders drooped. 'Just another Monday.'

Adam blinked, unsure what to say. He'd been expecting something along the lines of, *We all had lunch and went shopping and Auntie Jo told me loads of stuff about the past and it was a brilliant day!* Things always worked out better in his head than they did in real life. 'Anything happening on the betrothal front?'

'No!' Chloe's eyes had gone laser. 'Why do you keep going on about it? I don't have to do anything yet. Father told me not to rush into anything.'

Adam held his hands up, trying to appease her. 'OK, sorry! I was just asking!'

Chloe glared at him for a moment until she seemed to realise that he wasn't tormenting her. She hovered at the door, looking uncomfortable. 'Mother keeps telling me I should get betrothed to a Chinese Luman because they have so many souls. Either that or a French Luman. I don't know why she goes on about France so much. It's not like we go there very often so why does she want to marry me off there?'

To make peace, Adam realised with a sudden moment of clarity. It was like something out of his history class; all those warring kings and queens marrying their children off as bribes and peace offerings. Elise had betrayed her family in their eyes and now she was trying to find her way back. But having married for love herself, there was no way she would try to force Chloe into a betrothal she didn't want. He knew that in his gut. 'She won't make you do it. Trust me, she really won't.'

Chloe looked at him curiously. 'How do you know?'

'I just do.' Adam shrugged. 'What does Auntie Jo say about it all?'

'Auntie Jo doesn't say much to anybody these days.' Chloe's face darkened. 'She pretty much lives in the den.'

This wasn't really news to Adam. Toast and horror movies were the twin joys of Auntie Jo's existence. 'I thought she'd talk to you about Ciaron and stuff. I mean, I thought she was betrothed once?'

'She doesn't talk about it if she was. I don't want to end up like her though.' Chloe shuddered. 'I'll get betrothed to anybody rather than end up like that.'

'There's nothing wrong with Auntie Jo!' Adam felt a quick flare of anger. Why couldn't Chloe see that Auntie Jo cared as much about them as their parents did? Maybe she even cared more.

'Nothing *wrong* with her?' Chloe sounded incredulous. 'She sits there all day with her whisky bottle for company. You don't see anything wrong with *that*?'

'So she likes a drink!' Adam retorted, trying to ignore the prickle of unease he felt hearing this.

Chloe gave him a pitying look. 'Yeah, Adam. She likes a drink. She likes a drink the same way a junkie likes a fix. But you know, whatever.' She held her hand up, angry. 'Nobody listens to me anyway. I've told Father and he just disappears into his study. I told Mother too and she shouted at me. What am I supposed to *do*? Maybe I *should* just get betrothed and then I could go and live somewhere else, away from this *nut house*!' She stomped out, slamming his bedroom door behind her.

Adam looked at the door for a moment, then pulled out the pictures from under the duvet. He stared for a moment at Nathanial and Auntie Jo, their smiling, untroubled faces seeming to admonish him.

Things had been going so well. So why did it feel like his whole world was beginning to unravel?

As so often happened, when things went wrong they started small and snowballed from there. That evening at the dinner table Adam found it hard to eat. Everyone else was in a good mood, delighted to have another meal without being interrupted by a call-out. For Adam it was torture. He tried to focus on his plate but his eyes kept darting between his parents and Auntie Jo. He hated the thought that they were keeping secrets. It made him feel sick.

His plan for the days ahead had been simple. Get caught up on all his work. Spend some time with Melissa and enjoy the art show. Keep an eye on Luc and hope that Morta left them in peace for just a little longer. There were only two weeks of school left before Easter and then he could watch his wily brother twenty-four hours a day if necessary.

But now everything had changed. After dinner he made his excuses and fled upstairs, not wanting to spend an evening hanging out with Auntie Jo in the den. He didn't know what to say to her. He didn't even know who she *was* any more, when he looked at the photograph of who she'd once been.

Chloe was right – Auntie Jo was drinking too much. *Way* too much. Before, her hip flask had just seemed like a quirk; something as much a part of her as kaftans and toast. But recently she was drinking more than ever before – and that was only what he was seeing in the evenings. She could be drinking all day long when he was at school. So why was no one doing anything? Why did they think that was just how she was? She hadn't always been like that.

The mystery man was gnawing away at Adam. There was something so familiar about him. He pored over the photo, hoping inspiration would strike. Whoever he was, Auntie Jo had loved him – and whatever he had done, he was still a Luman. It seemed wrong that no one could talk about him or honour him. In his room Adam booted up his laptop and studied the memorial site, reading Auntie Jo's words: *We do not forget . . . we are not ashamed . . . our Light is your Light*. He clicked the comment button and watched his anonymous reply appear on the screen: *Our Light is his Light*.

Normally school was his refuge when things got crazy. But as Adam walked up the long school driveway on Tuesday morning he felt queasy. He was dreading seeing Spike. When he had a plan his friend was like a dog with a bone. There was no stopping him. It had been stupid deleting the picture; he realised that now. The photo didn't mean anything to Spike. He didn't know it was Adam's family. It had probably just picked up a hint of Adam's jawline in Nathanial or even Auntie Jo. Besides, it was still out there on the web. There was no way for Adam to delete it. All he could hope was that a billion other pictures would keep the programme busy.

He calmed down a bit in registration when he saw Melissa. She smiled and gave him a little wave across the desk. He grinned back at her. He wasn't up to playing it cool, the way Luc did. All that 'treat them mean' stuff seemed crazy. Maybe it worked on some girls – but Melissa was cool. If you 'treated her mean' she'd probably tell you where to stick it. He really wanted to get some more time to just hang out this week. He knew she was busy getting ready for the art show but every time he kissed her the world came back into alignment.

As it turned out, he was disappointed. Melissa and Archie were both tied up in the art room all through lunch – and for once even Archie was working. Adam made his way to the library to meet Spike and Dan. Spike greeted him like nothing was wrong but Adam's stomach was still rolling. This time it wasn't nerves – it was his death sense flaring. It flared again, after lunch and again on the bus home and again as he walked through the gate at home. As he reached the back door Aron was coming out. His face was tense. He jerked his head in greeting and stepped forward, disappearing into the Hinterland.

There was no need to ask. Adam could feel it in his gut. As

231

the week passed a few more souls died every day. It wasn't an avalanche yet but it was growing all the time. By Thursday night Aron and Nathanial were alternating call-outs and Elise was tight-lipped with fury as she put their plates in the oven.

Morta's reprieve was over – and there was nothing Adam could do.

Chapter 20

he day of the art show had finally arrived, providing Adam with a welcome distraction from the miseries of the Luman world and the frequent flares of his death sense. There was a definite buzz of excitement around the school, mainly because the local TV cameras were coming in. The visiting artist had turned out to be the eccentric Luna Kazuna, who had found fame running round London daubing black paint over road signs. She said it was to force visitors to stop and see the city in a different way. After painting over a stop sign caused a five-car pile-up she was forced to point her paintbrush in another direction and had ultimately ended up running her own gallery.

Archie was usually good at pretending not to care about stuff but even he had spent every lunchtime that week perfecting a piece for the display. He was coy about what he'd done but his friends knew it was called 'Perfect Love'. If it was typical of Archie it was probably going to top shelf rather than romantic.

Melissa was wired with excitement. Adam was pleased for her – but he was also a bit nervous. What had been supposed to be a school art show was in danger of becoming a media circus. He still hadn't seen Melissa's painting. What if it ended up splashed all over the television? Having survived her own scandal, there was a real chance Elise would fall down dead if her youngest son appeared on the evening news in a painting called 'Passion'. All he could do was keep his fingers crossed that Melissa's picture wouldn't end up on TV – not that he could ever admit this in a million years.

By the end of breaktime it seemed like most of the school was loitering out the front of the main building, waiting for their celebrity guest to arrive. The plan was that Luna Kazuna would do the judging first. The chosen pieces would be taken to one side and would then be unveiled for the whole school to see. The artists would get a small prize – and of course, they might also get their work into Luna Kazuna's gallery.

'She's here,' Dan hissed, shifting from foot to foot. A long, black car was sweeping up the gravel driveway into the school. A murmur of excitement rose from the mob. Adam and his friends had stayed up on the steps where they could see the whole thing. Melissa and Archie were in the hall waiting to meet the artist before the judging began. One of the local TV crews was already in position at the bottom of the steps (Adam was careful to keep a pillar between him and the cameraman) and another news van was chasing the black car up the drive. There were whoops and catcalls as the convoy reached the main building.

The Bulb was waiting, looking delighted at all the attention. He smoothed his bald pate and turned on a truly terrifying smile. Even the cameraman took an involuntary step back. The driver of the car stepped out first. He looked like a chauffeur from a film, only he had no hat and every visible scrap of skin was tattooed. He opened the rear door and a cloud of cigarette smoke billowed out, choking the people waiting at the bottom of the steps, The Bulb included. One pale, bare leg appeared from the fog, clad in an impossibly high black platform shoe. This was followed by another pale leg; and finally, as the driver offered his hand, the rest of Luna Kazuna followed – to stunned silence.

Dan was one of the first to find his voice, or at least part of it. 'She hasn't got any clothes on,' he squeaked. 'She forgot her clothes!'

Adam could understand why he had said that. Luna Kazuna was agonisingly thin. Just how thin was painfully obvious because her clothing mostly seemed to be made of net and every single rib was on display and ready to be counted. Her hair was black and hung to her navel on one side while the other half of her head was shaved and oiled until it was shiny. She was wearing the biggest sunglasses Adam had ever seen and her lips were slathered with black lipstick. She had at least put on some kind of stretchy black bandage across the bits she couldn't show on TV, but there wasn't much left to the imagination. Even Spike was gawking.

The Bulb made a heroic attempt to recover and scuttled forward, fawning for the cameras. 'My dear Ms Kazuna, such an honour to have you here today!'

'Call me Luna,' their visitor barked, in a voice that managed to be squeaky and steely at the same time. She took a last drag on her cigarette and flung it down on the gravel. Her tattooed minion stepped forward and ground it out with a size-fourteen shoe, glaring around, daring anyone to object. She held out her hand for The Bulb and with awkward chivalry he raised it to his lips. It looked like he was kissing a pale, dead fish. A titter of nervous laughter rippled through the crowd.

'Hello Luna,' Ms Havens said, restoring some kind of sanity to proceedings. 'Lovely to see you again. Thanks for coming along today.' The two women exchanged air kisses.

'She *knows* Luna Kazuna?' Dan whispered.

'They went to art college together. Something like that.' Adam *thought* that was what Melissa had told him. Ms Havens looked a bit out there by teacher standards – but beside Luna Kazuna she looked like the girl next door.

The local evening news reporter had been burbling his introduction into the camera and now he was determined to get an interview with the star of the show. He barged forward and bared his polished teeth in an equally polished smile, thrusting his microphone in Luna Kazuna's face. 'What are you here for today, Luna?'

'Call me Ms Kazuna,' the artist snapped. Her minion stepped forward, growling, looking ready to dismember the reporter, but Luna Kazuna patted his arm and he subsided like a well-trained dog. 'I am here for the art of course.'

The reporter was still keeping a wary eye on the chauffeur-slash-pet-werewolf. 'Lovely. And what are you hoping to see inside?'

'A lot of darkness. Teenagers are full of darkness. Beautiful darkness in every brush stroke. I remember it well. It excites me.'

'What is she *on*?' Dan muttered.

'Dunno.' Adam had a sinking feeling that Melissa was going to be disappointed with their visitor. He knew artists were supposed to be eccentric but Luna Kazuna was way beyond that and riding the train to crazy town.

The reporter was making one last desperate attempt to get some kind of sensible quote on camera. 'Some people have said that you're nothing more than a talentless, one-woman publicity machine. What's your response to that?'

Luna Kazuna stared at him, inscrutable behind her huge sunglasses. If she was angry she didn't betray herself with as much as a flicker of movement. 'My response is this.' Slowly her tongue slid out between her black lips and she blew an enormous raspberry.

There was a long silence before people started sniggering. It spread like wildfire through the crowd until everyone was laughing, teachers and pupils alike. A few people whooped and cheered. Adam grinned. Luna Kazuna might be as mad as a box of frogs but at least she was entertaining. The reporter was glaring all round him but the visitor herself never displayed a hint of emotion. Instead, she turned and swept up the stairs into the main building, followed by a grinning Ms Havens. The Bulb scurried behind, bowing, scraping and bellowing, 'Bell's gone! Get to class!'

There was a dull hour in geography before the message came through that pupils should gather in the assembly hall. A giddy horde swirled through the corridors, still laughing at the raspberry-blowing. Adam was filled with a mixture of excitement and nerves. Part of him really wanted Melissa to do well – it would be brilliant for her if she did – but what if this meant his face would be plastered all over the internet for Spike's software to find?

They squeezed into the assembly hall. Adam's year group were the youngest there so they were able to stand at the front and watch Luna Kazuna in action. She had slapped a nicotine patch on each arm and was pacing up and down the stage like a caged animal, wobbling occasionally on her platform shoes.

Ms Havens came in with the art students. Melissa was chatting to Archie and he laughed at something she said. Adam felt a quick and unexpected pang of jealousy. It was crazy but sometimes he still wondered what Melissa saw in him. She was so nice and so gorgeous and she seemed to like being around him. It had only been a month since they had started 'dating', but all their 'dates' were in school and he wasn't sure how much longer he could get away with doing that. Sooner or later she would want to meet up in the evenings; and even if he wasn't grounded forever he still wouldn't be able to act like a normal boyfriend. She was never going to be able to come round to his house or meet his family or just hang out in his room. What sort of future did they really have?

He tried to push those thoughts away as Archie and Melissa came over and focused on giving her the biggest grin he could. 'How did it go?'

'It was brilliant!' Melissa's eyes were shining. 'She's amazing.'

'Pretty cool,' Archie agreed.

Adam stared at them and he could see he wasn't the only one. 'Really?'

238

Dan wasn't as restrained. 'How was it brilliant? She's mental! The only brilliant bit was when she did this.' He stuck his tongue out and blew a raspberry.

Archie recoiled and wiped his face, swearing at Dan, but Melissa rolled her eyes. 'You didn't fall for all that, did you? All the "Woooo, I'm so crazy!" stuff?'

Spike raised an eyebrow. 'It didn't seem like an act. It was pretty convincing.'

Melissa grinned. 'She's actually really normal and nice. The Luna Kazuna thing is just her persona. She was telling us about it earlier. How she used to be a really good painter but nobody really noticed. So, she started doing crazy stuff to get attention and then people followed her online and started buying all her stuff. And then suddenly – wham! Everything took off. Now she has her own gallery and she can show whatever art she wants.' She lowered her voice but Adam could hear the excitement. 'Ms Havens thinks she's picked a few of the sixth formers for her new show. Can you believe it? Imagine getting your work in a gallery while you're still at school! And she said that once we're sixteen we can apply to go and do an internship in the gallery over the summer. I have to wait till next year but I'm totally going to do it!'

'That's brilliant,' Adam said – and he meant it. He loved it that Melissa had a dream and she was going for it, without being afraid. How amazing would it be to be able to just concentrate on doing the thing you loved the best? What must it be like being able to give all your energy and attention to one thing? Sometimes it felt like he spent all his time trying to juggle life and death, when all he wanted to think about was going to school, growing up, having a girlfriend, being a doctor. Having a normal life.

Where was all this negativity coming from? He tried to feel happy as The Bulb climbed back onto the stage. Behind him there were a dozen works of art on easels, hidden beneath large covers. The Bulb didn't have to say a thing; he just gave the hall one of his killer glares and a petrified silence rippled through the pupils from the front towards the back. After the usual faff with the microphone he managed to announce the names of the winners: three sixth formers who would each have three pieces of work displayed in Luna Kazuna's gallery. There were excited screams from the back and polite applause from everyone else. The winners walked up onto the stage, where they received a limp handshake and a smoky air kiss from the great woman.

At this point Ms Havens stepped forward. 'It's a huge achievement to get your work displayed in a gallery and congratulations to those chosen. However, I want to give a special mention to three other outstanding pieces of work; one by a fifth year, the other two by fourth years. I'm delighted to say these will also be displayed in Luna's gallery. The pieces are "Death and the Maiden" by Katie Kurtz; "Perfect Love" by Archie Maguire; and last but not least, "Passion" by Melissa Morgan.'

There were more screams of delight. Archie looked stunned, then grinned broadly as he went up on stage. Melissa was frozen to the spot, her hands clasped over her mouth until Adam gently touched her shoulder. She snapped out of it and ran up onto the stage beaming, joining the other two, who were already waiting by their easels. Luna Kazuna was talking to the second TV reporter as the cameraman videoed each piece in turn. His camera didn't linger on Archie's piece, although he did go back himself for a long, smirking look – confirming Adam's suspicion that it wasn't really fit for family viewing.

'It's your big moment,' Dan whispered. 'Hope she kept your clothes on!'

It was all happening so fast and it finally dawned on Adam that 'Passion' was about to be unveiled. He barely had time to gulp before The Bulb pulled away the sheet and revealed . . .

'What the hell is that?' Spike was squinting up at it.

Dan was bending his head so far sideways that his ear was touching his shoulder. 'I think I can see a hand if I look at it this way.'

Adam stared at the picture, bemused. He could hear fragments of Luna Kazuna's comments as she pointed at it for the camera. 'Passion . . . clear for all to see . . . Picasso-esque with a twist of Dali . . . A mature style . . . Full of darkness – but light too – and yet beautiful darkness. I love it!'

Adam wasn't sure how to feel about the painting itself. At first glance it just looked like lots of swirls of paint with the odd body part sneaking into the frame. Still, as he stared at it a bit longer he could see that in a strange way the whole thing seemed to come together. It was trying to give a message and he wasn't quite sure what that was, but there was something happy and confident about it. When he looked at Melissa shaking hands with Luna Kazuna he could see that same happiness and confidence glowing out of her. The painting said something about who she was and what was important to her – and he was in it.

'I like it,' Dan said suddenly. 'It's cool. Although let's face it, you're never going to be famous like that Mona Lisa woman. No one's going to walk up to you in the street and say, "Hey, you're the guy from the painting!" are they?'

'Nope,' Adam said cheerfully. He could live with that. He had a feeling that he didn't need to worry about Spike's software.

The whole school was still buzzing over lunchtime. The winners had to get photographs taken, so it was a while before Archie joined them in the library. He was trying to look casual but not doing a very good job. He was still carrying a huge board with his work attached for display. 'I have to take this up to art after lunch but I thought you might like to see it.'

He waited for Spike to move his laptop and placed the board on their usual table. Dan raised an eyebrow and summed up what they were all thinking. 'I don't think they'll be showing this on the news tonight.'

Archie grinned. 'Doesn't matter. It's going into the gallery, isn't it? Luna Kazuna said she liked the style. You had to pick a style or artist, so I went for a mixture of pop art and manga.'

'Pop art and perv art you mean,' Spike smirked. 'You're lucky this won't be on TV. Your gran would murder you.'

Archie's grin faltered slightly. 'Yeah, well, I probably won't tell my gran about the whole gallery thing. If she sees it and has another heart attack my mum will kill me.'

'What style did Melissa do hers in?' Adam was desperate to know.

'Oh, she went for the Cubists mostly. You know, Picasso's

lot? Everything kind of chopped up and rearranged. But she likes Dali too, crazy surreal stuff. Eyes on your toes and all that.' Archie pulled a face. 'It's not really my kind of thing but Ms Havens loves it.'

'It's not my kind of thing either,' Adam confessed. He was just grateful he would never in a million years be identifiable, even if it ended up famous some day.

'So what body parts *did* she get photos of?' Archie leered.

Spike snorted. 'It's not like it matters. If she was taking photos she must have some weird private collection because she didn't use them for her painting.'

'You're just jealous,' Dan piped up. 'You wish *you* had been her muse.'

Adam could see this whole conversation straying into territory he would rather avoid. He'd never managed to find out if Spike had, as Dan claimed, had his eye on Melissa. It was probably better to cut and run while he could. 'Yeah, I better go and see Melissa.'

'She'll be in good form. Make the most of it, mate.' Archie grinned.

Adam rolled his eyes and left them to squabble. He didn't know where Melissa would be – probably not the art rooms as Ms Havens had gone out for lunch with Luna Kazuna. After ten minutes of fruitless searching it was almost time for the bell. Adam went outside, trying to think up what he was going to say about the painting. He wanted to sound grateful that she'd picked him as her subject but he didn't exactly want to lie either. He would probably stick to saying that he'd never seen anything like it before . . .

243

But when he saw Melissa a second later all thoughts of the painting were pushed out of his mind. He'd expected to find her grinning from ear to ear. Instead, as she came round the side of the main building and walked towards him, he could see that she was crying. He ran over to meet her and put his hand on her cheek. 'What's wrong?'

Melissa looked up at him through tear-filled eyes. 'I just got a call. My friend from work was on her way in this morning and she got killed. It was an accident. A total freak accident.'

Chapter 21

elissa was crying in earnest now. Adam put his arms round her and pulled her in close until her head was resting on his shoulder. He felt her shoulders shaking and her tear-stained cheek against his neck. She clung onto him almost fiercely.

She pulled away a minute later. 'Sorry,' she whispered. 'I just can't believe it. It doesn't feel real.'

'It's OK,' Adam said, even though it wasn't. For a family somewhere it was never going to be OK again. He didn't want to ask but found he had to anyway. 'What happened?'

Melissa shook her head, bewildered. 'It was just a complete freak accident. She was on her way into work this morning and this guy in a lorry was unloading stuff. He had this trolley thing and the brake cable snapped and it rolled into her. It knocked her down into the road and a car . . .' She stopped and covered her mouth with her hand, the horror of it etched into her face. 'She didn't do anything! She was just going to work. She's only there on a gap year.' Her face crumpled. 'She was supposed to be going to university in September, to do

245

fashion. She was so excited about it!'

Adam stared at her mutely. *I killed your friend*, he thought. *I didn't mean to. I wasn't unloading the lorry or driving the car. But I made Morta angry and now your friend and lots of other people are dead. And I know I need to stop her but I don't know how.*

Melissa looked angry now. 'I texted her earlier. I texted them all, to tell them about my stupid painting and the gallery. And nobody replied at first and they probably didn't want to because they didn't want to spoil everything. As if it matters. As if a stupid painting and a stupid gallery matters!'

'It *does* matter!' Adam said. His heart was pounding. 'Of course it matters. That's why we get to be alive! We're supposed to do the things that make us happy and . . . live! Don't ever say it doesn't matter because it *does*.'

Clotho's face swam into his mind; the gentleness there when she talked about her work. *Every thread . . . every single human soul is precious.* How many more threads were going to be cut on a whim? How much longer was Morta going to get away with this? Rage boiled inside him. He'd felt paralysed before, knowing that Morta was killing people and not knowing what to do about it. Until now the deaths had felt far away and although he'd felt guilty he hadn't seen the effect of the deaths. Now in the face of Melissa's grief . . . He wanted to kill Morta and Darian and whoever or whatever had been stupid enough to let them get into positions of power.

The bell rang for the end of lunch. Melissa wiped her cheeks. 'I have to go to work tomorrow. It's going to be a nightmare.' She hesitated. 'Can we do something tonight? Just go and hang out somewhere? We could go back to Petrograd.'

Adam bit his lip. 'I really wish I could. I just . . . I can't. Not tonight. But I can ring you later.'

She shrugged but her disappointment was obvious. 'Don't worry about it. I'll see you on Monday.'

Adam caught her hand as she turned away and when she swung back towards him he kissed her. She tasted warm and salty and he would have done anything to take her back in time; back to an hour ago when she was happy and excited and thinking about the future with nothing but hope. 'I really can't tonight. I'm sorry.'

Her face softened. 'It's OK. What have you got to do? It sounds serious.'

Adam tried to smile. 'Yeah, I guess it is.' *I'm going to find a way to kill a Fate.*

Adam had two classes after lunch. He spent French drawing angry doodles with a black marker and after getting some odd looks from the girl beside him he realised he was never going to make it through his last class without going mad. Instead he slipped out of school, running down the drive towards the bus stop. It was maddeningly slow but he didn't dare to swoop. With so many call-outs his family would be in and out of the Hinterland and could easily spot him.

His head was like a revolving door all the way home. There had to be something he could do. He needed to find out how to get rid of Morta. Failing that, he would have to confess to Nathanial. Tell him everything. Tell him about being a Seer; about saving people; about going into the Realm of the Fates and seeing Darian and Morta conspiring. Adam could be executed of course – that was the law – but what was one life in the face of all the innocent people who were dying because of the Mortal Knife?

The thing was though . . . it wouldn't just be him. His family would be destroyed. Nathanial might well face the wrath of the Concilium too. Would his closeness to Heinrich be enough to save him? And what about Clotho? She had risked everything to come and see Adam and warn him he was in danger. What if they got rid of her too? Who would be left to care? Lachesis would be indifferent; she just measured the threads, wove them into the Tapestry of Lights and forgot about them. A new Clotho wouldn't dare to challenge Morta. She would be able to carry on wielding her knife for hundreds of years.

There had to be another way. Adam ran from the bus stop back to the house, hopping impatiently from foot to foot until the electric gates allowed him into the garden. His death sense had been flaring on and off all afternoon. There was a good chance his father and brothers were on call-outs. He scuttled towards the front of the house, trying not to crunch on the gravel, until he could peer into his father's study.

It was empty. Adam eased the front door open and left it ajar, not daring to close it tight. There was no noise in the house but that didn't mean no one was home. A quick peek revealed that the downstairs rooms were empty. Elise and Chloe were probably out and Auntie Jo was more than likely in her room sleeping. There was no point waiting. Do or die.

Adam slipped into Nathanial's study, feeling his heart beating faster. They were all banned from being in this room without Nathanial – a rule so sacrosanct that Nathanial had never put a lock on the door, trusting that it would be obeyed. The real prize was in the bookcase. This copy of *The Book of the Unknown Roads* had spent a long time in Mortson hands. It was a heavy leather-bound book, packed with the collected history and wisdom of the Luman world. The book was a mystery. The words came and went, constantly updated by High Lumen with knowledge gleaned from Lumen as they passed through their own Lights at the end of their lives, returning only briefly to the Hinterland to pass on their Keystones and anything new they had learned.

Right now there was no time to admire it. Adam sat cross-legged on the floor and touched his keystone to the book's cover. Every copy of *The Book of the Unknown Roads* was different. Sometimes the book seemed alive and it seemed to sense the blood or keystone of the person holding it, part of what protected the knowledge of the Luman world. If a book was stolen by casual thieves, they would simply see an old book with blank pages.

For now Adam was simply hoping the keystone would make the book cooperative. 'The Fates,' he whispered. 'I need to know about the Fates. How I can stop a Fate. How I can get there to do it.'

The pages lifted and turned, as though a breeze was stirring in the room. Adam scanned the first page it stopped on, written in a shaky, spidery hand as though the author had been very old or frail. There was nothing useful there – just a brief description of the roles of the Fates, stuff he already knew. The next few entries seemed no more helpful at first; they were random anecdotes about some of the ancient Fates. But as Adam skimmed through the stories he found one interesting line:

249

Harsh words were exchanged and Atropos severed the thread of Lachesis. New Fates were duly appointed.

Adam stopped and stared. The writer's tone was utterly dispassionate; he might have been talking about replacing a bulb or inserting a new battery. The important thing was that the Fates' threads could be cut like anyone else's. It was a start. Of course, he had no idea how he was going to find Morta's thread amidst billions of others but one thing at a time. He didn't allow himself to think about what he was really preparing to do – to kill another person – or even whether he could do it. He just concentrated on figuring out the practicalities.

Unfortunately a swift search through the next entries only confirmed one fact: there was no way for Adam to gain access to the Realm of the Fates unless he had a token from their realm. Frustrated, he slammed the book closed and shoved it back into the shelf. His mind raced. Maybe there were some tokens left after the Summoning. Maybe Nathanial had a big bag of them sitting around somewhere, just waiting for times like this. Adam threw open cupboard doors, pulled books aside, checked the drawers in his father's desk. He even lifted the rug and checked behind the pictures, hoping he would find some kind of safe – but it was all in vain. He'd known it would be.

He sank back against the wall, forcing himself to breathe and just think. *If I can't get to their realm it's all over. Unless I can get her to come here. Maybe I can set a trap, save someone, let Darian catch me. They'll catch me and kill me but maybe I can get her first.* It was stupid. Even as he thought it, he realised how stupid it was; as stupid as telling Nathanial the whole thing.

All it would do was destroy his family. And how could he cut Morta's thread without being in front of the Tapestry of Lights?

For an awful moment Adam felt like crying. It was pointless and pathetic but he felt *trapped*. All his good intentions, trying to save people, had gone so wrong. He'd managed to save a lot of souls before the Summoning. They were walking around today because of what he'd done. But Morta had killed so many more to exact her revenge and draw him out. How was he going to live with the guilt of knowing this? His throat was tight and he tried to swallow the ache away but it wouldn't go. He hadn't meant to hurt anyone. All he'd wanted was to help.

Angry at himself, he ground the heels of his palms into his eyes, rubbing them dry. He had to think – but not in here. He'd been here too long already. He took a quick glance around, hoping he hadn't moved anything, but the room still seemed calm and orderly, the way it always was. Adam stood by the desk and gently spun the antique globe with one finger. It had always been his favourite thing in the study when he was a kid. He closed his eyes and smelled the same familiar scents: old paper, beeswax polish, a faint, faint trace of Nathanial's aftershave. It smelled like safety and the life he used to have. Not quite fitting in with the Luman world, but not working against it, alone either.

He pressed his ear to the door, praying that the hall was empty. There wasn't a sound and he slipped outside, silent, easing the study door closed behind him. Adam rested his forehead against the cool wood, eyes closed, unable to let go of the door handle. Once he did, he was admitting defeat. He was admitting that there was nothing he could do and that

251

Morta could go on killing people until she got bored of hunting the rogue. He was admitting that he had played his part in helping a mass murderer.

'What are you doing, Adam?' Nathanial's voice was sharp.

Adam jumped. He let go of the handle and swung away in the direction of the voice. How long had he been standing there? He was so tired. 'Nothing. I . . . I thought you might be in there. I was going to knock.'

'Well, I wasn't but I'm going in now. Was there something you wanted to talk to me about?'

Adam hesitated. If he said no Nathanial would wonder why he was lurking in the hallway. If he said yes, he was going to have to think up something quickly. 'No, it's OK. I mean, it was nothing important. It can wait.'

Nathanial sighed and came towards him, resting a hand on his shoulder. 'It's OK, Adam. I'm sorry I snapped. I'm rather tired with all these call-outs. I don't have much time now I'm afraid but I think I know what this is about. I was speaking to your aunt and although I'm a little surprised, if you wish to be betrothed we'll arrange it. I'm assuming you have someone in mind?'

'Erm . . .' Just as Adam's brain needed to be working at full throttle, it was choking to a halt. 'Not really. I mean, kind of but –'

'Well there's not much point thinking about betrothal if you don't have someone in mind.' Nathanial was trying hard not to sound irritated but he wasn't quite succeeding. 'Your aunt also told me that she had been . . . indiscreet in her conversation with you. About some of the circumstances around your mother and I's betrothal?' At Adam's nod he grimaced. 'I'd appreciate it if you kept that information to yourself. There's no point dragging up old gossip. Let the past stay in the past. It's important not to harm Chloe's prospects.'

Adam nodded, feeling guilty all over again. Once his own part in recent events was revealed Chloe was going to be an outcast. They were all going to be outcasts. They would lose their home, their Keystones . . . The Mortsons would be too busy worrying about how they were going to eat to be worried about betrothals. He hesitated. 'Can I help you? I know there are lots of call-outs. I could help?'

Nathanial shook his head. 'Thank you but we're managing. It helps that Aron's of age now. If this continues we'll need to get Luc Marked too, although I'm not sure he's ready for it.' He bit his lip. 'It can't go on like this. The Concilium will have to intervene.' He seemed to be thinking out loud because his face changed when he remembered Adam was still there. 'I'm very tired Adam. Go and do your work. For school. Do it while you still can.' He stepped into the study and closed the door behind him hard.

Was it possible to die from guilt? Adam was beginning to wonder. It was growing and growing, like a toxic wave flowing through his veins, gnawing at the pit of his stomach, making his heart contract – and his fists clench. He felt sick. He went into the kitchen for a glass of water but to his dismay Aron was standing by the fridge, shovelling cheese into his mouth with one hand and bread with the other.

Aron jerked his head in greeting but didn't talk, concentrating on his food. He'd only just come of age but he already looked older. Tired too. He swallowed a mouthful and slumped down at the table, resting his forehead on his arms.

Adam stared at his older brother. They weren't close. They were so different. Aron did everything right. He was a Luman through and through and didn't want to be anything else. He would be happy to follow the path laid out for him: betrothal, marriage, children and maybe someday stepping into Nathanial's shoes and becoming High Luman. Their parents were proud of Aron. He had never disappointed them. Adam wished they could be friends, the way some brothers were but he knew he was an embarrassment to Aron. He cleared his throat. 'Do you want a drink?'

Aron's head lifted from the table and he blinked. 'What?'

'I could get you a drink. Or a cup of tea or something.'

Aron was staring at him like he'd lost the plot but he shook his head. 'No, it's all right. I need to go and get some sleep. I just can't be arsed going upstairs.'

'It's busy again, isn't it?' How could Aron not see it? How could he not *see* that Adam was responsible?

Aron gave a sharp, humourless laugh. 'Yeah, you could say that. If I hadn't been Marked, Father would have dropped dead by now.'

Adam hesitated. 'This morning . . . There was a girl died. Near Flip Street. My friend in school knew her. She worked in that shop Alter-Eden. She fell under a car.'

'Yeah, I know. Father and I did that job. That girl was really upset. It wasn't good.' Aron's jaw clenched and Adam saw his eyes well up, before he lowered his head and made a show of fixing his hair. It was a few seconds before he spoke again. 'Another girl died this afternoon, in Wales. Crossing a train

254

line. About your age. We could have done with Luc there. He's good with the girls. Pity he'd buggered off.'

'What do you mean buggered off?' There was a sharp edge to Adam's voice that startled them both.

Aron raised an eyebrow. 'What do you think I mean? He pissed off out. Probably out with his mates. He was here a couple of hours ago but he wasn't here when we got all those call-outs at once. Little prick.'

Adam stared at Aron, feeling his stomach clench tighter. Luc loved going out – but there was no way he would go off and leave them in the lurch. Not when he knew they were so busy. 'Did he say where he was going?'

Aron stood up and yawned. 'Course he didn't say. He's probably off meeting some bird.' He shook his head, half admiring and half rueful. 'One of these days he's going to get busted – and when he does he's dead. Mother will kill him.'

Not if someone else kills him first. Someone he was so desperate to meet that he walked out on the job. Adam watched Aron leave the kitchen, frozen with panic. He tried to be rational about it all – tried to tell himself that Luc was just being Luc and messing about – but he knew what had happened. Some part of him *knew*.

Adam ran upstairs. When he found the note in his bedroom it wasn't even a shock.

Chapter 22

dam's first thought was how young Luc's handwriting was. Luc had left school at eleven and had probably barely picked up a pen since, hence the childish, scrawling words on the back of one of Adam's test papers. His brother always seemed so much older than him. Nothing phased him and he never seemed afraid. Maybe that was why girls liked him so much. He didn't seem scared of them. And now, not being scared of them – even the ones he *should* be scared of – was going to get him killed.

You know where I'm going. She sent me a ring – hope she doesn't think I'm the marrying kind. If you're reading this I'm not back but I've probably died happy ;-)

Adam crushed the paper in his hand, fighting down hysterical laughter. Only Luc could write a note like that. Only Luc could think it was a game or a dare to be Summoned by the thread-cutter and see it as a chance to pull. His brother was probably dead by now and no one could reach him. No one would ever see him again. And it was all Adam's fault.

Adam picked up his pillow, hit the wall with it and then screamed into the feathers, pressing the pillow against his mouth, trying to get the tornado of feelings out of him before he exploded. He flung it back onto the bed and slumped down to the floor with something between a laugh and a sob. He wanted to smash things. He wanted to kill someone. He wanted to die and put the world out of its misery. He had messed everything up. There was no way back from this. It was *all* his fault.

He held the clenched-up paper against his mouth. What hurt the most was knowing there was nothing anyone could do. There was no way into the Realm of the Fates without a token. Maybe Heinrich had a stash but by the time the alarm was raised it would be too late anyway. Time moved differently there. The minutes or hours that Luc had been missing in the physical world could be days or weeks in the Realm of the Fates.

She sent me a ring. Adam leaned his head back on the edge of the bed and closed his eyes, desperate to come up with a plan. Colours danced behind his eyelids, then faded away into a dim greyness the colour of the Hinterland. *She sent me a ring.* There was no way to get into the Realm of the Fates without a token. What would happen if he just set off into the Hinterland and kept walking until he saw the doorway? Would it even appear? Or would he stand pushing it, shouting and screaming outside, unable to open it until the Hunter came and swallowed him? Maybe it would be a blessing, however futile.

She sent me a ring. The phrase looped and repeated through Adam's mind, incessant and irritating, a mosquito whine over

257

and over. A ring: a symbol of love. How ironic a psychopath like Morta would send a ring to the Luman she planned to kill. *A ring . . . a ring . . .* What token did she send to Darian when they met to hatch their plans? Did he get a ring too? *A ring . . . a ring . . . she sent me a ring . . . a ring . . . a ring . . . earring . . . a ring . . . earring . . .*

Adam's eyes opened. His whole body went rigid for a split second as the shock tracked through him, freezing him, making his breath stop. An earring. A token. Something from her realm. He remembered the faint sensation of it clipping the toe of his shoe. He could see it – black, polished, a tiny sphere on a metal spike, shoved into a pocket to avoid drawing attention to himself. He remembered his desperation to get home safely, unnoticed after Morta's warning to the Concilium and the Mortsons. An earring. His passport into Morta's realm.

Something shifted, allowing him to move. He hurled himself towards the wardrobe, half crawling, half staggering, reaching for the handle, opening the door and rising in one movement, hands pushing clothes aside until he found his suit. The jacket pockets were empty, so he threw it to the floor and pulled the trousers from their hanger. He remembered. He remembered the feeling of his hand sliding against the cool lining as he pushed the earring out of sight. He searched with his fingertips, waiting to feel the smooth stone or the sharp jag of the earring mount – but there was nothing.

It had to be there. Adam stopped, his heart thudding. He *knew* it had to be there. He tried to think. *The trousers were hanging there, undisturbed. The waistband and the hems were facing the ground. The pockets were upside down, so maybe the earring* . . . 'Fell, it fell on the ground,' he whispered aloud. He dropped on his knees and pulled clothes from the base of the wardrobe, flinging them behind him, his palms roaming over the soft grain of the wood until – there. His fingers scrabbled against the back corner of the wardrobe and then . . . he was holding it.

The black stone glimmered. He was looking at his key.

Adam kept his preparations to the minimum. He pulled on his coat over his blazer, out of some ancient impulse to stay warm, even though he wasn't going to need it. A crushed cereal bar at the bottom of his bag wasn't exactly survival rations but it would do in an emergency. Even as he was putting things together he knew a small voice at the back of his mind was telling him he was crazy. This wasn't going to be a long visit. Either he would get in and do what had to be done quickly – or he would die. It was that simple.

The note was the hardest bit. There wasn't time to go into detail, so he took Luc's note and scribbled the main details underneath. Where they were, why they were there – and what had happened if they didn't come back. Maybe it would act as a confession too: proving that his family hadn't known that he was a Seer. At first he just signed it 'Adam' but as he set it on his desk he realised it might be the last time he would speak to his family on this side of his Light, so he added 'love' before the Adam. And after a moment's hesitation, he scribbled a PS: *Tell Auntie Jo to stop drinking.* He allowed himself a brief grin. He'd probably get a clip on the ear for that when they met again on the Unknown Roads.

His smile faded. There was no more time. He looked around his bedroom, wondering if he would ever see it again. His reflection in the mirror was pale but he could just see the crest on his blazer, peeking out from beneath his coat. The little scrap of silvery-grey stitching gave him a burst of courage, just enough to get him through the bedroom door and down the stairs. He slipped out of the front door, veering away from his father's study window. Sam and Morty were roaming free and they ran over to greet him. He petted them roughly and muttered, 'Bye, boys,' pushing them away and stepping into the Hinterland. He could hear them whimpering.

Adam ran then. He had to get away from the house and everything that was so painfully familiar. Once the house and garden were out of sight it got easier. He unzipped the inside pocket of his blazer and carefully pulled out the precious earring, mentally rehearsing the steps. *Let the physical world fall away. See the true Hinterland. Find the doorway.* And as an afterthought: *Don't get eaten.*

Too quickly, the world went dim. Adam looked down at his feet and the way he seemed to be hovering in nothingness. It didn't freak him out this time. It was a pity he hadn't enjoyed himself more in the Hinterland but there was no time for regrets. He clenched the earring tightly in his hand and let his eyes roam through the grey half-light ahead. The Hunter crept into his thoughts but he gave that image a firm push away.

The doorway appeared – and Adam grimaced. Of course it wasn't going to be like the simple wooden doorway into Clotho's realm – that wasn't ostentatious enough for Morta. This doorway was black and highly polished, surrounded by an ornate lintel and carved pillars. It hinted at luxury and beauty on the other side. The handle was striking: a snarling leopard head with flat, obsidian eyes. Adam's fingers prickled as he reached for it, some primitive part of his brain screaming that it would bite him, but the handle turned smoothly. He took a deep breath and eased the door open.

He was back in the hallway of Morta's realm. There was the same marble floor, a cold sheen glimmering beneath the crystal chandelier. The last time Adam had been here there had been music in the air and tables covered in food, their hostess moving among them, laughing while her eyes flashed fire. Today the hallway felt cold and dead. There was no sign of Morta but the same velvet couches were dotted around and on one of them was his brother.

Adam sucked in a sharp breath. It was tempting to rush straight over but he forced himself to wait, listening carefully for any sign of movement. The silence was empty and terrible. He pulled the door closed, mindful of the Hunter and the Hinterland behind him. Only then did he move swiftly across the marble floor, his footsteps sounding horribly loud.

Luc was lying on a velvet-covered couch. The fabric was the colour of fresh blood; rich and dark like wine. Luc seemed terribly pale in contrast, the colour drained out of his face. His eyes were closed beneath his tousled mop of dark hair. He was wearing jeans and a white shirt that had been torn open. He might have been dead, but for the faint rise and fall of his chest. His torso was the same pale alabaster as his face – with one exception. There was a wound on his chest, right over the breastbone, just where a Luman would be Marked. It looked like someone had used a fine blade to draw a crude heart shape. It was crusted with dried blood.

At the sight of this all of Adam's rage flooded back, threatening to overwhelm him. It was the casual cruelty of it that got under his skin. His brother always seemed so confident and in control; more alive than anyone else he knew. Luc moved through life with a hint of a swagger and a smirk on the corner of his lips. To see him lying here so vulnerable hurt Adam in a way that took him by surprise. He had never really known how much he looked up to his brother until now. Seeing him like this was awful – as if he was an abandoned rag doll.

'Luc!' Adam hissed in his brother's ear, shaking his shoulder. 'Wake up!' There was no response. His first impulse was to drag Luc into the Hinterland and swoop them both home. Two things changed his mind. First of all, it would only be a temporary measure. When Morta realised Luc was gone all she had to do was cut his thread and he would be dead anyway. She could carry on her killing spree indefinitely. Adam didn't even know why she had brought Luc here, other than to toy with him. Maybe she was hoping he would confess something for Darian's benefit. Either way, the end results for his brother wouldn't be good.

Secondly – and more pressingly – Luc's keystone was missing. Adam slipped his hand beneath his brother's neck, hoping the chain had just snapped. He knew he was clutching at straws. There was no way Morta would leave her prisoner there with a way to escape. She had taken the keystone as a precaution. Adam's heart sank. With Luc's keystone he might have been able to swoop them both home, even with Luc unconscious.

Without it he didn't stand a chance. There was no escaping what needed to be done. He had to go and confront Morta.

The worst bit was leaving Luc there. He looked small and pale and broken. Adam clenched his fist around the earring, welcoming the sharp stab of the metal spike digging into his palm. It helped him to focus. *One step at a time*, he thought. *Find Morta first. She won't be expecting me. I'll have the advantage of surprise.* But another voice kicked in. This one was mocking. *And what will you do then, Adam? Are you going to kill her? Do you actually think you have what it takes to kill someone? Right there, while they stand in front of you? You, the one who wants to be a doctor and save lives. How ironic!*

Adam slammed an imaginary door in his head, shutting the voice up. It wasn't helping his concentration. He took a last look at his brother's prone form and forced himself to move. There were three doorways he could see. The first led into an enormous bedchamber. The bed was swathed in white sheets, like a vast slab of ice in the centre of the room. It was the only furniture. The walls were hung with tapestries, most of them dark with sinuous threads of colour shot through.

The room next door had nothing but a deep, marble bath sunk into the floor. Along the back edge there were glass bottles filled with oils and a single orchid bloomed in a stone pot. It was all rich and beautiful and cold. Clotho had managed to create a cosy space but it was obvious that Morta wasn't interested in making her realm homely. Luxurious, yes – but a den to rest in only briefly before she went back to work.

Adam returned to the hallway, miserably aware of Luc's prone form. There was only one double doorway left and he knew where it led to. In his heart of hearts he had known from the minute he got here where he would find Morta. She would be in the place she loved the best; the place where she got to revel in her own power. She would be in the vast circular chamber above, facing the Tapestry of Lights.

Adam stepped through the open door. In the darkness ahead he could just see the gleam of the metal steps spiralling upwards. Last time, Morta had illuminated torches along the wall – but Adam didn't want a welcoming party waiting for him. Instead, he raised his hand and imagined light coming from it. A second later his palms and fingertips lit up and a soft, golden glow radiated out from his hands, just enough to light the steps ahead of him. He grasped the handrail and began to climb, fast at first then slowing as he rose higher and higher. His head spun a little with the turns and this time there was no Nathanial behind him to break his fall. His trainers were quiet and sure on the steps and after a long time he had a sense that the stairway was coming to an end. There was a feeling above as if the air was opening up around him.

The first time he had seen the Tapestry of Lights the chamber had been in darkness until the Lumen reached the top of the stairs. This time Adam knew that Morta was already there: the glow from the billions of souls filled the chamber with light, which was now spilling down the staircase. There was no more need for the light in his hands and Adam allowed it to die away, missing the firefly comfort of it as soon as it was gone. He paused, feeling sick and afraid, then forced himself to lift one foot and then another. He crept up the last few stairs, bent double, keeping his head down until he was almost at the top. When he dared to raise his head he was confronted with an extraordinary sight.

Morta was working. She had her back to the stairwell, all her focus on the Tapestry of Lights. In one hand she held a long, thin hook; in the other the Mortal Knife. She was staring at a patch of lights in Europe. As Adam watched she raised the hand with the hook and the lights in the Tapestry got brighter; so bright that Adam had to turn away, spots dancing across his vision. When he was able to look again he could see that most of the lights had dimmed down, leaving only the palest, weakest lights. Morta lifted both arms and her body simply left the chamber floor. Adam felt his jaw go slack as she hovered in mid-air, leaning forward with the hook and catching a thread. She pulled it away from the Tapestry and with one quick movement the Mortal Knife darted forward and cut the thread. She used the hook to tease out the ends and they fluttered to the floor. Their glow faded away in seconds.

Someone had just died. They were probably in Spain, judging by the position on the 'map'. Even now, a Luman would be on their way to the scene to guide the soul into his or her Light. The only blessing was that the soul in question probably wasn't too shocked. Their thread had been wan and flickering. They were either very old or very sick. Either way, they probably knew they were dying. Was that better or worse? *Maybe they had a long and happy life. Maybe they were tired and ready to go. Maybe they were pleased when they saw a Luman waiting for them.* Older souls found it easier to shuck away their physical life. In the Hinterland they instinctively returned to the age they felt inside, not the age they saw reflected in the mirror.

They didn't cling to the bodies they had finally been freed from.

Morta was working with speed now, dipping and lunging, rising and falling in a strange, graceful dance. Thread upon thread met the tip of the Mortal Knife and darkened. There was no malice in what she was doing; she was simply being a professional. For the first time Adam could see some quality in her that helped explain why she had been chosen as a Fate. She was skilful and delicate and she worked quickly and carefully, never taking the wrong soul.

But just as Adam might have found some admiration she turned her attention to the Kingdom of Britain. Her body language changed. Adam could see her tension as she hovered in front of the tiny knot of lights. The rest of the Tapestry dimmed and this time the threads she was seeking were bright and strong, glowing with fire. She slashed with the knife almost carelessly and three people died, two in the south and one in the north, every one of them in the prime of their life.

There was a viciousness there that made Adam flinch. He drew in a sharp breath and clapped his hand to his mouth, trying to take the sound back – but Morta had heard it. Far from seeming alarmed she laughed and didn't bother turning round. 'Don't be shy, Darian. I thought you would be happy with what I left for you downstairs. Did you like my little gift?'

Adam scowled and stepped up into the chamber. 'You have crap taste in presents.'

Chapter 23

orta turned sharply and dropped to the floor in one movement. When she saw Adam her eyes opened wide and he had the satisfaction of seeing the shock register on her face – if only for a second. She recovered swiftly. 'You.' She studied Adam for a moment and shook her head, her face twisted, caught somewhere between a smile and a frown. 'This I did not see. You. The quiet one. The *clumsy* one.' She studied him for a long moment, then started to laugh. 'No wonder my new pet seemed so surprised. I didn't believe him but it seems he was telling the truth.'

'Let my brother go home. He didn't do anything.' Adam was trying to sound brave and calm and in control, like someone with a plan – but he could hear the faint quiver in his voice.

Judging by her smile Morta could hear it too. 'I think I'm going to keep him. He was flattered by my invitation at first. Maybe he'll forgive me when I explain it was a mix-up. Maybe I can make it up to him before I kill him.' She smiled. 'Maybe I should keep *you* a little while too.'

Adam couldn't help staring at her. She was so beautiful. Even now he could see that – her eyes, her mouth, her hair, the curve of her hips. Her beauty was like a cloak, covering the darkness inside her. He could feel himself responding to her, lethal though she was. For Luc, who loved a challenge, it was like a moth dancing helplessly into a flame. Thinking about his brother helped him to focus; remember why he had come. 'You don't deserve to be a Fate.'

'I don't *deserve* it?' Morta frowned. 'Why is that? Because I'm a woman? Because I was poor?'

'Of course not!' Adam was stung into answering her. 'You don't deserve it because you're evil! You're a psychopath! You kill people you don't have to kill. Heinrich told you that you didn't have to take all of your quota – but you do. And you're taking them all from Britain! It's not fair!'

Morta moved fast. One moment she was by the Tapestry of Lights; the next she was in front of him, her hand gripping his throat, nails digging into his skin. She was taller than him but he could see the fury in her eyes. 'It's not fair,' she whined, mocking him. Her laughter was harsh. 'Do you think it is *fair* that you were born a boy? A Mortson? Is it fair that you, who breaks our laws and can barely swoop, has a vault full of Keystones? Is it *fair* that my father – a Luman, just like yours – lived in a *favela* and could barely feed us? That I could not get betrothed because no one wanted a Luman from a *minor* family? Do you think anything in this world is fair, *child*?' She pushed him away and Adam coughed and gagged. He watched her move back towards the Tapestry of Lights through watery eyes. She was talking almost to herself now. 'I was a seamstress

268

and a slave but look at me now. I made a new life. And now I am going to take yours.'

Adam thought at lightning speed. *She doesn't know I've been here with Clotho; that I know how things work here. So I need the knife and I need it to stay in my hand and I need it NOW!*

There was a shocked cry and the Mortal Knife flew from Morta's hand. Adam barely had time to splay his fingers and catch it. The hilt was woven with fine silver and gold and the metal threads peeled away from the hilt and wrapped around his hand, lashing the knife against his palm. He held the knife up, trying to keep his hand from shaking. 'You're not going to take anyone's life. Ever again.'

To his dismay, rather than looking afraid, Morta cocked her head to one side and studied him. 'You've been here with someone else.' Her lip curled. 'I know it was her. I'll deal with her later.'

'Let my brother go home,' Adam said again, trying to buy some time. 'And stop killing people in Britain. Just go back to normal. The way things were before.'

Morta shook her head and looked at him almost pityingly. 'I don't take orders from men any more. Or boys. Least of all those who rob me of the souls that are rightfully mine.' She swept her hand towards the Tapestry behind her. Mocking him. 'What are you going to do, Adam? Are you going to cut my thread? Are you going to *end* me? Please, go ahead. I give you leave to try. You have a one in seven billion chance of finding me.'

'I could kill you.' It sounded like a lie even to his own ears.

'You could.' Morta nodded. 'Just like that.' She snapped her fingers. 'You could put the knife between my breasts and slide

269

it into my heart. Is that what you want to do?'

She was moving towards him. Adam held the Mortal Knife up, the point facing her. 'Don't come any closer,' he said but his voice was weak.

Morta smiled and kept walking. She moved so close that he could feel her breath on his face, smell an exotic, cloying perfume. He could feel the knife pressing against her breastbone. When she spoke she sounded almost kind. 'Are you going to Mark me, boy? Make me a Luman?'

He wasn't going to kill her. How could he ever have thought he could kill her? Adam stared at her mutely, hating her.

Her voice was soft and sinuous. 'It's not easy to do what I do, is it Adam? So easy to talk of killing someone, of cutting a thread. Not so easy when they are looking in your eyes. You don't have what it takes to do this – but I do.'

She turned suddenly and moved away, before Adam realised what was happening. At the same time she lifted one hand and made a summoning gesture. The wires around the knife snapped back sharply, lashing Adam's hand and wrist and he cried out as thin weals of blood sprang up on his skin. The knife hurtled through the air into Morta's hand. She was talking as she walked, never missing a beat. 'I'm bored of you now. It's time for you to step into your Light, little Luman. Your brother and your father will follow.' She paused and turned back to him, tapping the knife against her lips. 'Maybe I should let your eldest brother live. At least he can feed the women. I know what it is to starve. I don't like to see the women go hungry because their men have failed them. First your uncle, now your father and brother. Of course the shame will probably kill your mother anyway.' She shrugged and made for the Tapestry.

'Stop.' The voice rang with authority. Adam turned his head almost as fast as Morta did. Clotho was very calm. 'Enough now. This has gone too far.'

'Greetings, *sister*. What a pleasant surprise.' Morta's face transformed, her smile becoming a snarl. 'I should have seen your busy hand in all of this. I didn't think you would take such a chance with one of your precious souls. I'm impressed you could be so ruthless. Maybe you should have been the thread-cutter, not the spinner.'

'Enough, sister.' Clotho seemed to be struggling to find the right words. 'This has been a mistake – all of it. You cannot remain here but I do not wish to shame you. I know the pride in your soul. I know the pride you brought to your family. So . . . now it is time. Revoke your service. Go into your Light with honour.'

'You think I will walk away? That I will cut my thread after everything I endured to get here?' Morta laughed. 'You're a crazy old woman. Maybe we need more new blood around here.'

'I am giving you a choice. There is always a choice. Take it. Revoke your service and walk into your Light.' Clotho was pleading.

'*I* think it's time *your* service was revoked.' Morta pointed the Mortal Knife up high, to where the lights began to give way to the uninhabited darkness of the Poles. 'Sweden, yes? Just outside Stockholm. Ah, there you are!' One light shone out amidst the teeming mass of souls; a clear light that burned like white fire.

Clotho closed her eyes. She looked unimaginably sad. Adam

271

watched her, horrified. *She's going to die! She's going to just let Morta kill her and then there'll be no one to stop her!* He wanted to call out and beg Clotho to do something, anything at all to save them. Not just him; not just his family – but the whole world.

Then Clotho's eyes snapped open. 'I am sorry it has come to this, sister,' she said softly.

Morta seemed to know what was going to happen a split second before it unfolded. She launched herself into the air, the Mortal Knife heading straight for Clotho's thread – but the knife and its owner both fell to the ground. Morta threw herself at the blade and managed to grab it but as she stumbled forward she seemed to hit an invisible barrier. She looked at Clotho with pure hate. 'How are you doing this?'

There was no triumph in Clotho's voice. 'I have been in this realm for a very long time.' She swept a hand through the air in front of the Tapestry and the lights blinked out, darkness sweeping through the chamber. Only one soul remained illuminated, far west of Britain, across the Atlantic. A red and gold soul that twisted and spiralled and grew brighter and brighter, fierce enough to cast its own light into the chamber. 'Your soul passed through my hands. There was such very great potential.'

Morta was straining towards her but getting nowhere. 'You will *not* cut my thread,' she hissed. Before Clotho could react she threw the knife. Adam flinched but Clotho stood unharmed. It was Morta who twisted towards them, her smile savage in the red light for just a second before the Mortal Knife sliced through her thread and the chamber was plunged into darkness.

Adam stood frozen. He could hear the racing thud of his

own heartbeat. The chamber felt hollow now and cold. He was aware of the cavernous space all around him. Out of the darkness a woman's voice spoke, soft and sad. 'Atropos, known as Morta, has revoked her service and gone into her Light. Our Light is her Light.'

The silence that followed was expectant. Adam cleared his throat. 'Our Light is her Light,' he whispered.

Gradually the firefly points of light returned to the chamber walls, the brightest souls glowing first, then the cooler, quieter souls filling in the gaps until the great sphere was illuminated all around them once again. Adam found himself back at the centre of the globe. Clotho bent down and picked up the Mortal Knife – and something else. She moved towards him and when she got close she put out her hand and patted Adam's cheek. 'All is well now. You and your family are safe. Be at peace.'

Adam tasted salt on his lips. He realised he was crying, hot tears running down his face. He swiped his palms across his cheeks and stared at the ground, trying to make sense of what he'd just seen. 'I thought I had to kill her but I couldn't do it. I . . . didn't know she would end herself.' His stomach churned with guilt and relief.

'It was better that she went into her Light. There was no other way.' Clotho looked tired. For the first time, Adam could see some hint of her age in the stoop of her shoulders and the lines in her face. She straightened up and reached for Adam's hand. When she saw the weals in the flesh she frowned and swept her hand across it. A second later the pain had gone and the skin was back to normal. 'Come. We do not have much time.'

She led him back to the staircase and they climbed swiftly

down. Torches were burning brightly along the walls. There was no need for darkness now. It had only been a few minutes since Adam had crept up the stairs, full of fear. Now as they descended all he felt was numbness, listening to his feet patter on the steps over and over. Morta was dead. He was safe now. They were all safe now. He should be happy.

Clotho was in front and moving faster than him. He hurried after her, catching up as they reached the bottom of the staircase. They emerged into the marble hallway. It seemed even colder and brighter than before. Adam stared around, not quite able to shake the feeling that he was trapped in a nightmare. Only the sight of his brother lying on the velvet couch made it real. 'Is Luc going to be OK?'

Clotho moved swiftly across to Luc and bent down beside him. She rested a hand on his forehead and nodded. 'He must return to the physical world. His body and mind have been through trauma. He will take some time to heal.' She stroked Luc's cheek as tenderly as a mother with her baby. 'I remember this one.' Clotho smiled softly. 'He's going to surprise everyone, himself most of all.'

'Surprise people how?' Adam said. His voice sounded cracked and croaky.

Her smile faded. 'That depends on Luc. He has darkness and light, as all mortals do. Only he can choose his path.'

Adam hesitated. 'And what about me?' He was whispering, without meaning to. What he really wanted to do was shout and yell and scream, *'What about me? Will I always be the failure? The disappointment? The one who can't do anything right, even when I try?'*

Clotho looked at him with that strange, piercing gaze that seemed to see straight through him and into his soul. She knew what he was thinking; Adam could see that. 'You have nothing to fear, Adam. Life is brief and beautiful. Be the man you are meant to be. Be a clear light in the world. If you do that, your mortal life will cause you no regret and when the time comes you will step through your Light in peace.'

Adam nodded. Some of the painful pressure in his chest eased, even though she hadn't really answered him at all. What she'd told him was enough. He joined her at Luc's side and together they looked down at his sleeping brother. The blood crusted on Luc's chest was stark and horrible against his alabaster skin. Adam winced looking at it. 'Why did she do that?'

'Because she was scarred herself. She took her pain and chose to be cruel.' Clotho's face was expressionless. She passed her hand across the wound and it disappeared. The terrible paleness began to fade and colour rushed back into Luc's face. 'He will wake soon. Take him home.'

'How am I going to explain it to him?' Adam bit his lip. How much had Morta told him?

Clotho didn't answer. She slipped her hand beneath Luc's head. Luc lay there perfectly still; then without warning his body went rigid. His neck arched and his mouth opened in a silent scream, before his body fell back into repose. Clotho pulled her hand away. She looked ill. 'I have done what I can. Unweaving memory is a complex affair and I have little time. Fragments may remain for him, like a dream or a vision.' She reached into the pouch on the front of her dress

275

and pulled out Luc's keystone. A wave of her hand and it was safely back on Luc's neck. 'You must go now – but first I need the token.'

Adam frowned, confused, until he remembered what she meant. He slipped his hand into the pocket of his school trousers and pulled out the earring. Looking at it now gave him a mixture of revulsion and fascination. He felt a strange reluctance to hand it over. He would probably never see this place again. 'What if I need to come back here?'

'This is not a place for mortals, Adam. You may be here briefly for the next Summoning but the next Atropos will be chosen with care.' A faint smile touched her lips. 'As will the next Clotho.'

Adam stared at her. 'But . . . You didn't do anything wrong. They can't replace you!'

Clotho shook her head. 'Like Morta, the time has come for me to revoke my service. I have been here too long. I have my own path to walk now on the Unknown Roads and there is nothing for me to fear. I will go into my Light with honour.' She clasped Adam's cheeks in her hands and gently kissed his forehead. 'I am glad to have known you, Adam Mortson. Precious soul.' She smiled and for a second her eyes were bright. 'So, now you must go.'

Adam nodded, not trusting himself to speak. Between them, they helped Luc to his feet. He was stirring and murmuring and Adam knew they had to get out of there. Clotho moved her hand and a doorway appeared. She opened it, revealing the Hinterland beyond. Adam double-checked both his and Luc's keystones and stepped into the grey light. He turned and looked at Clotho one last time. 'I'll see you again someday?'

Clotho smiled. 'I hope that is so, Adam Mortson. Till we meet again on the Unknown Roads.' She bowed her head and closed the door one final time. Even as he watched, the doorway disappeared, leaving him and Luc alone at the centre of an infinite twilight.

It was time to go home. Adam took his own keystone and Luc's in his hand and hoped fervently that he could do this. Holding Luc's arm tight, he closed his eyes, took a deep breath and swooped.

Adam had never been more relieved to see their garden. How long had he been gone? Maybe just a few minutes. Morta hadn't killed anyone since her last vicious swipes at the Tapestry of Lights – but with a bit of luck Nathanial and Aron would still be away on their jobs. There was no way he wanted to explain why Luc was semi-conscious and stumbling like a drunk. He half led, half dragged his brother to the front door, pausing in the hall. He could hear his mother and Auntie Jo squabbling in the kitchen and Chloe thumping out something semi-recognisable on the piano. They must only just have come home. One more minute of luck was all he needed.

Luc was coming round. His eyes were slits and his legs seemed to be moving in different directions but a mixture of urgent pleas and a bit of manhandling got him to the top of the stairs. Adam opened Luc's bedroom door and tipped him onto the bed, scarpering before his brother could fully wake. He stood out on the landing for a second, getting his breath back, until he heard someone coming up the stairs. Panicking that all could still be lost, he hurtled into his bedroom, feeling his heart flutter with relief when he saw the note sitting just where he had left it. He managed to rip it into quarters and shove it in his pocket before Chloe knocked. 'Dinner's ready,' she chorused.

Adam flung open the door. 'I'm coming now. I'll wake Luc.'

Chloe raised an eyebrow. 'He's been *sleeping*? Father was looking for him earlier.' She rolled her eyes and flounced off downstairs.

Adam breathed out slowly, shredding the rest of the note in his pocket. Luc was going to have to explain his absence – but what would he remember? Hesitating, he knocked on his brother's door. There was a muffled groan from inside which he took as an invitation. He poked his head inside, trying to act like everything was normal. 'Dinner's ready.'

Luc raised his head up off the pillow and stared at him, as if he'd never seen him before. 'Yeah, OK. Thanks.'

Adam studied him, petrified that Luc would blurt something out; remember what he had seen. 'How are you? I mean, why are you in bed?'

Luc blinked and let his head slump back on the pillow. 'I don't know. I must have been tired.' He frowned and rubbed his eyes. 'I have just had the *trippiest* dream.'

Adam snorted. 'I'll bet you did,' he muttered.

Chapter 24

ver the next week life returned to something like normal – or as normal as it ever got for Adam. Nathanial was cagey about what had happened but Adam knew that shockwaves had gone through the Luman world. Although the number of sudden deaths had returned to normal, Nathanial was barely home, constantly attending meetings with Curators and High Lumen, who were all trying to get to the bottom of why not one but two Fates had revoked their service without any warning. He had no idea that the one person able to answer his question was sitting at the dinner table every evening, trying to look inconspicuous.

Adam watched his brother closely over the weekend. Luc seemed fine but quieter than usual. He stayed close to home instead of disappearing out the way he usually did. Elise and Chloe were pleased to have him around the house more. Only Auntie Jo seemed concerned at the sudden change in character. He was with them physically but sometimes it seemed like his thoughts were elsewhere. He would start talking about something, then tail off. Watching Luc come to a halt halfway through a sentence filled Adam with guilt. His brother seemed permanently confused. Was it from having his memories 'unwoven'? Would it pass? Clotho had said it would take time for Luc to recover. He hoped it wouldn't take long.

Going into school the Monday after Morta's demise was a truly strange experience. As he blinked around his classes, he marvelled that everything else still looked the same. There was the Buzzard, terrorising his biology classmates as usual. Poor Stinky Pete still sat at the front bench, directly in her firing line. Adam ignored her rants. She didn't seem as terrifying now after Morta.

It was the last week of school before Easter. Part of Adam was dreading the holidays, but as the week went on that changed. Ironically for once it was school where he began to feel like public enemy number one, instead of at home.

Firstly, Spike was quiet with him for several days. He avoided talking to Adam but as they sat in the library Adam could *feel* his friend's eyes boring into him. He wanted to ask what was wrong but it was risky with the other two there. Even Dan and Archie picked up on the atmosphere – impressive when they usually had the emotional radars of fruit flies. On Thursday, the day before they finished for Easter, they were at their usual table at breaktime. Conversation was at an all-time low. Eventually Archie sighed. 'I don't know what is going on with you two but seriously – sort it out, will you?'

'Yeah,' Dan piped up. 'It's like that old film we had to watch in English. Everyone kind of *staring* at each other and not *saying* anything.'

Adam grinned in spite of himself, although he cringed on the inside. He knew exactly what Dan meant. 'There's no problem with me.'

Spike didn't say anything. He didn't need to. His silence spoke volumes.

Dan and Archie exchanged glances. They knew that whatever it was it was bad, and with Spike in this frame of mind it wasn't the time to get on the wrong side of him. Archie announced, 'I'm going to art,' at the same time that Dan muttered, 'I need to go and get my physics file.' They stared at each other accusingly, before standing up and fleeing.

Adam sighed. 'OK, I don't know what's going on. What's your problem?'

Spike didn't look up. 'You tell me.'

Adam glared at him, exasperated. Whatever petty crime he had committed was nothing to what he'd done in the Realm of the Fates. It was hard to take it seriously. 'I'm not psychic.'

Spike looked up. There was a hardness in his face that Adam hadn't seen before. 'OK. Let me tell you a story. Once upon a time I spent a whole weekend working on a program to help me find a mysterious guy who magically escaped seconds before a bomb went off. Proof, if you like, that actual ninjas exist. Only my dickhead "mate" poked about at my laptop and erased a file – or a photo, to be exact. The same mate that didn't want me to find the ninja, right from the start.' He paused and waited for an answer. When none came he scowled. 'You're the dickhead, in case you didn't get it.'

Adam tried hard to look like someone honestly puzzled. 'I have no idea what you're talking –'

'I have the log. I can see exactly when it happened: in chemistry after school while I was doing the message for Suresh. I came back and found you messing about with my laptop.'

'I was looking at the photos,' Adam protested. 'I told you, I thought I knew the Jewish guy. Maybe I deleted one by accident.'

Spike shook his head. 'I don't think you did. You never wanted me to find out who the guy was, right from the start. You know I'm going to find out.' He stood up and closed the laptop. 'Last chance. Tell me.'

Adam tried to laugh. 'You're being crazy! You're making something out of nothing. I didn't mean to delete anything!'

Spike was studying him. 'You know, we've been mates for years now, and I don't know anything *about* you. I've never been to your house. You hardly ever meet up with us out of school. I don't even know what your parents do. For all I know your dad could be a diamond thief or a terrorist. Maybe *he* was the ninja.' Spike glared at him and pointed an accusing finger. 'I think you're hiding something. Something really big.'

Adam stared at him, paralysed. Spike was just throwing ideas into the air, not being serious. But what if he got serious? He made one last effort at pleading. 'Look, there's nothing going on. If I deleted something it was an accident. I'm sorry. But I'm not hiding anything.'

Spike looked at him with utter coldness. 'I'm going to find out what it is. I'll find the photo too. I'll run the whole search again from start to finish if I have to.' He turned and walked away.

Adam stood up and called after him. 'You do that!' He was shaking. He sat down and breathed out slowly. He hadn't planned for this. Maybe it *had* been a mistake deleting the photo and maybe it hadn't. He didn't know.

What he *did* know was that Spike would never find the photo. It was gone. He knew it was gone. Over the weekend he had returned to the memorial page, curious to see if Auntie Jo had seen his comment. He guessed she had because her reaction had been to delete the page and close the account. Her message to Lucian was gone.

By lunchtime he was desperate to see Melissa – but nervous too. She hadn't been in the day before because of her mum's hospital appointment. He'd made a special effort to text but she hadn't replied. Seeing her pale, tense face in registration that morning had already told him what he needed to know.

He found her just where he expected. She was outside the main building, waiting for him. He reached for her hand without a word, lacing his fingers through hers. Her hand felt small and fragile, but she tightened her grip and he felt the warmth and strength beneath her skin. They started walking, silent at first. He waited for her to speak.

She cleared her throat. 'So my mum has to go back to the hospital again. They want to do more tests. They found something they didn't like the look of.'

Adam closed his eyes. 'I'm sorry. But it's good that they're being careful. They might just find out that it's something small.' Why was he saying this? Why was he lying to her and lying to himself?

'I don't think it *is* good.' Melissa's voice was so quiet Adam could hardly hear her. 'The doctors were being really nice. Like, *too* nice.'

Adam wanted to throw his arms around her and hold her tight. He wanted to keep away those awful pictures in his mind; Melissa so pale and sad, holding a sick woman's hand. He stopped and turned towards her. 'Let them do the tests first before you start worrying.'

Melissa nodded. 'She's going back next week. She won't let me go. My aunt will be off work this time so she's going to go with her.' She let her head fall forward and rest on Adam's shoulder. 'I have to go to my friend's funeral next week too. My friend from work.' She looked up and gave him a watery smile. 'Happy holidays.'

Adam didn't know what to say. Instead, he kissed her. Her mouth was warm and soft and when he put his arms around her she pulled him in tight against her, hugging him fiercely. He felt her tongue brush against his and a wave of fire ran through his whole body. He pulled her in tighter, until there was no air left between them and kissed her harder, and harder, until he felt dizzy.

It was hard to tell who ended the kiss first. They shifted apart but not too far. Could she feel his heart beating? Her face tipped up and her eyes were huge and happier. Adam dropped a kiss on the end of her nose.

Melissa smiled. 'I was thinking we should meet up over the holidays? There's a really nice park near Alter-Eden. I could meet you after my shift on Tuesday.'

Adam's heart plummeted. He tried to keep his face expressionless. 'I'd really like to but I don't know if I can.'

She shrugged. 'That's OK. What about another day?'

'I have to do stuff over the holidays. With my family.' It wasn't a lie. It just wasn't the whole truth.

'Every single day?'

'Yeah, pretty much.' Her smile had faded. Adam felt a bolt of misery. 'I can ring you though. I'll ring you whenever I can.'

Melissa pulled away. He saw the flash of hurt and disappointment before she made her face impassive. 'OK.'

For a second Adam longed to tell her everything. *Everything*. Everything about his messed-up life, his messed-up family, the whole messed-up Luman world. The urge was so strong it crushed his chest, making it hard to breathe. He caught her hand, willing her to see how he felt about her. 'I want to see you. If I can get away I will. I promise.'

Melissa shook her head, bewildered. 'I don't get your family. Sometimes you make it sound like you're a prisoner when you're not at school.'

Adam looked at the ground. 'It's not like that. It's not their fault. It's just . . . complicated.' It was too hard to find words. He kissed her again, before he could blurt out something stupid.

But this time she pulled away. Her face was sad. 'Sometimes I feel like I could tell you anything. But sometimes . . . I feel like I don't even know you. Like you're keeping some big secret from me.'

Hearing this for the second time in one day made Adam want to weep. Instead, he reached for her other hand and pulled her in as close as he dared; close enough that he couldn't see her face. Close enough to put his lips against her ear and whisper. 'I tell you everything I can. It just . . . takes a while to get to know me. Just . . . trust me. Please. Trust me.'

The bell rang in the distance. When Adam found the courage to look at her again she met his eyes for a long time, searching for something. Finally she nodded. 'I do trust you. And if you want to do something over the holidays . . . you know where I am.' She stretched up and kissed him one more time.

Adam tried to freeze the moment in his head – her scent, her warmth, the way her mouth felt against his. As she walked away he couldn't help wondering if that had been their last kiss.

Adam was angry and depressed by the time he got home from school. Standing at the iron gate, he felt a momentary hatred for everything beyond it. He placed his palm on the electronic security pad, resisting the urge to punch it. He kicked his way up the path and when Sam and Morty came to greet him, he let them herd him into the paddock and present him with their favourite soft football.

He kicked the ball again and again, trying to shift the rage inside him – and when that didn't work he started running, letting the dogs chase him and wrestle him onto the grass. Finally, he pushed them away, sitting in a breathless heap. His blazer lining was torn. Any normal mother would have shouted and yelled at a damaged uniform but Elise wouldn't care. She'd slice it up herself if she got the chance.

He struggled to his feet, sweating and mucky. The anger was gone, replaced with numbness. He reached into his blazer pocket, the zip-up one on the inside. The photo was there, covered in clear plastic to keep it safe. Adam studied the faces, familiar now, all three of them – even Lucian's. A face not unlike the face Adam saw every day in the mirror.

A mystery solved because of Morta's cutting words in the Tapestry chamber, forgotten at first in his struggle to survive. Words half remembered in the night. Words that made Adam jolt awake, turn the light on and search for the photo so he could see the truth once and for all.

'Adam?' His father's voice called across the paddock.

Adam's first instinct was to hide. He was tired. Tired of all the lies and half-truths and secrets. Tired of false pride and disappointment and sadness washed down with whisky. He didn't want to see any of them. And yet in the end – who else did he have? Who else understood the world he lived in, if not his family?

Still clutching the photo, he walked towards the house. His father came round the long hedge and stopped when he saw him. From the shock on Nathanial's face Adam could only imagine how savage he looked. He didn't care. His family had been worried about appearances for too long.

Nathanial tried to smile. 'I thought the dogs sounded energetic. I was waiting for you to come into the house but they appeared back without you.' When Adam didn't speak, he cleared his throat. 'I wanted to give you some warning. We have another Summoning to attend. You won't be able to go to school tomorrow, I'm afraid. Although judging by your uniform, that's probably not a bad thing.'

'OK.' Adam shrugged. What else could he do? The Luman world always came first. He started to walk away when he felt his father's hand on his shoulder.

'Adam.' Instead of sounding angry Nathanial's voice was gentle. He waited, silent, until Adam was forced to look up and meet his eye. 'I know things have been difficult recently. It's been a difficult time for all of us. I haven't been here as much as I should have been – but I'm here now. If there's anything you want to talk about, I'm here.'

Adam stared at him. His father was waiting for questions. Questions about swooping or guiding or betrothals. Adam had a question all right – just not the one his father was expecting. He held up the photo and handed it to Nathanial. 'Who's the man in the picture? Not you, the other one.'

His father blinked. Nathanial didn't betray any other hint of shock. 'I suppose there's not much point asking where you got this, is there?' In the face of Adam's stubborn silence he sighed. 'It's your uncle. My brother Lucian.'

Adam nodded slowly. 'I thought it might be.' Morta's words had twisted and danced through his head for days, just as the Mortal Knife had danced between her fingertips. Words from the Summoning and words from their last, desperate confrontation. *I was told your family had some talent. Well, most of your family. Not every family member has shared your aspirations for greatness . . . I don't like to see the women go hungry because their men have failed them. First your uncle, now your father and brother.*

They stood side by side looking at the photo, taking in Nathanial's swagger, Auntie Jo's smile and Lucian's haunted eyes. Adam studied his uncle's face. 'His hair's a bit lighter but he looks like both of you. Both of you together.'

Nathanial gave a ghost smile. 'He was. People said he was more like your Auntie Jo in personality, although gentler. They used to fight like cat and dog when we were children but she adored him.'

Adam hardly dared to breathe, afraid that whatever he said next would stop Nathanial from saying any more. He had the feeling of standing on the edge of something; that if he said the wrong thing Nathanial would walk away and Adam would never find out what he needed to know. 'He's dead, isn't he?'

Nathanial nodded. 'I'm afraid so.'

'What happened to him?'

Nathanial closed his eyes for a moment, weighing something up. When he opened them they were cloudy. 'He decided to step into his Light before his time.'

Adam blinked. 'You mean he . . . killed himself.'

'Yes.'

There was a long pause. Pieces of the past tumbled and fell through Adam's mind, locking together. The shame and the scandal, betrothals broken. A Luman who had refused to live the life he was destined to lead. A picture formed, explaining a thousand different moments. Nathanial's painful sense of duty, Elise's perfectionism, Auntie Jo's long unhappiness. 'Why? Why did he do that?'

Nathanial sighed. 'We don't know for sure Adam. I know that he never felt at ease in our world. He was the eldest. He was supposed to be the next High Luman but things didn't come naturally to him. Maybe he felt too much. He cared about people. He couldn't detach and get on with the job. And at a certain point . . . perhaps he decided he'd had enough.'

Adam stared at him, mute. Nathanial might just as well have been describing him. Maybe Nathanial realised this because he gripped Adam's shoulder fiercely. 'You're not like him, Adam. Maybe in some ways. You have some of his qualities.'

He smiled. 'And you look like him too. But you're *not* him and that is *not* the path you will walk.'

Adam nodded. He knew that. He loved being alive. He couldn't imagine there *ever* being a time when he didn't want to be alive. The difference was, he had something beyond the Luman world that was *his*. He had school, his friends, his hopes and dreams. Maybe Melissa too. 'That's why Auntie Jo made you let me go to school?'

Nathanial nodded. 'She wanted you to have something to hold on to beyond our world. Just until you find your feet.'

'So why didn't you tell us about him?' Adam's anger rose up out of nowhere. His words poured out in a scalding wave. 'Why are you ashamed of him? It wasn't his fault! He must have been miserable! You must be ashamed of me too!'

'*No.*' Nathanial's hand tightened, his fingers digging into Adam's shoulder hard enough to bruise. 'I have *never* been ashamed of you. You are my son. Nothing will ever change that.' He paused, struggling to control himself. 'We were all devastated. Lucian didn't tell anyone his plans. He wasn't guided. He took no keystone with him. People said he was selfish. He was supposed to be the next High Luman.

'We're an old family but it nearly wasn't enough to save us. They could have stripped our Keystones. I was young and foolish but I worked and worked and finally I proved myself. It was Heinrich who made me High Luman. He knew what I'd done. And Elise gave me a chance. It took a long, long time but I brought us back.' Colour had flared in Nathanial's cheeks but he breathed in slowly. 'And now we're fine.'

Adam shook his head. 'Auntie Jo isn't fine. She's the opposite of fine. She's drinking herself to death.'

'That won't happen.' Nathanial closed his eyes. 'I won't let that happen. I promise you.'

Adam studied him for a long moment. He realised then that he believed him. His father had never let them down. 'You should have told us. You should have told us we had an uncle.'

Nathanial didn't try to hide the pain in his face. 'I loved my brother but we nearly lost everything. Your aunt Jo suffered the most. The past must stay in the past, for all our sakes – but most of all for Chloe's sake. Your aunt lost more than her brother. She lost her future too. I won't let that happen to my daughter.'

For just a second Adam saw the boy Nathanial had been. The second son. A happy, careless boy who had never wanted to be High Luman. The Luman world was unforgiving and Nathanial had worked hard to save them. Now all Adam could think about was how close he had come to dragging the family down into scandal again. 'I'm sorry.'

'For what?' Nathanial said.

'For being crap, I suppose,' Adam said. His voice was small. 'I'm sorry I'm no good at being a Luman. I do try. I just hate it. But I'll get better. Like you had to.'

'Some day you'll be a great Luman,' Nathanial said. His voice was quiet. 'You care about people Adam. That's why you find the job hard. But some day you'll realise this is just a different way of caring. It's the last way of showing care to each and every soul.'

Adam nodded. His throat was tight. He had his own way of showing care to souls – by helping them stay here as long as they could. He was going to keep helping them too because something stubborn in him wouldn't let him stop. He would be a doctor and he would have the life he wanted. But that didn't mean he couldn't show care to the ones he couldn't save too.

As if testing him, his death sense flared. He turned to his father. Nathanial closed his eyes for a second and sighed, like a man with the weight of the world on his shoulders. 'I believe it might be a hit and run. Would you like to come on the job with me?'

Adam swallowed down the sick, unhappy feeling that rose up. 'Yeah, OK.'

Nathanial reached into his pocket and produced a handkerchief. 'You might want to give your face a wipe before we go. No point alarming anyone.'

Adam shook his head and pulled a packet of tissues out of his pocket. 'Thanks but I'm OK.' And he realised suddenly that he *was* OK. He wasn't his uncle. He could do this. He could do this and still be himself; still be the other Adam.

Nathanial smiled. He put his hand on Adam's shoulder, and together father and son stepped into the twilight of the Hinterland.

Acknowledgements

Thanks as ever to my agent Gillie Russell and my editors Emily Thomas and Georgia Murray. Thanks also to EVERYONE at Team Hot Key, especially Jet and Jan for another brilliant cover and Meg, Livs and Sarah for looking after me in London and Dublin.

I am grateful to the pupils, staff and governors of Sperrin Integrated College, Magherafelt for their continued support with the books. Thanks also to everyone who cheered me on or made me laugh while I was writing: Rosie McClelland; the endlessly patient, talented and hilarious Flowerfield Writers; the Rosemary Drama Group, Belfast for the fairies and the funnies; and as ever the mighty PWA – Julie Agnew, Mandy Taggart – and most of all Bernie McGill for endless encouragement, cool-headed Beanie handling and emergency bun delivery.

Special thanks to my family and friends, especially my parents Derek and Patricia McCune and my parents-in-law Michael and Gretta Murphy. Your cheerleading means a lot.

Most of all, love and thanks to my husband Colm Murphy and our daughter Ellen. You are the people who make it all worthwhile.

D.J. McCune

D.J. McCune was born in Belfast and grew up in a seaside town just north of the city. As a child she liked making up stories and even wrote some down, including a thriller about a stolen wallaby.

D.J. McCune read Theology at Trinity College, Cambridge but mostly just read lots of books. She lives in Northern Ireland with her husband and daughter – and two cats with seven legs between them.

THE MORTAL KNIFE is the second book in the DEATH & CO. series.

If you'd like to know more you can find her at:

www.facebook.com/djmccuneauthor

http://debbiemccune.tumblr.com

Twitter @debbiemccune

The Young Graphic Artist Prize

For book one in the Death & Co. series, we worked with our friends at Movellas.com on The Young Graphic Artist Prize, and challenged their creative community to make a piece of art or character illustration around Death & Co. We were stunned with the quality and talent of the entrants – and picked a winner and two runners-up to be printed in THE MORTAL KNIFE. Their work follows on the next pages – keep an eye out for these talented Young Artists in the future! Thanks to all those who entered the competition.

Winner: Kathryn Kurtz

From the moment I read D.J. McCune's words, I had a clear image in my head of what everything looked like, and felt the need to commit these images to paper.

On one side was her keystone; on the
other, an old photo of a man.

Runner-up: Cassidy McClurkan

I saw this as a challenge since I have never created a sequential art piece. I thought this book offered the perfect opportunity.

Runner-up: Thuntha Soe

I took part in the competition because I really enjoyed Death &
Co., and the idea of being able to create a piece of work in response
to something that I'd liked reading was brilliant, and, actually,
a lot of fun in itself!

Adam Mortson